Taken In

Center Point
Large Print

Also by Elizabeth Lynn Casey and available from Center Point Large Print:

Dangerous Alterations
Reap What You Sew
Let It Sew
Remnants of Murder

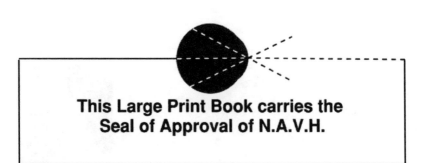

**This Large Print Book carries the
Seal of Approval of N.A.V.H.**

Taken In

Elizabeth Lynn Casey

CENTER POINT LARGE PRINT
THORNDIKE, MAINE

This Center Point Large Print edition
is published in the year 2015 by arrangement with
The Berkley Publishing Group, an imprint of
Penguin Publishing Group,
a division of Penguin Random House LLC.

The text of this Large Print edition is unabridged.
In other aspects, this book may vary
from the original edition.
Printed in the United States of America
on permanent paper.
Set in 16-point Times New Roman type.

ISBN: 978-1-62899-558-9

Library of Congress Cataloging-in-Publication Data

Casey, Elizabeth Lynn.
   Taken in / Elizabeth Lynn Casey. — Center Point Large Print edition.
      pages cm
   Summary: "When a trip to the Big Apple ends in murder, the sewing
circle searches for a killer who's rotten to the core"—Provided by
publisher.
   ISBN 978-1-62899-558-9 (library binding : alk. paper)
   1. Murder—Investigation—Fiction. 2. Large type books. I. Title.
PS3603.A8633T35 2015
813'.6—dc23
                                                                    2015003910

For the friends I've made
along my writing journey—thank you.
You've made each step sweeter
than I could have ever imagined.

Acknowledgments

A big thank-you to my friend Lynn Deardorff, whose suggestion of Flower Zipper Pins turned out to be the perfect project for the Sweet Briar crew during their trip to the Big Apple.

A heartfelt thank-you also goes to my beloved Aunt Mary, who has passed her love of the city on to me in so many ways.

And finally, a thank-you to my parents. Not only do they remember the day I came home from a friend's house (at the age of ten) determined to be a writer, but they also saved those first few writing attempts as if they never had any doubt I'd succeed.

Chapter 1

Life's memorable moments tended to offer their share of distinct sounds.

A well-earned promotion brought the clink of glasses and a heartfelt round of congratulations . . .

A broken heart brought crying jags and bewildered moans . . .

A marriage proposal brought squeals of delight, a few sniffles, and sometimes even a combination of the two . . .

And while Tori Sinclair had never been hours away from embarking on an all-expense-paid trip to New York City with six of her best friends before, she expected it to sound differently than it did as she stepped into Margaret Louise Davis's home with her suitcase in one hand and her air-line ticket in the other.

Tilting her head to the side, Tori strained to pick out the thump of luggage against stairs, the gasp over an almost-forgotten toiletry item, even a verbal claiming of the always-coveted window seat from some distant corner of her friend's home. Yet no matter how far she leaned or how utterly still she stood, she heard nothing more than the tick tock of the kitchen clock and the faintest hint of a sporadic tapping.

"Hello?" she called out as she set her powder blue carry-on beside a floral soft side bag and an ancient-looking maroon hard side suitcase tucked beneath Margaret Louise's foyer table. A quick peek at the luggage tag on each let her know that at least Rose Winters and Beatrice Tharrington had arrived. "Margaret Louise? Are you here?"

The creak of a door toward the back of the house was followed by a never-before-heard hushed version of a voice that always made her happy. "We're in here, Victoria . . . in my sewin' room. But come quick. There ain't much time."

Her mouth froze mid-smile as an image of Rose's eighty-year-old body, slumped atop Margaret Louise's sewing machine, sent her sprinting across the house with nary a thought to the brightly colored obstacles that littered her path with the promise of a sprained ankle if she misnavigated. "Is Rose okay? Did she fall? Is she sick?" she managed to ask as she skidded to a stop beside her friend.

"Rose is fine, Victoria." Margaret Louise rested a plump and reassuring hand on Tori's shoulder while simultaneously guiding her gaze toward the beloved matriarch of their sewing circle. Sure enough, leaning toward the screen of Margaret Louise's desktop computer was the diminutive white-haired woman that reminded Tori of her own late great-grandmother in everything from strength of spirit to shared tidbits of wisdom.

"She's havin' a hootenanny in here lendin' her smarts to Operation Dixie."

Tori worked to steady her breath as she took in Beatrice's typing, Rose's fevered dictation, and the handsome gray-haired gentleman that smiled out at them from the nearly monitor-sized snapshot. "Operation Dixie?"

Dixie Dunn was, well, Dixie Dunn. Stout in mind and body, Dixie had served as head librarian of Sweet Briar Public Library for more than four decades. Her job, as she liked to remind everyone within a fifty-mile radius, was unceremoniously snatched from her still-able hands when she was forced into retirement by the library board. The fact that Tori's hiring came *after* the board's decision mattered naught to the seventy-something, who'd spent the next year or so glaring at the same newcomer the rest of her sewing circle had embraced with open arms.

Fortunately, time and a handful of olive branch offerings—including riding to Dixie's rescue after both a fire and a dead body—had eased virtually all of Dixie's resentment toward Tori and the two had become friends. Still, mention of the woman's name tended to give her pause. Especially when it was said in conjunction with the mischievous glint Tori now saw in Margaret Louise's eyes. "We"—Margaret Louise pulled her hand from Tori's shoulder and waved it toward Rose and Beatrice—"think most of Dixie's belly-

9

achin' comes from bein' lonely. When Nina came back from maternity leave, Dixie's volunteerin' at the library wasn't needed no more. And as much as she likes to toot her horn 'bout her involvement with Home Fare and the shut-ins, she still ain't happy. Not like she *should* be anyway."

"That's why she needs a bloke." Beatrice glanced over her shoulder at Tori, the hint of crimson on her pale skin a perfect accompaniment to the shy smile that flickered across the young nanny's face. Employed by a wealthy Sweet Briar family, the British girl's departure from her teen years four years ago gave her the honor of being Rose's opposing bookend when it came to the age range within the Sweet Briar Ladies Society Sewing Circle.

Tori inched her way into the small, eight-by-eight-foot room until she was close enough to see that the man on the computer screen had brilliant blue eyes, was listed as seventy-two years old, and had the kind of face stubble that instantly elevated his appeal into the alluring category. "I really think you should leave the whole notion of dating up to Dixie. Maybe she doesn't want a man in her life right now. Or maybe her tastes are different than yours."

Margaret Louise unzipped the jacket of her polyester jogging suit halfway down her rounded stomach, shaking her head emphatically as she did. "Don't you worry that pretty head of yours none, Victoria. Dixie already knows 'bout John Dreyer. In fact, they're gonna meet face-to-face over breakfast tomorrow mornin'."

Her focus ricocheted off the man and landed squarely on Margaret Louise. "But we'll be in the city tomorrow, remember?"

"And so will John, on account of that's where he's livin'." Margaret Louise rocked back on the soles of her Keds and clapped her hands with glee. "Why, it's hard to think this is anything but a match made in heaven, ain't it?"

Tori looked at the screen again, the incessant tapping of Beatrice's fingers against the keyboard making it difficult to think, let alone truly process the situation. "Okay, so what are the three of you doing in here with his profile and picture on *your* screen?"

"Makin' sure Dixie's got the best bait on her hook, that's what." Margaret Louise nudged her chin in Rose's direction. "Rose is Dixie's smarts. Beatrice is Dixie's quiet charm. And me? I make it sound as if she's a pro in the kitchen."

"Yeah, yeah . . . that's good," Rose said, grabbing hold of Beatrice's upper arm with one hand while gesturing toward the screen with her other. "Now, tell him I backpacked through Europe as a teenager and that I'm considering doing it again!"

Tori watched in horror as Beatrice nodded then typed Rose's words into the rapidly scrolling text box in the bottom-left-hand corner of the screen.

"Oh! Oh! And be sure to add that I'll pack my backpack with an array of healthy homemade treats to share with other backpackers." Margaret Louise beamed as Beatrice made the addition. "That way he gets domestic and charmin' all at the same time!"

"Are you guys crazy? You can't do that! Dixie would be—"

"Hello? Where is everybody?" Dixie's voice rang out from the front of the house, kicking off a flurry of activity that had John's breathtaking blue eyes disappearing from the computer screen in a single blink of Tori's eye. Gone was the keyboard, the notebook with Dixie's user name and password for the senior online dating site, and the self-satisfied smiles from the faces of Tori's meddling friends.

A final check of the room for any remaining evidence of their misdeeds was followed by the scraping sound of Rose's chair as she pushed back and struggled to her feet with a rare burst of speed usually reserved for dessert time at the group's weekly sewing meeting.

"We're comin'," Margaret Louise bellowed. Then, lowering her voice for the benefit of those in her study, she spoke around the side of her index finger. "Now remember. Don't breathe a word."

For the second time in as many minutes, Tori

opened her mouth to protest, only to have her second attempt at the same sentiment ripped from the air by Rose's bony elbow. "You're young, Victoria. You're in love with a wonderful man. You don't know what it's like to be old and alone."

"Come tomorrow, when they finally meet over tea and scones, Dixie will be on her own," Beatrice whispered. "This just gets them started."

"Started in lies, you mean," Tori murmured before bringing up the rear of the parade that was now crossing the same toy-strewn room she'd navigated like a world-class skier less than ten minutes earlier. What Rose, Beatrice, and Margaret Louise were doing was wrong. Setting Dixie up to meet John under such false pretenses was handicapping any chance the woman had at something real.

But any and all thoughts of calling the trio on the carpet disappeared the second Dixie came into view. She was standing beside her awkwardly large black carry-on with the most genuine look of childlike joy Tori had ever seen on her face.

Sure, she'd seen Dixie smile while talking about books.

And yes, she'd seen Dixie smile when lavished with praise for just about anything.

But the smile on her friend's face at that exact moment was different. It started with her mouth but it kept on going—claiming the woman's eyes, cheeks, and virtually every other part of her five-foot-four, linebacker-like frame.

Was it really so terrible for Rose, Beatrice, and Margaret Louise to help Dixie along in an area where she'd had no experience since losing her husband fifteen years earlier?

Yes. Because it's not real . . .

"Oh, shut up."

Four sets of eyes beneath four sets of elevated eyebrows turned in Tori's direction.

Uh-oh.

She waved her hands back and forth. "I—I wasn't talking to any of you."

Rose scowled. "No one else is here, Victoria."

A succession of loud thumps from just outside the front door saved her from having to admit she'd been arguing with herself, and she was grateful. Right or wrong, Dixie's exuberant mood would make the flight to New York City easier on whoever pulled duty as her seatmate.

"Would it be too much trouble for any of you to stop your endless chitchat long enough to assist me with my bags?" Leona's perfectly made-up brown eyes peered through her stylish glasses at them from the other side of the screen door, an irritated expression marring her otherwise beautiful face.

She felt the weight of Leona's irritation as it moved across each and every face before landing squarely on hers. With a shot, Tori sprang into action. "Oh. Sure. I can help." She stepped around her friends and through the door Leona held open with a bored hand, only to come to a statue-like freeze at the mountain of luggage atop Margaret Louise's front porch.

Her mouth gaped open.

Margaret Louise's fraternal twin shook her head of salon-softened gray hair. "How many times have I told you not to let your jaw slack like that, dear? It's a very unbecoming look for anyone, let alone someone who does so little to enhance their features—positive or otherwise."

She knew she should say something to defend herself, or at the very least, wait a beat or two until Rose could jump in and begin trading barbs with her biggest adversary, but she didn't. All she could focus on at that moment was the luggage.

Three bulging bags to be checked.

Four questionable-sized carry-ons.

And one very pampered garden-variety bunny with a bejeweled bow around her neck.

For a three-day trip.

"Leona, you can't bring all those bags!"

Instantly, Leona's chin rose into the air above Paris's soft, velvety ears. "And why not?"

"Because we want the plane to actually get off the runway?" Rose quipped from her spot in the doorway between Beatrice and Margaret Louise.

Ever the mediator, Beatrice's voice, quiet and sweet, rushed to smooth the fight-inducing words. "You look so lovely in everything you wear, Leona, I'm most certain you don't need all of the things you packed."

Leona's anger-filled eyes left Rose just long enough to take in the British girl with a knowing nod before returning to her nemesis with flaring nostrils. "I figured at least *one* of the two of us should dress like something other than a housecoat-wearing, feet-shuffling, backwoods-living bumpkin."

Silence permeated the air for all of about two seconds before Rose returned the volley. "And you think a teeny-bopper-clothes-wearing, street-walking, man-hungry floozy is better?"

Leona's mouth gaped, then recovered, then gaped again.

"Pssst, Twin?" Margaret Louise mock-whispered. "I can see your partials when you do that."

Unable to hold it back any longer, Tori laughed, the tension brought on by her friends' shenanigans regarding Dixie all but a distant memory against the promise of three fun-filled days in the Big Apple. The fact that the trip coincided with their appearance tomorrow on the nationally syndi-cated morning television sensa-tion, *Taped with Melly and Kenneth*, only made it more exciting.

The death glare that had been aimed solely at Rose until that moment grew to include Tori as well. But before Leona could give words to her anger, Margaret Louise waved off the negative vibes. "I got a call from Zelman this mornin'."

"Who's Zelman?" Beatrice asked.

"He's the guy who makes sure that Melly and Kenneth's show goes off without a hitch each day." Margaret Louise pushed off the door frame and motioned everyone back inside. "He said a limo will pick us up at the hotel at one o'clock tomorrow afternoon and bring us to the studio."

Beatrice patted the purse draped over her arm. "I have the picture of Georgina they requested."

"And I have one of Melissa, too." Margaret Louise unzipped the front of her own carry-on and reached into the side compartment, retrieving an eight-by-ten portrait of her daughter-in-law, her son, and her eight grandchildren, including Matthew, the twelve-week-old addition. "Can't you just imagine all them oohs and ahhs when folks see this picture? Why, I'm bettin' the phones will be ringin' off the hook at the studio with folks wantin' to know more 'bout them."

"I sure wish Georgina and Melissa could come. It won't feel quite right without them being there."

Heads nodded around the room at Dixie's words but stopped as Tori reminded them of the reason Georgina Hayes—the town's mayor—and Melissa Davis couldn't attend. "You know Georgina, she can't miss a town council meeting. And Matthew is too young for Melissa to leave behind, no matter how badly she wishes she could come."

"Well, we'll just have to make sure we tell them all about it," Rose said amid a sudden coughing fit.

Beatrice straightened up, waving a camera as she did. "And *show* them."

"Look who I found out on the sidewalk looking all wistful!"

All heads turned back toward the door, the sight of the final sewing circle member and her lone suitcase filling the doorway a nanosecond before yet another familiar face came into view just beyond Debbie Calhoun's shoulder.

Tori planted a warm kiss on her sewing sister's cheek then stepped into Milo Wentworth's waiting arms.

"I came to see you off. I hope that's okay?"

She couldn't help but smile at the butterflies that still flapped in her stomach every time her fiancé was near. It was one of many signs that this time she'd made the right choice in future husbands, after finding her first fiancé in the coat closet of the reception hall with her then-best friend.

"It's perfect," she murmured against his chest before stepping back and grabbing hold of her bag. When Milo tried to take it from her, she shook her head and nodded toward the front porch and the security line nightmare they were sure to have thanks to Leona. "I've got this one."

Slowly, bag by bag, Milo got them down to the

sidewalk and the first of several limos tasked with delivering the seven prize package winners to XYZ Studios on Manhattan's Upper West Side. Tori had known this day was coming for three weeks now, yet still, she found the whole thing hard to believe.

She—Tori Sinclair? A guest on a major television program? With six of her best friends in the whole world? In New York City, of all places?

It was a pinch-worthy moment for sure.

"I was hopin' you'd both come to see us off." Margaret Louise's booming voice pulled Tori from her woolgathering in time to see Melissa and Georgina approach the limo from the opposite side of the street. In Melissa's arms was baby number eight, sleeping soundly.

Hugs were exchanged, cheeks were kissed, and pictures were taken before it was time to say good-bye.

"Have fun," Melissa called.

Shifting her straw hat forward on her head, Georgina nodded. "Now remember, if you find yourselves with any quiet time, I sure could use your help with those flower pins we talked about the other day. They'll make a mighty nice addition to the Mother's Day Picnic on the Green."

"We'll do our best," Tori promised.

"Oh, and remember we want to hear every last detail when you get back." Then, with a pointed look in Leona's direction, Georgina added, "And I do mean every last detail."

Tori shot a look at Margaret Louise and then Rose to see if they knew what was going on between the pair, but saw the same confusion on their faces she knew was on her own.

Oblivious to the silent messages passing between Leona and the mayor with a side order of knowing smirks, Beatrice lifted her camera into the air once again, a shy smile playing at the corners of her thin lips. "I'll take pictures of everything—the buildings, the people, the shows, and maybe even a real live dead body or two."

Debbie's left brow rose in amusement. "A real live dead body or two?"

"Right-o! We *are* going to New York City, are we not?"

Chapter 2

Tightening the belt around the waist of her plush white robe, Tori wandered into the tiny common area located in the center of the trio of bedrooms assigned to them by XYZ Studios. The hotel itself was grand, with ornate ceilings in the lobby, pristinely polished wood appointments in the hallways, and employees dressed to perfection, with impeccable manners and a desire to please.

The bedrooms themselves were a slightly different story.

They were nice, of course. Fancy, even. But as Leona had aptly stated upon her hasty return to the registration desk just moments after checking in, they weren't much bigger than a mouse hole.

Especially if you ended up sharing said mouse hole with Margaret Louise Davis, World-Class Snorer.

Tori rounded the back side of the floral love seat and dropped onto the empty cushion beside Leona, the aroma wafting from her friend's ceramic mug making her salivate. "Where'd you get that? And how do I get one, too?"

"Dial nine, dear. Ask for Luigi." Leona lowered the mug to her lap and traced its rim with her index finger. "Call from the phone in my room and he'll be at the door in no time."

Tori smiled through the persistent throbbing behind her eyes. "Adding to your list of male admirers, I take it?"

"Luigi just knows an attractive woman when he sees one." Leona glanced toward one of the bedrooms and then back down at her mug, her hand trembling ever so slightly as she hunched forward and raised the steaming liquid to her lips once again. "Though, frankly, it's beginning to seem as if doing the hard work doesn't matter anymore."

"What are you talking about?" she asked,

surprised by the hint of defeat in Leona's voice. "What hard work? And what doesn't it matter for?"

Slowly, deliberately, Leona peered at Tori over the top of her coffee cup, her eyes narrowing behind her morning glasses. "Does Milo know you look like that when you first wake up?"

"Like what?"

"Like *that*," Leona repeated in a voice tinged with horror. "The dark circles, the rumpled hair, the hint of dried drool at the edge of your mouth?"

She felt her mouth beginning to gape but reined it back in before Leona could add that to the list as well. "Leona, I just woke up. Though, in all fairness, that implies I actually slept through the night . . . which I didn't."

Leona rolled her eyes skyward. "The constant traffic noises and occasional siren from a passing fire truck is part of city life, dear. You, of all people, should know that after living in"— Leona's right nostril lifted ever so slightly in conjunction with her next word—"*Chicago,* of all places. I'm quite certain those noises were only amplified there. Especially the sirens."

"It wasn't the city noises, Leona," she protested around the yawn she could no longer hold at bay. "It was your sister's snoring."

"Oh. That."

"Why didn't you warn me?"

"You didn't ask, dear." Leona set her coffee cup on the side table then bent forward to shower

Paris with air kisses as the bunny hopped into the room. "How's Mommy's precious angel this morning? Did you sleep well?"

She tried not to laugh as Leona lifted the bunny into the air in much the way Melissa would lift baby Matthew. "Does Debbie snore?"

"No."

"Does Beatrice?"

"No."

"Then Paris slept fine." Tori pushed aside the momentary envy she felt for the long-eared creature and focused, instead, on the conversation she thought they were having before the apparent bags under her eyes came into play. "So what was this about hard work and Luigi the room service guy?"

Slowly, Leona lowered Paris to her lap and rested a flawlessly manicured hand atop the animal's back. "Now, don't get me wrong. This"—Leona's hand left Paris long enough to indicate herself—"doesn't take a lot of work. Natural beauty is natural beauty, after all. But even with such a gift, I put actual *thought* into my clothes, my attitude, and the perception I wish to portray to those around me."

"Okay . . ." She didn't know where, exactly, Leona was going with her diatribe, but knew there was a point to be made and hell to be paid if Tori interrupted or was seen as anything less than enthralled.

Leona, of course, continued. "So it makes sense why men find me desirable. Why wouldn't they?"

At a loss for what to say, Tori merely nodded while simultaneously stifling the laugh she knew would earn her a death glare if she were to let it out.

"Yet there are still a contingent of men who seem to be okay with women who"—Leona paused just long enough to run her gaze from the top of Tori's sleep-tousled hair to the tips of Tori's well-worn white slippers—"don't care about their perception quite so much."

She started to remind Leona about Margaret Louise's snoring and her subsequent lack of sleep but closed her mouth when the reason for the woman's angst finally took center stage. "Take this man—John—who Dixie is meeting for breakfast this morning. All he's seen of her so far is a postage stamp–sized picture. That's it. Yet despite that—and the fact that it's not even an attractive picture to begin with—he's invited her to meet him for coffee at some bookstore café on West Fifty-eighth."

"Actually it's changed to breakfast. At the Waldorf Astoria."

Leona's jaw went slack. "Dixie is going to breakfast at the *Waldorf Astoria?*"

At Tori's nod, Leona pulled her jaw in tight. "Obviously the man is blind."

"Leona, stop! Dixie *is* an attractive woman in her own way."

"I don't know how housecoats and moccasins can be seen as attractive and alluring in *any* way, especially to a man who breakfasts at the Waldorf!"

Tori pushed off the sofa and made her way over to the one bedroom from which no one had emerged yet. Putting her ear to the door, she listened for any sign that either Dixie or Rose was awake and listening. When she heard nothing, she returned to the sofa and Leona, who was still babbling away. "All I can think is that this John character must be neighbors with the chef. Either that, or he's no prize himself."

"You haven't seen his picture yet?" she asked, surprised.

Leona shook her head emphatically. "I have not. In fact, I didn't even know about him until the plane ride yesterday."

"You'll have to ask Margaret Louise to pull up his picture for you later . . ." She let her words trail off as her mind wandered back to the scene she'd stumbled across in the aforementioned's study the previous day.

"You've seen him, dear?"

She nodded.

"He's mousy, yes?"

"No."

Leona's brow rose ever so slightly. "Nerdy?"

"No."

A hint of a smile played at the corners of Leona's collagen-enhanced lips. "Homely?"

"Not in the slightest. In fact, he's quite handsome."

"H-hand-handsome?" Leona stammered.

"He has a nice smile and absolutely gorgeous blue eyes." She dropped her own voice an octave or two as she searched Leona's dumbstruck face. "But I take it that's not what you wanted to hear?"

"I—I just can't believe . . . oh never mind." Leona wrapped her arms around Paris and scooted forward on the sofa cushion in indication of her pending exit. "Desperate can be wrapped in a handsome package every once in a while, I imagine."

"Desperate?"

"What other explanation can there be for a man to seek out Dixie? Especially *online* of all places, where anyone can make themselves sound scintillating?"

She closed her eyes momentarily against the image of Rose, Beatrice, and Margaret Louise creating a cyber-version of Dixie that was sure to sound very different across a table at the Waldorf Astoria. And for the umpteenth time since she'd caught them in the act, she couldn't help but feel they'd done Dixie a disservice.

Leona rose to her feet, tossing back her shoulders as she did. "That alone says he's oblivious to the definition of discerning. Which, on a side note, is probably a good thing considering he's meeting her in less than an hour and she's still fast asleep and drooling all over her pillow, no doubt."

"Lots of people meet each other online these days, Leona. It's the wave of the future, actually."

"Oh, shut up, dear." Leona fairly pranced across the sitting room, only to stop mid-step at the knock on the other side of the door. "Oooh, perhaps Luigi came back with a rose . . ."

Poofing her hair from the ends, Leona took one bejeweled hand from around Paris and used it to open the door.

"Delivery from XYZ Studios."

Tori joined a beaming Leona at the door as a man, dressed in the hotel's black suit with red appointments, held a gift basket with candy and flowers in their direction. "Welcome to New York City. Your limousine driver will meet you in the lobby at one o'clock this afternoon to take you across town to the studio for taping. Until then, we hope you have a restful morning. Please let us know if there's anything we can do to assist you in that regard."

Leona gave a few well-timed bats of her eyelashes as she set Paris at her feet and retrieved the basket from the man's outstretched hands. "How lovely of you to bring this up to us," she fairly cooed. "Oh, and it's so heavy."

"Let me get that for you, miss."

Leona stepped aside just enough to let the man pass, but not enough to eliminate all chance for physical contact. "Thank you"—her gaze dropped to the gold name tag on the front of the man's jacket—"*Samuel.*"

The doorman set the basket down on a long marble-topped table beside the door then turned back to Leona, his awareness of Tori virtually nil. "Is there anything else I can do for you at the moment?"

Sliding her gaze to the table long enough to take in the array of treats, Leona smiled up at Samuel. "The limo will be here at one, you said?"

At his nod, Leona stepped closer to the man and increased the wattage on her smile. "Can you tell me how I might find the Waldorf Astoria?"

She'd tried to protest, to remind her friends that Dixie was a grown woman and perfectly capable of handling a breakfast date on her own, but she'd been outvoted five to one.

Margaret Louise, Beatrice, and Rose, of course, already knew what John looked like thanks to their separate and combined stints as Cyber Dixie over the past few weeks. As a result, their curiosity as to how the date was going was more about self-satisfaction and the desire to see the fruits of their labor than anything else.

Debbie, being Debbie, went along for the ride,

her excitement over being in New York making her agreeable to just about anything.

Leona, on the other hand, was motivated by one thing, and one thing only . . .

Good old-fashioned nosiness with a side order of underlying jealousy that the woman would never admit aloud.

"Would you slow down, please?" Rose mumbled as she stepped onto the sidewalk beside Tori and stopped to take a breath. "I'm not used to all this walking."

Tori waved to her friends to stop then stepped closer to the elderly woman. "Rose? Are you okay? I can hail us a cab and we can go back to the hotel if you'd like."

"No, no. I'll be fine. I just need a moment is all."

Leona looked left and right, and then, when she was certain no one was watching, she stamped her foot on the sidewalk. "We don't have time to stop. Dixie has already been gone more than an hour. Surely she can't hold a man's interest any longer than that."

"Put a sock in it, Twin." Margaret Louise moved in beside Rose and Tori, a look of concern crossing her face. "Rose, we can turn back if you want. We can just wait for Dixie to tell us the details herself."

"I'll be fine," Rose hissed. "I just need a moment."

Beatrice plucked her purse off her shoulder and

rummaged around inside, withdrawing her camera from its depths. "This is perfect. It'll give me a chance to take a picture for Georgina and Melissa." The young woman flipped on her camera and then rummaged in her purse a second time. "I just need my—oh, here it is."

Rose's eyes narrowed. "Tell me that's not what I think it is . . ."

Beatrice looked from the figure in her hand to Rose and back again. "Is there a problem?"

"That's your Kenny Rogers bobblehead, ain't it?" Margaret Louise chimed in.

Beatrice nodded. "I thought it would be something familiar for Georgina and Melissa when we're showing them pictures from our trip."

Ever the diplomat when it came to their sewing circle, Margaret Louise rubbed her chin between her thumb and her forefinger. "Well now, don't you think seein' one of us in the picture would be somethin' familiar?"

A beat or two of silence was followed by a shrug of Beatrice's narrow shoulders. "It will make the picture more special."

Before she could think of something to say, Rose leaned in, her breath warm against Tori's ear. "And that, Victoria, is why I refused to share a room with Leona on this trip. Being trapped behind a closed door with that woman can make anyone lose their mind, even someone as young as Beatrice."

Tori allowed her laugh to propel her forward past a gaped-mouth, eavesdropping Leona. "I'll hold Kenny when you take the picture," Tori offered. "I'm sure Georgina and Melissa will be excited to see the skyscrapers—"

"So what's *your* excuse for being feeble brained, you old goat?"

Margaret Louise shot her hand up between Leona and Rose. "Oh no, you don't. This trip is 'bout friendship. And celebratin' Victoria's upcomin' weddin'. Not you two cluckin' at each other like a bunch of barnyard chickens."

"Amen," Debbie whispered just loud enough for all to hear.

Five or six shots—and a volley or two of evil glares between Rose and Leona—later, they were on their way again, the Waldorf Astoria soon rising before them majestically.

"Do you think it's goin' okay?" Margaret Louise pondered aloud as they approached the front door. "Do you think he's fallin' in love with her?"

"If he's desperate enough to resort to the computer to find a date, I would imagine anything is possible." Leona waved off their gasps in favor of smiling at the doorman, who greeted them from his position just outside the famed hotel. "Good morning!"

"Good morning, ladies. Are you here for breakfast?"

At Debbie's nod, he pointed at Paris. "I'm sorry, no pets allowed."

Leona's hand found the man's forearm and squeezed once, twice. "Don't you worry, Paris fits inside my sister's tote bag. No one will notice, yet *I* will most certainly remember your thoughtfulness." She deposited Paris into Margaret Louise's bag then batted her eyes up at the doorman once again.

Slowly, his gaze moved down Leona's polished form before reengaging eye contact and opening the door for their admittance. "Enjoy your breakfast."

They gathered just inside the lobby and took a moment to get their bearings, the spectacle that was Leona paling quickly against the beauty that was the famed Waldorf Astoria's lobby.

"I have to take a photograph of this," Beatrice insisted, only to have her hand smacked from her purse by Rose.

"Kenny isn't allowed in the Waldorf."

"But Paris—"

"Kenny isn't allowed in the Waldorf," Rose repeated.

The clatter of silverware in the distance aided in their collective decision to turn left and then right, their steps coming closer together as the elegant breakfast restaurant sprang into view.

"Oooh, lookee there! They're sittin' right there." Margaret Louise motioned everyone behind a large potted tree then pointed to a table near the edge of the dining room.

Rose rested her hand slightly above that of a steely-eyed woman in her mid to late seventies who was also standing behind the plant for some reason, widening the view of the restaurant for both of them while simultaneously directing the gazes of her friends with the lift of her chin. "Why, he looks positively smitten with Dixie."

A squeal rose up from Beatrice's throat just before the quiet clap of her hands. "I knew John was the perfect bloke for Dixie!"

"Let me see," Leona groused, pushing her way to the front of the group, only to gasp so loudly she sent Ms. Steely Eye in search of some much-needed personal space and everyone else ducking for cover behind the ill-fitting planter. "No, no, no . . ."

Tori took in the bewildered faces of her friends before focusing entirely on Margaret Louise's red-faced sister. "Leona? Are you okay?"

"It can't be . . . *him* . . ."

She grabbed Leona's hand and turned the woman to her, the shock on her friend's face sending an odd little chill down her spine. "It can't be who, Leona?"

Looking back through the still-parted branches, Leona's shoulders sank in defeat. *"Paris."*

Chapter 3

Tori peered past her own reflection to study Leona in the makeup chair across the room, the rapt attention of her friend's style crew seemingly unnoticed by the queen of attention mongers. There was no eyelash batting at the male hair stylist, no words of advice given to the makeup artist, and no snide barbs aimed at the elderly woman seated to her left.

No, Leona simply sat still, staring straight ahead and working her bottom lip like a still-dateless teenage girl on the last day of prom ticket sales.

"You have beautiful hair, Victoria."

She pulled her gaze back to her own reflection and nodded her approval of the final product. "Wow. Any chance you'd like to give up your job here and come to Sweet Briar, South Carolina, with me?"

If the stylist answered, she didn't hear, as Zelman—the producer of *Taped with Melly and Kenneth*—stepped into the room and clapped his hands together. "Ladies, I must say you all look lovely this afternoon."

At their chorus of gratitude, he continued, the jovial personality he emitted on camera throughout the syndicated talk show taking a backseat to a more no-nonsense, let's-get-the-show-on-the-road sort of attitude. "I know you've all been briefed on what's going to happen during your segment, but are there any questions you have for me before we start taping? Anything that's unclear?"

"Can I sit next to Kenneth?" Margaret Louise hoisted her tote bag onto her lap and patted its exterior. "I baked him some of my famous cupcakes right before we left Sweet Briar and I'd sure like to give 'em to him before they lose their freshness."

Zelman consulted the clipboard in his assistant's hands. "I take it you're the baker of the group then?"

Margaret Louise's thick shoulders rose and fell in a shrug. "I like to bake and I like to cook, but Debbie here"—she swept her hand toward the makeup chair on her other side—"she's the one who actually owns her own bakery. She's the professional."

"Debbie"—he liberated the guest list from the petite woman at his side—"Calhoun. You're the one Ms. Davis described as unstoppable."

Debbie's narrow face reddened instantly. "I wouldn't say unstoppable."

"We would," said Rose, Beatrice, Margaret Louise, and Tori in unison.

Zelman grinned then took a step toward the frailest of the group. "Okay, and you must be Rose, yes?"

"What gave it away? My blue veins or the fact my skin no longer fits my body?" Rose leaned forward in her chair and coughed so loud it echoed around the room. When her lungs were clear, she waved away the discomfort on Zelman's face. "Don't mind me. I'm old and I have no filter but I assure you I will behave on set."

Beatrice slid off her chair and stood. "And I'm Beatrice. The nanny from England. And this is Dixie."

Dixie, who hadn't stopped smiling since returning to the hotel from her date with John, ran a trembling hand down the front of her lavender housecoat. "I'm the librarian who lost her job when Victoria came to town."

Zelman looked back down at his notes, his finger quickly moving down the page and then slowly from left to right. "The librarian who will make sure to tell you she lost her job when Victoria came to town," he read aloud. "Yup. I've got you right here in Ms. Davis's letter."

"And that's Leona," Beatrice added, pointing toward the chair across the room from Tori. "And Paris."

"Paris?" Zelman glanced down at his notes. "I don't have a Paris on the list."

Leona shot her sister with a death glare. "You didn't mention Paris in your letter?"

Margaret Louise waved away the oversight with a pudgy hand. "Paris is my sister's pet bunny."

Zelman blinked once, twice. "I see that."

"She goes wherever Leona goes," Margaret Louise clarified.

"And Leona is"—he stared at Paris for what seemed like an eternity then took in his notes once again—"the sewing circle member who doesn't sew, right?"

Spinning around in her chair, Leona managed a smile for the producer that stopped just short of its usual flirtatiousness. "I'm the cultured one who just happens to be two weeks away from taping the very first episode of my very own cable television fashion program."

"She's also the most rude and egocentric member of the group," Rose offered helpfully. "But pay her no mind. None of us do."

Overpowered by her need to keep World War III at bay until after they were safely back in their Manhattan hotel room, Tori leapt off her chair and thrust a hand in Zelman's direction. "And I'm Tori, the bride-to-be."

"The extra pretty one, just like I told you in my letter," Margaret Louise chimed in. "Inside and out."

Again, Leona glowered at her sister, but this time it was short-lived as Zelman handed the clipboard back to his assistant and motioned for everyone to follow him down the long hall that would eventually lead them to the set of *Taped with Melly and Kenneth*.

"As you know from watching the show, the first twenty minutes is the time when our hosts chat about their previous day as well as whatever they feel like discussing. Then we'll go to our latest contest." They slowed along with Zelman as he approached an open door on the left, about halfway down the hallway. "After that, they'll announce your group. Janie, here"—he pointed to his assistant—"will come get you here in the Green Room and escort you to the edge of the stage. You'll come on, take your seats with Melly and Kenneth, and answer whatever they ask over the next ten minutes or so before it's time to fetch the next guest from the Green Room."

Beatrice leaned forward, unbridled excitement stretching her otherwise subdued features. "Is it Kenny?"

"Kenny?" Zelman echoed.

"Rogers."

Rose pushed her way to the front of the group and smacked a hand over Beatrice's mouth. "Don't mind her, she's young."

"I must confess, I'm mighty curious 'bout the next guest, too." Margaret Louise peeked into the empty room then back at Zelman. "Is it a movie star?"

Zelman shook his head. "Nope. An author."

"Who?" Dixie demanded.

"Gavin Rollins."

Dixie tapped her index finger against her chin

then turned to Tori. "Gavin Rollins? Do you know that name?"

She opened her mouth to answer, only to have Zelman fill in the blanks. "He's the author of that new blockbuster, *Finding Love After Sixty-Five*."

"So it must be fiction?" Rose quipped.

Zelman cracked a smile. "Nope."

"A public service warning?"

"Nope."

Rose's bony arms flew into the air. "I'm out of guesses."

"It's more of a step-by-step guide, interspersed with real-life stories of post-retirement happily ever afters," Margaret Louise explained, earning herself a nod from the producer. "Heck, he might even be inspired to write one of them sequels if he sits next to Dixie in that Green Room for more 'n a minute or two."

Tori's legs felt like rubber as she led the way across the stage to Melly Pipa and Kenneth Donaldson, their warm smiles and the studio audience's polite applause adding to the dream-like fog clouding her head and making her feel as if her alarm clock were going to rouse her at any minute.

But it didn't.

Instead, she accepted a hug from Melly and a kiss on the cheek from Kenneth then stepped aside as each of her friends did the same.

"Welcome, ladies," Melly said, gesturing toward the semicircle of chairs set up to her left. "We've been looking forward to your visit all week, haven't we, Kenneth?"

The six-foot-ten former linebacker pulled his lingering gaze from Leona and fixed it on his diminutive co-host. "Uhhh . . . yes . . . we have." At Melly's raised eyebrow, he managed to shake off Leona's spell long enough to concentrate on the cue card beside the camera. "This has been one of my favorite sweepstakes so far simply because you made the selection process super easy."

"It's not every day a group of friends spans the kind of age range you do." Melly reached behind her chair and retrieved a letter from the host chat table. "Let me read the audience a little of the letter we received here at the studio. But before I do, which one of you is Margaret Louise?"

Like a shot, Margaret Louise's plump hand was in the air waving from side to side. "That's me."

Melly nodded then began to read, "Dear Melly and Kenneth. My name is—"

"B'fore you read that, I'd like to show everyone this picture." Margaret Louise reached inside the jacket of her polyester running suit and extracted the eight-by-ten glossy she'd packed especially for that moment. Then, holding the portrait toward the camera with her left hand, she beckoned the cameraman to come closer with her right. "This here, is my son, Jake. He's the spittin' image of his daddy. And this here is my daughter-in-law, Melissa. I couldn't love her any more if I'd popped her out myself."

Lowering the letter to her lap, Melly let out a laugh. "If you popped her out, eh?" She turned to Kenneth just long enough to point a finger in Margaret Louise's direction. "I like this woman! She says it like it is, just like I do!"

"Lord help us all," Kenneth groaned playfully.

Margaret Louise cleared her throat and continued on, her index finger guiding the television audience's gaze to each of her grandbabies. "And these are my grandbabies—Jake Junior, Julia, Tommy, Kate, Lulu, Sally, Molly, and the brand-new youngin', Matthew."

Melly leaned forward on her high-top stool and conducted a silent count. "That's *eight* kids! Oh. Wow. I can hardly keep up with *two!*" She turned to Kenneth, who was, once again, engaged in meaningful eye contact with Leona. "Can you imagine me having *eight* kids?"

"And Melissa, their mum, still finds time to sew in our group," Beatrice offered.

"I don't sew with *two* kids!" Zelman's finger moved counterclockwise beside the camera, prompting Melly to return to the letter in her lap. "Okay, so where was I? Ahhh, here we go . . . 'My name is Margaret Louise Davis, and I'm writing to you from Sweet Briar, South Carolina. When

41

people think of friends, they picture folks of the same age—jogging together, going to movies together, and talking on the phone for hours. But when I think of my friends—my *best* friends—I see something very different. Some of us have been married and widowed, some of us are retired and looking for hobbies to keep us busy, some of us work full-time while juggling mother-hood, and some of us are really just starting out, choosing paths the rest of us traveled a lifetime ago. We shouldn't work as friends, but we do. And it all started with a sewing needle—a sewing needle we each picked up for very different reasons.' "

Melly set the letter back on her lap. "That letter gives me goose bumps every time I read it. And now here you all are, such a visually varied group, yet you're all best friends. Amazing."

"Do you ever fight?" Kenneth asked.

"Not really, no. 'Cept, of course, for the spats between my pigheaded twin sister and Rose, right here." Margaret Louise slipped an arm around Rose's shoulders. "But they ain't serious. And as much as they might squeal otherwise, we see right through their bickerin' and posturin'."

Leona opened her mouth in protest but shut it as Kenneth posed another question. "Did you all start in your sewing circle at the same time?"

Dixie took that one. "Margaret Louise, Rose, Georgina—one of our two members who couldn't

42

make the trip—and myself started the group along with the late Charlotte Devereaux many years ago. Margaret Louise's daughter-in-law, Melissa, started about three years ago, along with Debbie and Beatrice."

"And Leona and Victoria?" Melly inquired. "When did they start sewing with the group?"

Rose snorted. "Leona doesn't sew. She just eavesdrops and annoys everyone around her." Then retracting her bristles, the matriarch of the group continued. "But Victoria here, she has a way of bringing us all together like a family. She's made us all nicer somehow."

Heads nodded to the left and right of Tori, kicking off a mistiness in her eyes that necessitated a rapid blink or two. "I moved to Sweet Briar as a way to start fresh in life," she explained as Melly gave her the floor. "I'd lost my great-grandmother, my personal life was in upheaval, and I was in desperate need of a change. Moving to Sweet Briar—where I found my dream job, my future husband, and met all of these amazing women—was, hands down, the smartest decision I've ever made."

"Stop! Stop! You're going to make me cry!" Melly widened her eyes as she took in the camera then turned back to Tori. "Being one of the younger ones in the group, do you feel as if you learn a lot about life and love from these women?"

"Absolutely."

"And we learn from the younger ones, too." Dixie shifted in her seat to afford a better view of Melly and Kenneth.

"Hmmm, that's interesting. How so?"

"Well, when Victoria first came to Sweet Briar, I was rather . . ."

"Cranky?" Rose offered.

Margaret Louise narrowed her eyes in thought. "Close-minded?"

"Bitter," Leona stated.

Ignoring her peers, Dixie continued, "Set in my ways. I knew life one way—the way I'd lived it for seventy years at that point. Victoria opened my eyes. Made me see so many things in a different way, including myself. For that—and for the steadfast loyalty of each and every one of these women seated here beside me—I am truly blessed."

"Wow. Makes me want to run right out and form a club myself." Melly tucked the letter beside her hip and clasped her hands in her lap. "I'd like to take a few more moments to get to know each of you and share some of the pictures you brought with our studio audience. Then when we're done, maybe some of you will join the ranks of our next guest's fans—women just like you who are ready for a new chapter in their life," Melly said by way of a segment transition that brought her focus back to the camera at the edge of the stage. "A chapter that could include finding love again, just like Gavin Rollins writes about in his blockbuster sensation, *Finding Love After Sixty-Five.*"

A smile bright enough to rival every camera light in the room crept across Dixie's face. "I think I may have started that chapter over breakfast this morning."

Chapter 4

Tori did her best to keep pace with Leona and Margaret Louise as they made their way from the elevator to the front door of the hotel, but short of running, it was difficult. Leona was on a mission involving a man, and there would be no asking her to slow down. Then again, the doorman posted just inside the revolving glass door could be handsome, muscular, and single . . .

She looked up just before she smacked into Leona from behind, the woman's sudden halt just shy of the exit, allowing Tori to catch her breath while her stylish friend basked in the glow of approval from not one, but *two* uniformed hotel employees.

"Margaret Louise?" Tori stepped closer to the grandmother of eight and lowered her voice. "Do you really think we should be tracking

John down without speaking to Dixie first?"

"You know my twin. When she gets somethin' in that thick head of hers, there ain't no talkin' sense with her. Especially when it's 'bout a man."

"But he's Dixie's man now. Or could be if Leona would stay out of it."

"I know, Victoria. I know. But it's the way it always is with—"

Leona's elbow found its way into Tori's side. "Samuel and Ryan would like to know if they should hail us a cab."

"Hail us a cab?" Margaret Louise pushed at the air with both palms. "Are you pullin' my leg? My knuckles are still white from the taxi we took after spyin' on Dixie! Why, if that plastic thinga-bobbin hadn't been between us and that driver, I'd have smacked him over the head with my bag after he nearly ran over that woman with the stroller."

"My sister, here, is from the backwoods of South Carolina. She's having trouble adjusting to the way things are done in this wonderful city." Leona rested her well-moisturized hand on the taller of the two doormen and flashed her pearly white capped teeth up at him. "Do you have another suggestion for how we could get to West Sixty-eighth between Columbus and Central Park West?"

Five minutes later, they were underground and

shoulder to shoulder with a dozen or so other people, awaiting the arrival of the first of two subways that would take them to their destination. Margaret Louise looked around, clearly mesmerized by her first experience on a subway platform, while Leona pulled Paris and her purse closer to her body.

"Leona?"

"Yes, dear."

She tried to formulate the best way to pose her question but finally gave up and just let it flow, unchecked. "Assuming John is indeed Paris's namesake the way you claim, why, after six-plus years of never mentioning him beyond his part in her moniker, are you suddenly so interested in him that we have to spend a few hours of our limited time in the city trying to track him down? It makes no sense to me."

"Is it so far out of the realm of possibility to consider I might be trying to protect Dixie from having her heart broken?"

Margaret Louise's laugh echoed around them. "I'm not sure what you were seein', Twin, but that man looked mighty taken by Dixie 'cross that table this mornin'."

"And that alone doesn't send up warning bells for you?" Leona spat through clenched teeth.

"No . . . why would it?" Tori asked, confused.

"You saw John. You saw those eyes and that smile. There's no way someone who looks like that could be taken by someone who looks like Dixie. Certainly not after having spent time with"—Leona threw back her shoulders, elevating her bosom as she did—*"me."*

"You mean someone who didn't even know his name was John until this morning?" Margaret Louise teased before turning her attention to the approaching subway. "Oooh, goody! It's here! It's here!"

The doors swished open in front of them, and a throng of people exited the train. "When we get inside this thing, sit quietly," Leona hissed. "Don't make eye contact. We're not in Sweet Briar, Margaret Louise!"

When the doorway was clear, they stepped inside and quickly claimed three seats in the middle of the subway car. All around them passengers were reading, listening to music, studying scripts, and in some cases, closing their eyes.

"Now, to address your comment, I knew John's name . . . at one time. I just misplaced it against a backdrop that includes far too many suitors to keep track of on a moment's notice," Leona said quietly. "But I remembered enough. And I recognized him the second I saw him this morning."

"But even you, yourself, said you had one dinner with him. That's hardly enough to stake a claim on him now."

Leona's eyes widened in horror. "Stake a claim

on him? Is that what you think I'm doing, dear?"

"Well, isn't it?" Tori waved her hand across her lap, the frustration she was feeling inside making its way into her voice. "Isn't that why you suddenly have a need to see him after all this time? Because *Dixie* might actually end up with him?"

A voice from their left prevented Leona from answering. "Good evening, everyone! My name is Wurly Rhoades, and I'm here to play you a song on my ukulele."

Not a single head moved around them. People who'd been reading continued to read. People who'd been listening to music continued to listen to music. People who'd been engaged in conversation with the person next to them continued talking. And those who'd been sitting with their eyes closed merely shifted in their seats and turned their heads in the opposite direction.

"Did you hear that, everyone? Wurly is goin' to play a song for us, isn't that nice?" Margaret Louise clapped her hands. "You go ahead, Wurly, we're waitin'."

Leona threw an elbow into her sister's side and followed it up with a foot stomp. "Didn't I tell you to keep quiet?" Leona whispered. "Don't engage him. Don't look at him. Just do what everyone else is doing."

Following her sister's pointed gaze around the subway car, Margaret Louise's shoulders slumped, the surprised-tinged sadness on her face making Tori wish she could live in her friend's world rather than the real one. But still, she knew Leona was right and did her best to distract the kindhearted woman. "Look, Leona, I don't know what your deal is, but John looked happy with Dixie this morning."

"Which is why my antennae are pinging loudly."

"That's a Beatles song you're playin', ain't it, Wurly. That's real nice." Margaret Louise dug her hand into her tote and pulled out Beatrice's camera and the Kenny Rogers bobblehead. Turning, she shoved the camera in Tori's hand and stood as the subway bumped and swayed along the tracks. "Beatrice wants me takin' pictures so take one of Kenny and me with Wurly! Melissa will love this one!"

Leona covered her face with her hand and turned her legs away from Tori, whispering as she did. "That sister of mine is going to get us killed."

"It's just a picture, Leona. What harm can that do?" Tori lifted the camera to eye level and snapped a picture of her friend and the subway musician just as the subway came to a stop and passengers around them jumped to their feet. "Besides, Margaret Louise is right. Melissa will get a kick out of this. Georgina, too."

"If we're still alive to show them the photograph when this is all over . . ."

"Quit your bellyachin', Twin." Margaret Louise dropped Beatrice's bobblehead into her tote and sat back down in time to clap for Wurly's final few notes. "That was a treat, Wurly. An absolute treat."

The shaggy-haired man flashed a crooked smile in their direction then pulled off his hat and held it out in front of Margaret Louise, an expectant look widening his otherwise hooded dark eyes.

"Why, thank you, Wurly, but I'm not much of a hat wearer. Besides, it looks real good on you."

Wurly's mouth hung open for a count of ten, then slowly shut as he shook his head and wandered farther down the car, muttering under his breath as he did.

"He wasn't trying to give you his hat," Leona hissed through clenched teeth. "He was trying to get you to give him money."

Margaret Louise drew back in her seat. "Money? For playin' that little ditty of his?"

Leona's answer came the way of an exasperated eye roll.

Instantly, Margaret Louise's hand dug into her purse, only to get smacked away by her sister. "Oh no you don't. Are you trying to get us mugged?"

"No, I'm just tryin' to pay him like you said."

"Too late!" The subway lurched to a stop, prompting Leona to reach across Tori and dig her nails into her sister's upper arm. "It's time to get off."

They made it out of their seats and through the door just as it was closing, the roar of the fast-moving subways around them making it difficult to hear much of anything.

Tori peered up at the sign above the closest staircase. "What's the next train we want?"

"We don't. We're walking the rest of the way." Leona shot one final glare at her sister then made her way up the stairs. "I'd rather take my chances walking through the park than ride on another subway with"—she turned around and pointed at the plump woman two steps behind Tori—"*that* one. She made me look like a—a . . . *tourist*."

"You *are* a tourist, Leona."

This time it was Tori who bore the full brunt of Leona's glare. "I'm a *traveler*. There's a difference, dear."

They emerged onto street level and crossed at the light, the lushness of the trees in Central Park calling to them with a sense of familiarity. But Leona retained point and had them skirting the edges of the park in favor of the Fifty-ninth Street sidewalk. "Dixie will be getting out of her hair appointment in the next ten minutes or so, and I don't want her getting back to the hotel room and calling *John* with some ludicrous idea to move up their dinner date before I have a chance to see him."

"What exactly are you hoping to accomplish,

Leona?" Tori quickened her pace until she was in step with Leona.

"The man I met in Paris all those years ago had standards. Goals. Obviously something has changed."

"Because he was enjoyin' Dixie's company?"

"As a matter of fact, yes." Leona's chin jutted upward as they turned right on Central Park West. "Dixie is far too simple for the man I remember. She's a retired librarian of all things. She does nothing except sit around and deliver an occasional meal to the infirmed. I can't imagine anything she had to say about herself being interesting enough to make him suggest that date this morning."

Tori's feet automatically slowed but not enough to compensate for Margaret Louise's sudden stop. "Maybe he found her ability in a kitchen to be commendable."

Leona turned around. "What ability? She makes soup seven days a week."

Margaret Louise's cheeks grew crimson. "She's . . . well read."

"In high school classics and children's books maybe."

"Maybe it was her—her charm!" Margaret Louise said, looking down at Beatrice's camera.

"Since when is bitter and snappy considered charming?"

"It works for you, Twin."

Uh-oh.

She rushed to head Leona's hissy fit off at the pass. "Okay, your point is taken, Leona. But *something* attracted him to Dixie, right? Does it really matter what it was?"

"It might." Leona stopped at the nearest light and crossed at the signal, her stylish shoes clicking against the pavement. "I'll know more soon."

They turned left and then right, the parade of flashing police lights stealing their attention from the street sign they'd been seeking. A turn at the corner revealed more lights, a mob of onlookers, and a line of police tape that ran from one side of Sixty-eighth Street to the other.

"Quick! Take our picture!" Margaret Louise shoved Beatrice's camera into Tori's hand and backed up to the edge of the yellow tape, the bobblehead in her hand. "This will be a good one! Real New Yorkish."

Shaking her head, Leona stalked away, leaving Margaret Louise and Tori to fend for themselves.

"I don't know why her panties are in such a bunch, do you, Victoria?"

Tori followed Margaret Louise's line of vision just in time to see Leona disappear into a crowd of uniformed officers. "Because Dixie had a date this morning and Leona didn't?"

"I'd like to say that's not it, but I can't." Margaret Louise dropped the bobblehead back into her bag and took the now-zippered camera bag from Tori's outstretched hand. Then, turning to an elderly woman to her right, she got down to business. "Any idea what's goin' on 'round here?"

The woman, whom Tori judged to be about Margaret Louise's age, nodded sadly. "I've lived on this street since I was a little girl and never, in all that time, have we had a murder. Until now, that is."

"There was a murder?" Margaret Louise gasped, her eyes wide. "A real live New York City murder?"

Tori stepped forward, quieting any further talk from Margaret Louise with a well-placed hand to her friend's back. "Did you see anything?"

The woman shook her head. "No, but I heard it."

"You heard the gunshot?" Margaret Louise prompted.

"I heard his body hitting the road from"—the woman lifted her index finger into the air to indicate the third floor of a brownstone midway down the block—"up there."

Tori and Margaret Louise sucked in their breath in unison.

"I live in the apartment just below his."

"I'm so sorry," Tori said, her gaze moving past the woman, past the tape line, and toward the vicinity of the policeman speaking to Leona on the other side of the street, an inexplicable chill making its way through her body as she did. "Is there anything we can—"

"I know I shouldn't be surprised. It was only a matter of time before one of those women wised up to his ways and exacted revenge."

She saw Leona point up to the balcony in question, watched as the cop nodded in response, and then swallowed hard as her friend dropped her chin to her chest.

Uh-oh.

"Did you know his name?" Tori asked despite the eerie feeling she already knew the answer.

"Dreyer. John Dreyer."

Chapter 5

Tori pulled Dixie's door shut and ventured into the sitting area of their pricey suite, the helplessness she'd felt while comforting her nemesis-turned-friend finally taking its toll.

"How is she?" Margaret Louise asked, patting the vacant yet narrow cushion beside her own wide frame.

Accepting the invitation, Tori sank onto the cozy sofa and released the breath she'd been holding for entirely too long. "I wasn't sure it was ever going to happen, but she finally fell asleep."

Debbie *tsk*ed softly under her breath. "We hated hearing her cry the way she was. Somehow crying and Dixie don't go together very well."

Tori rested her head against the sofa back and closed her eyes. "No. They don't."

"Victoria, why don't you head on into bed now yourself?" Debbie reached across the end table that separated her chair from the sofa and patted Tori's shoulder. "You must be exhausted after being up all night with Dixie."

She forced her eyes open, shaking her head as she did. "No, I'll be fine. Our show is going to air in"—she peeked at her watch through the sleepy haze—"ten minutes. I don't want to miss that."

"It's a shame Dixie will miss it." Beatrice worried her bottom lip between her teeth.

"Melissa is tapin' it at home so Dixie can watch it then," Margaret Louise offered. "When she's feelin' better."

"Think we'll ever see her smile again the way she did over that breakfast table yesterday morning?"

"I sure hope so, Beatrice." Margaret Louise lifted the remote control from the coffee table and aimed it at the flat screen television on the other side of the room. "But I'll tell you what. This whole thing shores up what my daddy used to say."

Rose shuffled through the bathroom door. "What's that?"

"One day you're drinkin' wine, the next day you're pickin' grapes."

Leona, who'd remained silent to that point, shifted on the love seat that sat at an angle to the sofa. "What's that one you always say about owning up to your mistakes sooner rather than later?"

"The easiest way to eat crow is while it's still warm, 'cause the colder it gets, the harder it is to swallow? Is that the one, Twin?"

Leona nodded. "That's one you need to share with Dixie when she wakes up."

All eyes turned toward Margaret Louise's flawlessly dressed sister. Rose was the first to speak. "Why on earth does Dixie need to hear that?"

"Because she needs to realize that whoever pushed John off that balcony did her a favor."

Debbie's gasp mingled with Beatrice's. "Leona!"

"Oh, here we go again—the matches are being readied." Then, before anyone could ask what she meant, Leona continued, her voice a study in boredom. "Go ahead. Burn me at the stake. What else is new?"

Tori held off the torrent of anger from her fellow sewing sisters with the palm of her hand and addressed Leona. "Did you not hear Dixie sobbing all night?"

Leona brought her own hand toward her face

for a quick inspection of her nails. "How could I not?"

"Did you not see how beautiful her smile was yesterday as she sat across from that man over breakfast?"

Slowly, Leona lowered her hand, bringing her gaze to rest squarely on Tori's. "You know I did, dear."

"Then how can you sit there and say what she's going through is for the best? And imply, in a not-so-disguised way, that she had it coming to her?" She heard the anger in her voice, yet had no desire to try and soften it. Leona was out of line. "Dixie is devastated."

"That's because she doesn't know the whole story yet and she thinks she's truly heartbroken. But she's not. Not in the way she would have been if John had been able to continue down his all-too-familiar path."

"Familiar path?" Beatrice echoed.

Leona's gaze shifted to the nanny, but her words, her tone, made it obvious she was addressing them all. "The one that had him *using* Dixie while making her think she meant something."

Rose pointed a bony finger at Leona. "When will you realize you're not the only woman capable of being admired by a man?"

"You think that's what this is about, you old goat?"

"I *know* that's what this is about. It's all

anything is ever about where you're concerned, Leona Elkin." Rose lowered herself onto the couch and pulled the flaps of her sweater more closely against her body. "You can't handle the fact that someone who once found you attractive found Dixie to be attractive, too."

"Heck, I reckon he even found parts of me, and Beatrice, and you attractive, too, Rose, now didn't he?" Margaret Louise puffed her chest out with pride then returned her focus to the television and the channel she'd just located. "It's time for all y'all to hush now. *Taped with Melly and Kenneth* is 'bout to start!"

For a moment, Tori wasn't entirely sure the promise of watching their segment on a nationally syndicated talk show was enough to call a cease-fire in the ongoing war of glares between Rose and Leona, but eventually it was, Leona's eye roll and Rose's answering snort serving as the parting shot from both sides. Yet even as they reluctantly turned toward the television, Tori couldn't help but spend a few extra moments picking through Leona's words and comparing them to those of John's downstairs neighbor.

"Today on *Taped with Melly and Kenneth*, we'll be looking for and finding love in all the right places—in your kitchen, on your next date, with the help of a blockbuster book, and even down south, where the love between friends knows no bounds."

Margaret Louise clapped her hands together, nearly drowning out Debbie and Beatrice's collective squeal. "You hear that? That down south part? I bet they're talkin' 'bout us!"

"You really think so, Margaret Louise? Because from where I'm sitting, I see lots of boundaries in our group," Leona snipped. "And they're always stacked at *my* feet."

"Do us a favor then and trip on them, will you?" Then before anyone could speak, Rose pointed at the television as the camera panned in to reveal the show's hosts seated behind their opening segment table. "Here we go . . ."

Twenty minutes later, after much chitchat and crazy antics, the hosts turned to the interview portion of their show. "Kenneth and I are delighted to have Gavin Rollins on the show today to talk about his blockbuster sensation, *Finding Love After Sixty-Five*. C'mon out here, Gavin!"

"Now wait just a cotton-pickin' moment," Margaret Louise said. "That fella' came *after* us yesterday."

Leona rolled her eyes skyward. "And they put him before us today. That's why it's *taped*, Margaret Louise. So they can make changes and edit before it's put on the air." Then, lifting Paris onto her lap, she addressed her furry bunny with a second dose of boredom. "Is it any wonder why *I'm* the one who has her own cable television program debuting in the fall?"

"Shut your pie hole, Twin."

"I couldn't have said it better myself, Margaret Louise." Rose shot a defiant look in Leona's direction, then returned her focus to the screen in time to see Gavin Rollins appear in the guest chair to Melly's right. "Now listen up, everyone."

They leaned forward in their respective chairs, their attention riveted on the screen as the man they'd chatted with over sandwiches and fruit salad in the studio's Green Room prior to the show took his turn in front of the camera.

"Welcome to the show, Gavin." Melly picked the man's book off her lap and held it up. "I have to say, Gavin, you make the prospect of finding love after sixty-five sound both scary and possible."

"And that's because it's both." Gavin settled into his high-back stool, unbuttoning his suit coat as he did. "But my book, *Finding Love After Sixty-Five*, can show you how to avoid the first in order to achieve the second."

Kenneth puffed out his expansive linebacker chest and leaned forward. "I have to tell you, Gavin, if someone took advantage of my mother's vulnerabilities the way you speak of in your book, I'd be locked up."

Melly's eyes widened. "I know, right?" Then, turning to the guest, she indicated the book once again. "We'd be naïve if we didn't realize there are scam artists in this world. They come out of the woodwork when there's a national disaster or tragedy in the hope they can prosper off others' misery. But to scam an elderly woman who's looking for love? It just blows my mind."

"They're out there," Gavin said, nodding, his emerald green eyes looking out at the audience. "And what makes them particularly dangerous is that it's a rare occasion to find one of their victims who will speak up."

Kenneth raked a hand down his face. "I read that in your book and it made me mad all over again. I mean, what would a seventy- or eighty-something have to be embarrassed about in that situation? They weren't the louse."

"We're all just kids at heart, that's why," Melly mused. "Who wants to admit they were duped at the prom? Or stood up at the altar? It's humiliating." Then with a sideways glance at her co-host, she took a moment to bring the point home for their viewers. "Were you ever duped in love, Kenneth?"

"I plead the Fifth."

Melly gestured toward the guest. "Which backs up your point, doesn't it, Gavin?"

"It does, indeed. But as my mother always said, to be forewarned is to be forearmed. I don't want to see anyone's heart broken by con artists. It's part of the reason I wrote this book in the first place."

"And the other part?" Melly prompted.

"To give people hope for life's next chapter. A chapter that doesn't have to be lived alone."

Tori glanced around the room at her friends, three of the five women present falling into Gavin Rollins's target demographic. And sure enough, each one of them sported a version of the same look—hope.

On Margaret Louise's face, that hope was for someone else, like Rose or Georgina. After all, *her* life as a long-widowed woman with a grown son and eight beloved grandchildren was full enough.

On Rose's face, the hope took on an almost wistful quality. As if being in her mid-eighties put any chance of finding a mate just out of reach.

And on Leona, the hope was clothed in longstanding confidence. Leona knew there was romance after sixty-five. And in her world, it was more a given than a hope.

Tori closed her eyes against the image of Dixie that came next—the hope her friend had worn prior to the news of John's death making her heart ache. It was as if she'd witnessed firsthand the obliteration of Dixie's hope and joy.

She swallowed once, twice, then forced her eyes to open, to focus on the television screen as Melly asked viewers to stay with them as they went to commercial, the promise of a "friendship tale like no other" upping the excitement in the room in short order.

"We're next!" Margaret Louise linked hands with Beatrice and Debbie and smiled triumphantly. "We're next! Can you believe it?"

Sure enough, after a handful of commercials, Melly and Kenneth appeared on the screen once again, with Melly's voice coming from the speakers on either side.

"My name is Margaret Louise Davis and I'm writing to you from Sweet Briar, South Carolina. When people think of friends, they picture folks of the same age—jogging together, going to movies together, and talking on the phone for hours. But when I think of my friends—my best friends—I see something very different. Some of us have been married and widowed, some of us are retired and looking for hobbies to keep us busy, some of us work full-time while juggling motherhood, and some of us are really just starting out, choosing paths the rest of us traveled a lifetime ago. We shouldn't work as friends, but we do. And it all started with a sewing needle—a sewing needle we each picked up for very different reasons."

Then, one by one, Melly and Kenneth introduced them to the audience—the sound of applause holding steady as Tori, Margaret Louise, and the rest of the gang made their way onto the stage. The questions they were each asked and the answers they each gave were exactly the way Tori remembered them from the day before, yet somehow, watching the interview as a spectator rather than a participant made it all the more poignant.

There, in front of her face, were some of the most important people in her life. People who had opened their arms to her at a time she needed it most. People she'd known only a little over two years, yet felt as if she'd known a lifetime.

There was Margaret Louise, her trusted confidante and sidekick . . .

There was Debbie, the kindhearted entrepreneur and mother of two who unknowingly made Tori strive to be better—a better librarian, a better fiancée, a better friend . . .

There was Beatrice, her quiet friend who reminded her that listening was every bit as important as talking . . .

There was Rose, who touched her heart in a way it hadn't been touched since her great-grandmother had been alive . . .

There was Leona, who kept her on her toes and made her laugh even when that wasn't the intention . . .

And there was Dixie, the woman who'd singlehandedly taught her that blue skies were behind every dark cloud . . .

Dixie.

She blinked against the same tears she saw misting in more than a few pairs of eyes in the room and willed herself instead to enjoy the experience of watching her friends and herself on the television screen, silliness and all.

"For that—and for the steadfast loyalty of each and every one of these women seated here beside me—I am truly blessed."

One by one, each head on the screen bobbed in the aftermath of Dixie's words. And like clockwork, each head present in the living room of their hotel suite bobbed as well.

They were blessed.

Each and every one of them.

As their segment faded to black amid a smattering of live sniffles, Leona cleared her throat, scooted to the edge of her chair, and stood. "I'll be right back. I just want to check on Dixie and make sure she's doing okay."

Chapter 6

Under any other circumstances, Tori would have jumped at the opportunity to rib Leona for the creases that managed to push their way through the artful handiwork of the most sought after dermatologist in all of South Carolina. But considering the likely reason for those creases, Tori opted to pass on her one and only prospect for a little verbal payback in favor of nailing down an answer she'd been craving all afternoon.

"How is she?" Tori blurted out as she stepped through the door of the hotel suite with an armload of bags and Rose's forearm tucked securely inside her own.

Margaret Louise followed closely behind, flanked on either side by Debbie and Beatrice. "She been eatin'?"

"She hasn't moved since you left." Slowly, Leona pushed off the sofa with Paris in her arms, the creases across her forehead and around her eyes deepening even more. "In fact, she was so still for so long I actually went all the way into her room and rested my hand on her back to make sure she was still breathing."

Debbie set her own menagerie of colorful shopping bags on the entryway table and held a piece of carrot stick from their lunch in Paris's direction. "The body has a way of shutting down when it becomes overwhelmed. Sleep is important right now. It'll help her deal with all of this a little easier when she finally wakes."

Leona's slender shoulders rose and fell in a rare shrug, her stance and overall demeanor in keeping with the unfamiliar wrinkles that made her look far closer to her sixty-five years than ever before. "I suppose." She gestured toward the bags on the table, the bags in Tori's hand, and the sliver of Kenny's plastic head bobbing just above the opening of Beatrice's purse. "Where did you go? What did you do?"

Margaret Louise dropped onto the nearest chair and hoisted her left foot onto her knee, her pudgy hands making short work of the buckle that stood between her sandaled feet and a much-needed massage. "Why, I think I just walked more 'n the last three hours than I have in my entire life."

"You could stand to do a little more of that at home, too. It would be good for your"—Leona let her gaze drop slowly down her sister's pleasantly plump frame—"*heart.*"

"I ain't sure how pantin' can be good for my heart, Twin, but I'll keep it in mind." With her left hand kneading away at the bottom of her foot, Margaret Louise gestured toward Beatrice with the other. "We sure got a lot of pictures to show Melissa and Georgina when we get back home. Sightseein' ones, fancy people ones, and some you just have to see to believe—like the one with the man who had pink hair, purple shoes, lime green pants, and earlobes that were clear down to his chin! You want to see?"

"I think I'll pass." Leona wiped the underside of Paris's mouth with a crisp white handkerchief then set it on the table beside Debbie's bags. "What did you buy?"

Debbie looked down at her bags, fingering each one as she ticked off her purchases. "A T-shirt for Jackson, a necklace for Susannah, and a really nice signing pen for Colby."

"And for yourself?"

Debbie waved her hands side to side, pulling her head back as she did. "Nothing. Things here are far too expensive. Anything I really need I can get in Sweet Briar."

"But they won't be from New York."

"That's okay, Leona. Sweet Briar is fine with me."

Leona rolled her eyes then turned to Tori. "Let me guess. You bought something for Milo, right?"

"I tried to, but I haven't found just the right thing yet." She pointed to the bags on her arm. "These are actually Rose's."

Leona's left brow arched upward at Rose. "Oh? I didn't know Bengay came in a soft pink shopping bag. Or is that to carry the slippers you usually wear morning, noon, and night?"

"No. It's for the duct tape I purchased for your always-flapping mouth," Rose quipped. "But now that I'm standing here, looking at you, I realize I should have gone with the extra-wide size."

Tori laughed despite her best efforts, her desire to remain neutral during Rose and Leona's show-downs not always easy to fulfill. Especially when Rose was a master at the comical comebacks.

Leona's gaped mouth shut just long enough to twist in anger at Tori. "You find this nasty old goat to be funny, dear?"

"I can't speak for Victoria, Twin, but I sure as

shootin' found it funny." Margaret Louise turned to first Debbie and then Beatrice, their smartly placed hands a poor disguise for their own reactions. "Yes siree, it's just as I 'spected. *Everyone* thinks Rose made a funny."

Leona's foot came down hard on the carpeted floor. "I can't win with all of you, can I? I stay behind to look after Dixie while you all go off gallivanting, and *this* is how I'm treated upon your return?"

Four heads slowly lowered in shame, Rose's following suit with the help of Tori's gentle hand.

Leona, seeing an opportunity to ride the martyr train a little longer, continued on, the wounded tone to her voice akin to the smack of a rolled newspaper on their noses. "Of everyone here, *I'm* the one who needed this trip to New York City. I'm far too cultured and intelligent for life in Sweet Briar. But I gave that all up to be closer to you, Margaret Louise. And even though my mind is wasting away in that one-horse open town, I stay as my gift to you, Victoria."

"Your gift?" Tori echoed during a fast upward glance.

"Of course. If it weren't for me, you'd still be plucking your eyebrows by hand and missing more than seventy percent of those stray hairs."

Debbie's shoulders began to shake, bringing Leona's full attention in her direction. "And you, Debbie Calhoun? If it weren't for my being in

Sweet Briar, all those handsome reporters who come to town to interview your husband wouldn't ask to come back with each new book release."

Beatrice stepped in closer to Rose, cowering unnoticed under Leona's reproachful stare. "And Rose? You'd be drooling away in some rest home, the victim of an unchallenged mind. Because *I* keep you sharp. My intelligence keeps you sharp."

Rose's response was unintelligible behind Tori's hand, and for that, Tori was glad. The last thing they needed was for Dixie to wake to their battle sounds. She said as much to Leona and Rose, their grudging agreement quickly drowned out by a hard knocking sound just over their shoulders.

"Did you order room service, Twin?" Margaret Louise asked.

Leona shook her head then pushed her way to the door, smoothing her hands down her form-fitting skirt as she did. "No. But I'm not usually the one who summons men. They just flock to me all on their own."

Wrapping her bejeweled hand around the doorknob, Leona yanked it open, a smug smile stretching her lips wide. "Mmmm," she fairly purred as her lashes began to bat. "See? They flock."

Five heads craned around and over Leona's shoulder to take in the handsome, well-built, uniformed police officer eyeing them from the hallway. One by one he took in each of their faces, his thoughts—save for the momentary appreciation shown Leona—unreadable.

Finally, he spoke, his gaze coming to rest once again on Leona. "Are you Dixie Dunn?"

Leona's shoulders slumped along with her jaw, Rose's laugh igniting the indignant sputtering that followed. "Of—of course I'm not *Dixie Dunn*. I have class . . . I have standards . . . I have—"

The man held his badge up for all to see. "I'm Detective Jay Pollop of the NYPD. I'm here to speak with Dixie Dunn."

Tori gently pushed her way past a still-sputtering Leona and held out her hand. "I'm Victoria Sinclair, Dixie's friend. Can I ask what this is about? Dixie is sleeping."

"It's in regards to the murder of John Dreyer. Wake her."

Chapter 7

"If you don't quit all that pacin' back 'n forth, Victoria, you're gonna wear a hole in that fancy carpet." Margaret Louise patted the empty chair to her left. "And I for one don't have the money to replace a rug that's probably worth more 'n my car."

Tori turned around and made yet another pass in front of the still-closed door that separated them from the conversation between their friend and Detective Pollop, then sank onto the chair with a sigh. "I think one of us should have gone in there with him and held her hand while he fills her in on John's death. She's been through enough already."

"She didn't want us in there, Victoria, remember?" Rose's arthritic hand, calmed by the movement of her sewing needle, worked on the sample for their flower pin project. "She'll be all right. Dixie has rebounded from worse in her lifetime. She'll mourn, of course, but the fact remains she spent just one morning with the man."

"I still can't get over the fact he was really murdered," Debbie mused over a late afternoon cup of coffee. "I'm shocked."

"I'm not." All eyes turned in Leona's direction, the woman's pallor still reflective of the trauma of being mistaken for a woman nearly ten years her senior. "Frankly, it was only a matter of time, if you ask me."

"Why?" It was a question Tori had wanted to ask since they'd set off to find John after their taping at the studio the day before, but she'd refrained when the discovery of his body moved Dixie to the forefront of her concerns. "What was so awful about this guy that you'd actually say something like that out loud?"

Leona looked down at the man's nose-twitching namesake then leaned the back of her head against the sofa. "The first time I saw John was in a bookstore coffee shop."

"Was it that lovely little one closest to the Eiffel Tower?" Beatrice asked as she set down the novel she'd been reading in order to listen more closely.

A pregnant pause was soon followed by a shifting of Leona's legs. "Um . . . not that one, no."

"But you met him in Paris, right?"

Leona pinned the British girl with a death stare then continued with her story. "What caught my eye about John was how enthralled he was by his companion."

"With *you* in the room, Twin?" Margaret Louise teased. "How is that possible?"

Turning to Tori, Leona made a face. "Do you want to hear my answer about John or don't you?"

"Yes I do." Then to Margaret Louise, Tori said, "Please. Can we let Leona speak?"

Satisfied, Leona took center stage once again. "There he was, sitting across the table from this older woman who obviously wasn't in the habit of being in the company of a male."

"Why do you say that?" Rose asked.

"She was awkward, for starters."

"Okay . . ."

Leona's gaze swung back to Tori. "And she

fidgeted constantly. Like a middle school girl talking to a boy for the first time. Only this particular boy was handsome. *Extremely* handsome."

Rose, Margaret Louise, and Beatrice exchanged looks, their heads nodding in unison amid dreamy thoughts of the man's eyes and facial structure.

"He had this day-old stubble on his face that day that made knees weaken around him." Leona looked down at Paris and blew her a kiss. "That's why, when I saw my precious baby for the first time, I instantly thought of John, even though I couldn't recall his name at the time. His whiskers and his eyes were enough to transport me back to . . ."

"Paris!" Beatrice aided.

Again, Leona pinned the nanny with a stare before moving on with her story. "The next day, I went back to that same store to purchase a book I decided I wanted to try. He was there. Again. With the same enthralled look on his face."

"I s'pose he must have liked her fidgetin', huh?"

"You might think that," Leona countered her sister's comment, "if the woman seated across from him was the same woman. But it wasn't."

Tori blinked once, twice, her mind working to absorb everything Leona was saying.

"It was the same thing again on the third day.

Same enthralled look aimed at yet another older, obviously infatuated woman." Leona set Paris on the floor and watched as she hopped over to Debbie's feet, the memory of the earlier carrot still alive and well in the rabbit's thoughts. "That's when I knew he was a gamer. A well-groomed, clearly well-off gamer. The young man behind the counter simply filled in the blanks when I asked."

"What blanks?" Tori asked.

"The fact that John's clothes and expensive car were *because* of the women he chose. Single women who wanted companionship badly enough they were blind to the ways of a real live —albeit attractive—con artist like John Dreyer."

"But—but he was so well read," Rose wailed. "He knew all the classics and could speak intelligently about them!"

"And he knew about the kind of places I've always wanted to visit," Beatrice added glumly.

Margaret Louise slumped in her spot. "He knew his way around a kitchen better than any man I've ever known."

Leona's left brow rose, followed seconds later by her right. "And if you'd said you were into skydiving, he'd have told you about all his many encounters with that, too." Then, dumbing her voice down to a pitch and pace in keeping with a preschool teacher, Leona continued, "That's what a con artist does. He cons you into thinking he's something he's not, luring you in until you believe he's something special and start showering him with gifts in order to keep such a wonderful man."

"But Dixie isn't wealthy. She needs every cent of her social security check to make ends meet." Tori looked to Rose for confirmation, her elderly friend's head nodding almost immediately.

Leona pushed off her chair and wandered around the room, stopping briefly outside Dixie's door before continuing her aimless path. "That's the part that doesn't make sense."

"Maybe the bloke changed since you saw him in Paris, Leona. Maybe he's no longer a wanker."

Tori began to nod along with Beatrice's supposition, but stopped as a very different conversation drifted through her thoughts . . .

"I know I shouldn't be surprised. It was only a matter of time before one of those women wised up to his ways and exacted revenge."

"Well, could it be possible, Leona?" Debbie posed. "Could he have changed?"

Leona opened her mouth to answer, but it was Tori who actually spoke. "From what I was told by his neighbor at the crime scene, it doesn't sound like it. In fact, this woman seemed to not only know about his ways, but pointed to them as a reason for his fall."

"If that nice policeman is callin' it murder, then it was a *push,* Victoria."

"And it probably was. Behavior like that has a way of catching up with you eventually." Leona stopped halfway through her third lap around the room, bent delicately at the waist, and retrieved Paris from the floor. "But louse or not, John was still the visual inspiration by which I named this precious little girl."

"You thought she was a boy when you named her, Twin."

"Does it matter?" Leona hissed at her sister. "It was still my inspiration. How can I sit idly by while his killer is on the loose?"

Margaret Louise linked her arms across her ample chest and laughed. "Then you best get crackin', Twin. The limousine will be here tomorrow afternoon 'round two o'clock to collect us and get us back to the air—"

A click on the far side of the room brought Leona's hand to her hair and an order for quiet from her lips. "He's coming!"

"He?" Debbie echoed just as Detective Pollop emerged with an ashen-faced Dixie.

Tori leapt to her feet. "Dixie, are you . . ." The words trailed from her mouth as a flash of silver caught her gaze and pulled it from Dixie's pasty white complexion to her handcuffed hands.

"Wait! What are you doing?"

The detective led Dixie through the sitting area and over to the door, his gait slowing long enough to answer Tori's question. "Your friend has been arrested for the murder of John Dreyer."

Gasps rang up around the room, igniting a torrent of tears from Dixie in response. Neither was loud enough, though, to abate the sudden roar of fear and rage in Tori's ears. "You're arresting *Dixie?* For *murder?*"

"I'm taking her downtown for processing." Detective Pollop opened the door, ushered Dixie into the hall, then looked back over his shoulder with a solemn expression. "You might want to hire your friend an attorney. She's going to need one."

Chapter 8

Tori was exhausted by the time she let herself into the still-lit hotel suite at nearly ten o'clock that night, the stress of the police station and the depression over her friend's plight leaving her stranded in utter helplessness.

"Oh, thank God you're here," Rose said as she shuffled her way to the door with a speed that hadn't been seen in years. "Where is Dixie? Is she okay?"

They were the questions Tori had been dreading hearing since she stepped out of the station with the cold hard answers in tow. To leave one brokenhearted and terrified friend, only to be the one who set off those same helpless emotions in the five women now staring at her, waiting, was more than a little difficult.

"She's—" Tori stopped, swallowed, and began again. "Dixie is still in jail. And she'll remain there until her arraignment in the morning."

"Her *arraignment?*" Debbie whispered amid the gasps of their friends. "You can't be serious."

Tori's sigh was long yet depleted as she slumped against the closest wall. "I'm afraid I am."

"But how on God's green earth can they possibly think our Dixie was involved?" Margaret Louise challenged.

"Not involved . . . *responsible.*"

"But this is *Dixie* we're speaking of."

Leona rolled her eyes in Beatrice's general direction. "We all know good and well that Dixie can get mighty nasty when things don't go her way. Just look at the way she treated Victoria when she came to Sweet Briar."

Five mouths gaped wide with Tori being the first to recover well enough to speak. "She may have made nasty comments and shot some evil death glares in my direction, Leona, but that doesn't make her any more capable of murder than the rest of us and you know that!"

Leona took three steps backward and lowered herself to the edge of the nearest armchair. "I wasn't saying she was capable of murder. I was just putting the halo Beatrice was trying to put on Dixie's head in perspective."

Rose was the next to recover. "I can't figure you out, Leona Elkin. Just this morning you volunteered to stay behind and look after Dixie. Now she's behind bars and you're upset that Beatrice believes in Dixie's innocence?" Then, before Leona could respond, Rose lowered her voice to a well-defined hiss. "Just do us all a favor and shut up. *Please.*"

"What can you tell us?" Debbie said, pulling everyone's focus back to Tori. "They can't possibly think she's capable of murder just because she had breakfast with him earlier that day, can they? I mean, she was so happy. So was he. And Dixie was here . . . in the room . . . with Beatrice, Rose, and me when he was pushed."

"That's right! She was!" Rose clapped her trembling hands together. "There's no way she could have been responsible. She had an alibi!'

Beatrice nodded emphatically, pointing at the couch as she did. "We sat right there and talked about her breakfast with John right up until the moment she, um . . ."

Debbie closed her eyes and gave voice to the part of the story Beatrice found herself unable to utter aloud. "Left to have her hair done by a woman she didn't know."

"Who told her she was flying out first thing this morning to take a hair-styling job onboard a Mediterranean cruise line for the next six months," Rose supplied sadly.

Tori spoke around the lump creeping up her throat. "That unverified gap in time, plus the fact that she slept away the effects of her appointment upon news of John's death, will be Dixie's first stumbling block at the arraignment."

Margaret Louise shifted her weight more evenly across her legs. "You mean she's got more than one?"

This was the part of the conversation Tori had been dreading. Somehow, even knowing she was merely serving as the messenger, she couldn't help but feel as if she was also the one holding the hammer above the final nail in Dixie's proverbial coffin. But she had to tell. Dixie needed all the support she could get.

"When that detective went into Dixie's room, she gave him permission to look through her things." She closed her eyes against the regret she shouldered for not insisting she be part of their talk, and filled in the rest of the blanks. "He found something. Something that apparently links her to the crime scene."

"Look, I'm sorry, but I don't care if Dixie was on the street where he died." Debbie's face took on a never-before-seen aura of disgust that prompted Rose to nod along. "That doesn't mean anything."

"But the missing piece of a torn scarf does. At least as far as the police are concerned."

"What are you talkin' 'bout, Victoria?"

She pushed off the wall and made her way over to the couch, where Margaret Louise had sought refuge from legs that had grown noticeably weak. "From what I was able to gather, the police found a torn scarf near the balcony of John's apartment. The other half was found in Dixie's handbag."

More than anything, Tori wanted one of her friends to jump up, to offer a counterpoint explanation as to why the scarf had been found in Dixie's purse. But just as an alternate reason had eluded her in the police station, so, too, did it elude Debbie . . . and Rose . . . and Margaret Louise . . . and Beatrice.

Tori swallowed. Hard.

She'd known all along they'd be as stunned as she'd been. But still, she'd held out hope. Hope that one of them would say something that could rid her heart of the suffocating reality that had her bracing for the worst.

Dixie was in trouble.

Big trouble.

"Why are you all looking like that?" Leona finally said, the bewilderment in her voice little match for the bewilderment—and raw disgust— she wore across every facet of her face.

Rose was the first to speak, anger lacing each and every word. "Because we're worried for our friend? Is that so hard for you to understand?"

Leona matched Rose's ending sneer with one

of her own. "I get the worry. This is going to be a battle. But it's a battle we're going to win."

"D-did you hear what Victoria just told us, Leona?" Debbie sputtered.

"Of course I heard her. I'm not deaf. But I also know every single one of you watches *FBI Manhunt* every Thursday night at eight o'clock."

Tori slowly raised her gaze to meet Leona's. "Do you have a point, Leona?"

"What did Dixie say about the scarf?"

"She couldn't explain it." Mentally, Tori revisited the moment she asked Dixie about the torn fabric, the former librarian's wide-eyed fear rivaled only by unmistakable confusion.

"Of course she couldn't," Leona said.

"Would you quit talkin' in circles, Twin? You're only makin' things worse."

Leona looked from Tori to her sister and back again, before widening her gaze to include Debbie, Rose, and Beatrice, as well. "Dixie can't explain the torn scarf because she didn't put it there."

And just like that, Leona singlehandedly removed the hammer and nail from Tori's hand. "It was planted on her," Tori whispered.

Slowly, dramatically, Leona rested her hands in her lap. "Exactly. Which means it's *our* job to figure out who did the planting and why."

"But why would someone do that?" Debbie protested through the sudden silence.

Keeping her focus locked on Leona, Tori gave the answer she should have come to on her own while sitting across a table from Dixie at the police station. "To draw attention away from the real killer."

Leaning forward across her lap, Rose buried her face inside frail hands while Beatrice stared off in the distance.

"How is Dixie holding up?"

Rose let her hands slip back to her lap as she, along with everyone else, waited for Tori's answer.

"She's terrified, Debbie. Absolutely terri—"

A strangled sob cut Tori off mid-word. "This is all my fault! I stuck my nose where it didn't belong and now Dixie feels like a rubber-nosed woodpecker in a petrified forest!"

Tori blinked once, twice. "Margaret Louise?"

"It was my idea to get her datin' again. She tried to argue, tried to tell me she was doin' just fine with her volunteerin', but I was sure she was wrong. I was sure she needed a friend to help her with that smile she's lost little by little over the years. And now I wiped it clear off her face once and for all thanks to my meddlin'."

Rose peered down at her lap. "You didn't meddle alone. I was right there, dirtying up the waters, too."

"Me three," Beatrice said sadly.

"But it was my idea to get her lookin' at that

datin' site," Margaret Louise said. "And it was my idea to make her look like she knew somethin' 'bout cookin' besides pourin' soup in a pot and openin' a sleeve of crackers."

"And it was my idea to help her sound more intelligent since she was spending much too much time blushing the few times they *did* actually interact online," Rose chimed in. "I should have just minded my own business and let Dixie show her true colors when she was ready to show them."

"I don't know why I thought I could be more charming than Dixie," Beatrice wailed.

"Because *I* said you were." Margaret Louise exhaled a rush of air from between her thinning lips. "Don't you blame yourself for this mess, Beatrice. You were just tryin' to help me on *my* quest for Dixie's true happiness."

It was Leona who finally cut through the parade of self-recriminations coming from her sister's mouth. "I don't care if you made Dixie sound like the Queen of England, Margaret Louise. None of you were sitting at that breakfast table yesterday morning. None of you were on the receiving end of John's smile."

"But you said yourself he was a con artist," Debbie reminded.

"A con artist when there was something to gain from the con."

Tori held off any further comments with her hand. "What are you saying, Leona?"

"I don't care how Rose or Beatrice or my sister polished up Dixie's image. She was still wearing a floral housecoat when she met John. And we all know that Dixie can't get through a conversation without relaying how she got ousted from her job at the library to make room for Victoria."

"So?"

Leona pinned first her sister and then Tori with a pointed look. "It doesn't take a rocket scientist to know librarians don't make a lot of money. Retired librarians make even less."

"Your point, Leona?" Rose demanded in a bored voice.

"Dixie said John wanted to see her again, right?"

As heads nodded to her left and right, Leona continued, "That says to me that, despite all lack of reason, John was actually interested in Dixie. The Dixie who showed up across the table from him at breakfast and remained with him for more than an hour and a half."

Tori considered calling Leona on the backhanded slap volleyed in Dixie's direction, but let it go. After all, it was shared for the sole purpose of freeing Margaret Louise, Rose, and Beatrice from guilt's paralyzing effects.

At any other time and any other place, she might have considered pulling Leona aside and commending her for her selflessness. But now was not the time.

All that mattered was getting all six of them on the same page where Dixie was concerned.

"Someone set Dixie up for this murder," Leona fairly purred. "Someone with an axe to grind where John was concerned. Our singular focus needs to be on finding that person."

"I couldn't agree more." Feeling her energy begin to rebound alongside the first glimmer of hope in hours, Tori stood and turned to face her friends. "We all need to put on our thinking caps and come up with some ideas as to who that person might be."

Debbie took the ball and ran. "The easy guess would be one of the women this guy has bilked over recent weeks."

"Revenge is always a good motive," Tori said by way of agreement.

"But so is money, is it not?"

Tori took in Beatrice's words along with everyone else. "It is. But in the case of the women he bilks, I think they'd seek revenge *because* of the money."

"But surely some of the women this bloke has taken up with have children of their own."

"I'm not following you."

"Think of the Queen. When she passes, the throne will be left to her successor—Prince Charles, will it not?"

"Assuming he's still of sound mind," Tori said.

"And if an elderly woman has a fair amount of money, it is quite likely it will go to her heirs, yes?"

"Yes but . . ." The words petered from her lips as the meaning behind Beatrice's took root. "Wait. You're right. Behind a duped and heartbroken woman can be a whole army of protective soldiers. Children, siblings, neighbors, et cetera."

"Children, siblings, and even neighbors who may have been counting on a monetary inheritance that no longer exists because of John Dreyer and his con artist ways."

Tori stared at Beatrice as the young woman's words settled in her thoughts, Leona's head bobbing in her peripheral vision.

"The church mouse does indeed pay attention, doesn't she?" Leona drawled.

Ignoring Leona's latest barb, Rose lifted her hands upward in exasperation. "How on earth are we going to figure out who this man was seeing when he's lying on a slab with a name tag wrapped around his big toe?"

Tori lifted her wrist to the light and noted the late hour. "First, we get a good night's sleep. Then, starting first thing tomorrow morning, we start turning over rocks—big rocks, little rocks, and everything in between. The key to Dixie's freedom is out there somewhere and it's up to the six of us to find it. Fast."

Chapter 9

"You have to eat, Victoria." Rose halted her French toast–laden fork inches from her mouth. "You have to keep up your strength."

She knew Rose was right, knew Dixie was counting on her and everyone else assembled around the table to find the truth, but it was hard. They were in a strange city, far from home, with a mammoth-sized problem to solve and little to no idea of where exactly to start.

"The folks at XYZ Studios were most accommodatin' when I called this mornin' to tell 'em we'd be stayin' on a few days." Margaret Louise chased her ham and cheese omelet around her plate with her fork, smiling triumphantly as she delivered it to her mouth. "In fact, would you believe Melly actually called back herself and said they'd pick up the tab for the hotel for the rest of the week?"

Beatrice looked up from her tea. "They will?"

"Seems that little thing was so taken by our friendship that she wants to make it easier for us to help Dixie." Margaret Louise laid down her fork, pointed at Tori's largely uneaten breakfast, then swapped plates at the nod of agreement she sought. "Course they might want to send that sweet camera fella with us when we actually get to springin' Dixie."

She bit her lip to keep from correcting Margaret Louise's use of the word *when*. Semantics weren't necessary at this stage of the game. Especially when the insertion of *if* could have damaging effects on morale.

"Are they picking up the tab for this meal?" Rose pointed her fork around the same breakfast restaurant they'd spied through the branches of a potted plant forty-eight hours earlier. "Because I *do* have to eat once we get back home to Sweet Briar."

Debbie waved away the elderly woman's concern. "This is Colby's treat."

Beatrice and Rose sighed in unison then joined in the chorus of appreciation that spread around the table with as much enthusiasm as they could muster in light of Dixie's plight.

"Oh, oh . . . there he is!" Margaret Louise pushed Tori's plate off to the side and pointed at the tall, dark-haired waiter they'd been hoping to see since arriving nearly thirty minutes earlier. "Should I call him over?"

At Tori's nod, Margaret Louise's hand shot into the air. "Woo-hoo, young man, over here . . ."

Leona dropped her head into her hands in embarrassment as the waiter glanced in their direction, then hurried over. "Yes, ma'am? Would you like me to call your server?"

"No. You're the one we've been waitin' to see."

His brows rose. "Oh?"

Margaret Louise guided his attention toward Tori. "Go ahead, Victoria, ask him."

Sensing the waiter's confusion, Tori lifted her purse from the floor beside her chair and retrieved the printout of John's face that Margaret Louise had managed to score from the computer in the hotel lobby. Holding it out, she looked from the waiter to the picture and back again. "Do you remember this man? You waited on him at that table over there"—she pointed with her free hand to the table where Dixie had been smiling so beautifully just two days earlier—"with a friend of ours."

Instantly, the waiter's hands were splayed waist-high. "I don't want any trouble. I'm just a waiter, trying to work off my student loans."

"Please. I'm not looking for trouble—for you or for me. I just want to know if you remember him and whether you've seen him in here before. That's it." She heard the earnestness in her voice, saw the way it affected the waiter, who relaxed his shoulders and overall stance enough to warrant a second and more prolonged look at the picture in her hand.

"Uh, yeah. I sort of remember him. My female co-workers were all gushing about the way he looked at his breakfast companion."

Tori set the picture to the side of Margaret

Louise's empty plate and dug into her purse a second time. This time, when she produced a picture of Dixie, the waiter simply nodded. "Yeah, that's her."

"Ever see him before?"

Again he looked at the picture of John, the shake of his head coming fairly quickly. "Can't say that I have. Why? Is he in trouble for something?"

The tip of Beatrice's chin began to tremble as she leaned to her left to look at Dixie's snapshot. "No. But *she* is."

"I'm sorry to hear that. She was a nice lady. Very friendly and happy." Then stepping back from the table, he hooked his thumb in the direction of an impatient diner one section over. "I gotta go. Good luck with your friend."

And then he was gone, his relatively few answers useless in the grand scheme of things.

"What are we going to do?" Debbie asked. "We know nothing more than we did when we sat down."

Leona sipped her tea then set the cup back on its saucer. "While I can't begin to understand what it was about Dixie that possessed John to change his usual tactics, the fact remains that he did have a routine. One that, according to Dixie's original understanding, hasn't changed since I first saw him all those years ago."

"In Paris, right?"

Somehow, someway, Tori managed to divert Leona's stare from Beatrice back to the table at large. "What are you talking about, Leona?"

With all the drama of a leading lady, Leona lifted her napkin from her lap and folded it carefully beside her plate, the tangible weight of everyone's attention bringing a small smirk to the corners of her collagen-enhanced lips. "If you actually listened to me yesterday, you'll remember that it was at a bookstore café where I first saw John."

Tori leaned forward. "Go on."

"The same bookstore café where I continued to see him each day for the next several days . . ."

"You're wasting our time, Leona," Rose admonished. "Who cares where you saw John in *Paris?* We're in New York. Worried about *Dixie.*"

She let Leona's words filter through her head, the meaning behind them becoming crystal clear. "Wait. I get it. John started his con in the same place all the time—a place where the personnel knew him and were content staying mum about his antics."

Leona curtailed her glare at Rose long enough to nod at Tori.

"And if I remember correctly, John's original plan for meeting Dixie was at a—"

"Bookstore café!" Margaret Louise finished, wide-eyed. Then, turning to her sister, she smiled. "I'm not sure why you sat such a long time with your mouth open waitin' for a chicken to fly in, but at least it finally did."

The glare moved on to Margaret Louise. "Excuse me?"

"Why didn't you say somethin' sooner?"

"Would anyone have listened if I did?" Leona stepped into her well-worn martyr attire just long enough to send a few guilt-ridden eyes to the floor. "But don't worry, I'm used to it."

"Does anyone remember where that bookstore was?" Debbie asked, looking up once again. "Maybe that was his comfort spot here in New York."

When no one answered, Leona's smirk returned. "West Fifty-eighth Street."

"Do you think maybe someone there will be able to point us in the direction of the person who really did this?" Beatrice asked as Debbie signaled for the check. "The one who planted the torn scarf on Dixie?"

"We can hope." Tori folded the picture of John into fourths and returned it, along with Dixie's, back to her purse. "If nothing else, maybe we can start to figure out who some of John's other cons were."

Rose glanced at her watch then slowly back at Tori, the worry she held for Dixie aging her all the more. "There's something I don't understand about all of this."

"What's that, Rose?"

"You said that scarf was in Dixie's purse, right?"

At Tori's nod, Rose continued, the confusion in her voice doing double time across her weathered face. "Dixie was back from the hair salon before you returned with news of John's death."

She tried to follow Rose's train of thought, but it was hard. Her focus wasn't inside the Waldorf Astoria any longer. "I'm sorry, Rose, but I'm not following what you're saying . . ."

"I know Dixie was at the hair salon. I saw her hair before and after, and there's no question she had it done." Rose waited to continue until after the waitress assigned to their table had picked up Debbie's credit card and disappeared through the swinging doors at the back of the restaurant. "Then once you came back and told her, she never left her room until she was removed from it by that detective."

Since everything at that moment was simply a verification of facts they already knew, she nodded along with everyone else.

"Don't you see?" Rose uttered, clearly frustrated with Tori's lack of response. "It doesn't make any sense."

"What don't make sense, Rose?" Margaret Louise prompted.

"If that scarf was torn during the act of murder, how did it end up in Dixie's purse when she wasn't anywhere near that man's apartment?"

Tori stared at Rose as the woman's question

finally took hold. There was no plausible answer anywhere in sight. A quick glance at each of their friends yielded the same dumbstruck look she felt etched across her own face.

"I missed that." Beatrice turned to Tori and waited.

But like Beatrice, the timing of the scarf's placement inside Dixie's purse hadn't dawned on her, either.

Margaret Louise nudged her chin in Leona's direction then placed her hands on the table and lowered her normally boisterous voice the best she could. "My daddy used to have a sayin' that summed up situations like this in short order."

"What was that?" Tori asked.

"You 'member, Twin?"

Leona looked past her sister just long enough to bat her eyelashes at a handsome doorman in the hotel's famed lobby, her mouth curving upward in a seductive smile as he puffed out his well-built chest in response. "Daddy used to say all sorts of things."

"He'd say, 'If your cat had kittens in the doghouse, would that make 'em puppies?' " Margaret Louise shared. "That fits here, don't it?"

"I'm not sure," Tori said honestly. "How does that tie into the torn scarf?"

Acutely aware of the supposition she held, Margaret Louise leaned forward, gesturing for

Rose, Debbie, Beatrice, Leona, and Tori to follow suit. When they did, she got to the bottom of what she was trying to say. "Just because that torn scarf had somethin' to do with the crime scene don't mean it had to be planted *after* John was pushed."

When no one responded, Margaret Louise continued, the pride she felt over her theory making her large brown eyes sparkle with excitement. "What I'm sayin' is maybe that scarf was planted in Dixie's purse *before* the actual killin'. By someone who knew exactly what they were goin' to do and how they were goin' to get away with doin' it."

"But the tear points between the piece found in John's apartment and the piece found in Dixie's purse have to match," Debbie challenged, "or they couldn't use it as evidence against Dixie."

"I agree. But that don't mean that scarf wasn't torn that way long before John was pushed."

"But—"

Margaret Louise quieted Debbie's argument with a gentle hand on her shoulder. "It wouldn't be hard to put one torn piece in Dixie's purse and drop the second piece in John's apartment. Why, now that I think 'bout it, I'm pretty sure they did somethin' like that on *FBI Manhunt* 'bout two seasons ago. Only they used part of a diary instead of a scarf on that episode."

A chill skittered down Tori's spine as the

enormity of what Margaret Louise was trying to say finally hit her with a one-two punch . . .

John's murder was not only premeditated, but so, too, was Dixie's setup as the prime suspect.

Chapter 10

It took only a glance at each of her friends to know Dixie's predicament was taking its toll. Rose's footfalls were slower, her shoulders more slumped. The hearty laughter that was synonymous with Margaret Louise was infrequent. Debbie, who wore cheerfulness like a favorite sweatshirt, kept her eyes on the ground. Beatrice's camera and Bobblehead Kenny remained in the nanny's purse, despite the many landmarks they passed en route to West Fifty-eighth Street.

But it was Leona, perhaps, who showed the greatest wear and tear from the former librarian's official murder charge the previous afternoon. In fact, for the first time since Tori had met Leona, the sixty-something was void of all makeup.

No false eyelashes.

No artfully applied rouge.

No outfit-matching lipstick.

And not so much as a hint of hairspray across a single, solitary strand of her salon-softened gray hair . . .

Tori wrapped her arm around Leona as they reached Columbus Circle, the utter silence of the group enough to make her want to pull her hair out by the roots. "You're looking a little pale this morning, Leona. Would you like to borrow some of my blush?" She slipped her free hand inside her shoulder-mounted purse and felt around. "Ever since that lecture you gave me last fall about color, I've been pretty good about keeping some makeup on me at all times."

Leona stopped walking and stared up at Tori. "How can you be thinking about makeup at a time like this?"

She felt her mouth drop open, but no words came out. Instead, she snapped her fingers in Margaret Louise's direction, summoning her cohort in crime for a much-needed second pair of eyes.

"What is it, Victoria? Is somethin' wrong?"

"Who is this masked marvel?" she asked, pointing at Leona.

Instantly, Margaret Louise's hand was on Tori's forehead, checking for a temperature that wasn't there. "Victoria? Are you havin' a spell of some sort?"

"She's just being insensitive and hypocritical, that's all." Leona pulled Paris close in her arms, planting a kiss between the bunny's long ears as she did. "Can you imagine Victoria critiquing *my* looks?" Then, lowering the rabbit to her bosom, Leona narrowed her eyes squarely at Tori. "If you will recall, we were supposed to be back in Sweet Briar today—the tenth day of my cycle."

"Your cycle?" Tori echoed in shock. "You still get—"

"She's talkin' 'bout her beauty cycle, Victoria." Margaret Louise laughed her first real laugh of the day. "Every ten days, my sister allows her face to breathe. Today is the tenth day."

"Is this a new thing?"

"Not unless fifty years constitutes new in your book, dear," Leona mumbled.

Tori looked from Margaret Louise to Leona and back. "I've never seen her without makeup. Ever."

"That's because you don't see her on the tenth day."

"She doesn't work on the tenth day?"

"Nope."

"She doesn't date on the tenth day?"

"Nope." Margaret Louise grinned. "But flirtin' over the phone is okay, ain't it, Twin?"

At Leona's knowing nod, Tori stepped closer to Margaret Louise. "What about sewing circle meetings back home? Are you going to tell me they've never fallen on the tenth day in this beauty cycle?"

"Those are the meetin's she don't come to."

She thought back over the last two years, to the meetings Leona had missed for one reason or another. "Wait. You mean those times when Paris has needed a good night's sleep . . . or she's had to go over the inventory at the antique shop . . . or her nails were wet? Those were actually these—these makeup-free days?"

"Silly, ain't it? But it's like my daddy always said, 'You can't tell much 'bout a chicken potpie 'til you cut through the crust.' "

Rose joined the circle from whatever location she'd been listening from. "So what you're telling us, Margaret Louise, is that Leona is human like the rest of us? Or as human as she can be underneath all that meanness?"

"Meanness? *Meanness?*" Leona hissed. "I say something to Victoria about her raccoon eyes at a meeting, and I am nearly stoned. I refer to Beatrice as Mary Poppins and I'm vilified. If I don't gush over everything that comes out of my sister's kitchen, I'm accused of being jealous. I call you"—she pointed at Rose—"an old goat after you've humiliated me in front of everyone, and I'm admonished for being cruel. Yet Victoria invites everyone to mock my tried-and-true beauty ritual and that's okay? Sounds like your standard for meanness, you old goat, is rather one-sided."

Feeling suddenly one foot tall, Victoria held up her hands in surrender. "Leona, I wasn't questioning you to be mean. I was worried about you. I've never seen you without makeup in all the time I've known you. You lecture me on this same matter all the time. So it stands to reason I'd be concerned and then, as Margaret Louise explained the truth, curious, too."

Leona opened her mouth to respond but closed it as Debbie's index finger brought their focus back to the original task that had them traveling the streets of Manhattan by foot in the first place. "Look! There it is!"

Sure enough, less than four storefronts away, was McCormick's Books & Café, the original destination for Dixie and John's first meeting. And like clockwork, the apprehension that had plagued each one of them prior to the brief distraction offered by Leona's makeup-less face returned. In spades.

Only this time, instead of the silent manifestations that had accompanied their walk to that point, the worry took an audible form.

"Victoria, what happens if this turns out to be a dead end?" Rose said, her voice trembling. "I don't know if Dixie can stay in that horrid jail cell much longer."

Debbie pulled her gaze up long enough to nod along with Rose's assessment.

Beatrice's lower lip quivered. "All I wanted to do in that courthouse this morning was hug her, but there wasn't any time. They just snapped those bloody handcuffs on her and carted her off like a common criminal."

"If I've learned anything in the past two years helpin' Victoria, it's that there's always a trail of breadcrumbs to the truth," Margaret Louise said. "You just gotta keep the crows from gettin' to 'em first."

Leona began walking, her purposeful stride inviting all to follow. "Men like John are predictable when they've found a script that works. We'll find something here, I'm sure."

"But if he switched his and Dixie's meetin' to the Waldorf at the last minute, don't that make you think he was lookin' for a new script?"

"Maybe. Maybe not." Paris's ears perked above the line of Leona's swinging arm. "But my gut says we start here."

Two minutes later they were in McCormick's, the smell of books eliciting a momentary sigh of contentment from both Tori and Rose.

"Welcome to McCormick's, ladies! My name is Charles. If there's anything—and I do mean *anything*—I can do to make your visit to paradise better, let me know . . ." The twenty-something popped his spiky, red-haired head out from behind a giant poster-sized book placard and clapped his slender hands together. "Oh! Oh! I know you! I know *all* of you!"

Then, with a series of hops not unlike the ones Paris utilized to make her way from carrot treat to carrot treat, Charles stopped just inches from where they stood. "Now give me a minute, okay?

I can do this . . . Oh! Oh!" The young man flapped his hands up and down. "You"—he pointed at Margaret Louise—"you're the one who likes to cook!"

Looking left then right, he lowered his voice to a high-pitched whisper. "I have to tell you, *moonshine* in sweet potato pie is genius, pure genius!"

Margaret Louise beamed as he moved on to Debbie. "While your color scheme of blue and white is delightful for your pastry bags and tea-cups, have you ever considered adding a touch of pink? Perhaps as a contrasting color? You could make your sales receipts pink. Or maybe the doilies I imagine you must put on each plate."

"I *do* use doilies . . ." Debbie mused as she slipped into thought.

Reaching out, Charles took Leona's non-Paris-holding hand in his and squealed. "A fellow skin cycler! I am so—so glad to see someone with my sensibilities! And Oh! Oh! This must be Paris." He nuzzled his nose against Paris's. "She is simply precious. Precious, I say!"

Then, with his one hand still holding Leona's, he nudged his chin in Rose's direction and smiled approvingly. "Everyone here will tell you I wiped my eyes more than a few times when Victoria, here, was saying how you've helped ease the pain of her great-grandmother's passing. Touching . . . so, so touching."

He took a moment to wipe his eyes with his free hand then released his hold on Leona and hopped back to the register, winking at Tori as he did. When he reached it, he spun around, clapped his hands in a quick, yet deliberate beat, and ran his finger down the side of an autographed black-and-white photograph framed and hung on a nearby wall. "Beatrice, you *have* to see this."

Slowly, shyly, Beatrice took a step forward, a squeal erupting from her lips and spreading an even bigger smile across Charles's. "Oh my gosh! He was *here?* Kenny was here in this store?"

"Five months ago. Can you *believe* it?" He took one last look at the photograph then fixed his glance on the whole of them as a group once again. "I've been watching *Taped with Melly and Kenneth* for three years now and never have they had as wonderful a friend segment as they did with all of—"

Charles stopped, lifted his finger in a mental count, then dropped it back down to his side. "Really, ladies, don't you think Dixie should play hard to get just a little? I realize she's been without a man for quite some time, but there's no harm in turning down a date once in a while. Makes her more mysterious that way."

Leona's head nodded in approval. "I like the way you think, Charles. Your mother raised you right."

He snapped his fingers in a quick triangle

shape. "You're darn straight she did!" Then, turning to Tori, he said, "So what did she wear? Something spectacular, I hope?"

"Stripes are never spectacular, Charles. You know that."

His mouth snapped open. "Tell me you're kidding. Tell me you did *not* let her leave your hotel room in stripes, Leona."

"No, they gave them to her there."

Charles nibbled on the pinky of his right hand then stopped himself when he realized what he was doing. "Call in the search party. You lost me."

Beatrice tore her focus from the autographed picture of her idol and fixed it instead on Charles, her eyes wide with worry. "Dixie is in . . . jail," she said, lowering her voice to a whisper for the last word.

"What?" Charles held his hand to his heart and staggered back a step. "You can't be serious? What happened?"

"Her bloke was"—Beatrice looked left and right then lowered her voice still further—"*murdered* a few blocks from here the day before our show aired."

His hand moved to his mouth. "Hold the phone. Are you saying *John Dreyer* was her bloke?"

Tori heard the gasps that mingled with her own. "You knew John?"

"As much as anyone can truly know a snake as he's slithering along the ground . . ." Charles leaned against the edge of the counter and rolled his eyes with stage-worthy drama. "So all the time Dixie was blushing over her new friend, she was talking about *him?*" At their collective nod, he *tsk*ed loudly. "Men who prey on vulnerable women like that should be taken out into the woods and shot."

"Or pushed from a three-story balcony," Leona mused with a hint of boredom.

Charles laughed. "So true."

Tori took note of the various customers looking at or reading books around the store, her heart pumping loudly in her chest. "Dixie didn't do it, Charles. But someone has gone to great lengths to make it look as if she did. That's why she's sitting in a jail downtown. That's why we're here, in your shop, instead of heading back to Sweet Briar like we were supposed to." She took a deep breath in an effort to head off the emotion she felt building behind her eyes. "We need to know everything you can tell us about John—how you knew him, how he operated, who he preyed on. Basically everything and anything you think might help us prove Dixie's innocence."

A rapid blink gave way to a misting in Charles's eyes as he waved the splayed fingers of his right hand in a fan against his face. "You want *my* help? To rescue Dixie and reunite the Sweet Briar Seven? Oh my gosh, I *can't* believe this is really happening to me!"

Rose, who'd remained wide-eyed and silent since Charles introduced himself, finally shook her head in disbelief. "You must live a very sheltered life, young man, if you think *we're* exciting."

Charles wiggled his fingers at Rose and laughed. "Once we get Dixie back where she belongs, I'll bake you my world-famous lasagna and you can meet my roommate. He calls himself Double-Oh-Seven for his supposed prowess with the ladies. But between you, me, and the stylist with the exquisite eyes who saw straight through my hair to my very essence yesterday afternoon, he's really more of a Double-Oh-Dud. At least in my world anyway."

"Then why do you room with him?" Beatrice asked.

"We're the same size. He has great clothes. What can I say?"

"You can say you'll help us, Charles," Tori pleaded in frustration. "You can say you'll help us track down some of these women John wronged in the hopes one of them holds the key to the truth. *Please?*"

"D-o-n-e." Charles slowly, deliberately, ticked off each letter he said with an ardent finger. *"Done."*

Chapter 11

Tori looked up at the clock on the far wall and felt her shoulders tense. While she was all for using every avenue available to help Dixie, waiting for Charles to finish his shift was proving to be harder than she'd imagined.

She wanted to track down each and every woman John had scammed in recent months. She wanted to talk to the family members of those women. She wanted to find the person who'd pushed him over his apartment's balcony and be there with the biggest hug ever when Dixie was set free.

Yet even as she took a second and third glance at the time, she knew Charles was a necessary ingredient in the plan. He knew the city. He was familiar enough with John. He'd seen the parade of women the man had preyed on in a devious quest to live well. And Charles was more than willing to help.

Really, with all of those factors in play, how hard was it to wait another thirty minutes?

"We're gonna get her out, Victoria." Margaret Louise leaned across the two-person table they'd claimed at the edge of the café and patted Tori's hand. "Just you wait 'n see. I've got me a good feelin' 'bout Charles."

Tori allowed her gaze to move from the clock to Margaret Louise. "I know. I just want to get her out *now,* you know?"

"We will."

She tried to find solace in her friend's certainty, but it was hard. Instead, she forced herself to focus on something else for a while. "I'm not sure I've ever seen your sister so happy before," Tori mused while eyeing Leona across the store. "She's literally glowing."

Margaret Louise laughed. "That's 'cause she's finally found herself a kindred spirit. Someone who cares 'bout hair and makeup as much as she does."

Debbie leaned against the nearest wall and took a sip of her latte. "When I passed by them a few minutes ago, Charles was telling Leona about some hair convention he went to last weekend and how Leona would have made a wonderful hair model."

"Was that why she was batting her lashes so hard?" Rose mumbled from behind the book she was reading in a nearby armchair. "I thought maybe she was trying to achieve liftoff."

Beatrice poked her head around the back of her camera and made a face. "I've been so troubled about Dixie that I haven't been taking as many pictures as I was the first two days we were here. Melissa and Georgina are going to be disappointed."

"I'm sure the judge would have let you take a picture of Bobblehead Kenny next to his gavel."

"Rose!" Tori said sharply.

The matriarch merely shrugged her shoulders and flipped to the next page of her book, her brows furrowing as she did.

Tori rushed to soften Rose's sarcasm with a smile in the nanny's direction. "I'm sure they'll love the pictures you already have, Beatrice. Really."

After a momentary hesitation, Beatrice resumed her slow scroll through the photographs she'd snapped thus far, allowing Tori to focus solely on a clearly troubled Rose. "Rose? Is something wrong?"

Rose's head lolled to the side of the chair, prompting Tori to jump to her feet and bridge the small gap between them in a matter of seconds. "Rose? Rose? Are you okay?"

Lifting her head, Rose closed her eyes and sighed. "If it wasn't for me, Dixie wouldn't be in this mess."

"What are you talking about?" Tori asked as she squatted down beside Rose, took hold of her arm, and checked her pulse.

Rose's eyes flew open. "I'm not dying, Victoria. I'm—I'm just chastising myself for being a horrible friend and sticking my nose where it didn't belong, is all."

"I stuck my honker in every bit as much as you

did, Rose." Margaret Louise's smile slipped from her face.

For the briefest of moments, Tori contemplated reminding the women that she had tried to tell them their meddling in Dixie's life was a mistake, but let it go. I-told-you-so's at this point in the game didn't do anyone any good. Instead, she searched for something that would put Dixie's dilemma in perspective.

"We've been through this already. Pointing fingers at this point takes us off task. The only thing we should be worried about right now is how to get Dixie out of this mess—"

Rose pointed at the book in her hand and began reading aloud. "The reason we see so many singles in the sixty-five and older group is because of a small handful of mistakes they make."

Tori bobbed her head to the right, instantly recognizing the title and cover that graced Rose's lap as the elderly woman continued reading. " 'Those who refuse to change their patterns and never leave their homes remain lonely. Those who take a chance and attend a senior singles group, whether online or in person, often under-mine their efforts by appearing too needy or too anxious. Some even go to the extreme of making up a persona they believe will further their chances of finding a match only to discover they can't keep up the farce or that they've attracted the wrong sort of mate, bringing on a sense of defeat and a fear of trying again.' "

"That's exactly what we did, ain't it?" Margaret Louise moped. "Only instead of just bein' defeated as Gavin warned, Dixie is defeated, heartbroken, and livin' a complete nightmare. And it's all because of us . . ."

Rose's frail shoulders slumped forward in tandem with Margaret Louise's robust ones and Beatrice's diminutive ones, blanketing their corner of the bookstore in the kind of defeat that could be paralyzing if it went unchecked.

Dixie didn't need paralyzing.

Dixie needed help.

"Obviously you're not the first ones to make a mistake like this. If you were, Gavin Rollins wouldn't have a book, now would he?" Tori rose to her feet and looked around the store, the presence of a short, stocky girl behind the counter next to Charles giving her some hope that the start of their search was finally near. "But if you keep bemoaning all your mistakes, you're not going to be a whole lot of help in finding a solution. So please, stop. Let's focus on finding the truth, releasing Dixie, and getting back home to Melissa and Georgina and everyone else."

Beatrice nodded then handed her camera to Tori. "When it comes time to show them this picture, you'll have to explain it since I was back at the hotel with Rose and Debbie when you took this."

Tori glanced down at the camera and the shot of John's street as it looked with yellow crime scene tape blocking access to residents and passersby alike. "If I'd known all the excitement was about John, I wouldn't have taken this shot."

Margaret Louise leaned in for a closer look, her head nodding along with Tori's words as she did. "When we took it, I thought it would be real big city–like. But all it did was document the beginnin' of Dixie's nightmare while showin' how small the world is, even in a big city like this."

"How small the world is?" Tori echoed.

"You're darn tootin'. Why, think of all them people we saw on the way to spy on Dixie and John that first mornin'. Think of all them people in the audience when we were tapin' with Melly and Kenneth. Think of all them people on the subway that afternoon on the way"—Margaret Louise gestured toward the picture illuminated on the viewfinder of Beatrice's camera—"to this street with Leona. Think of all them people we passed on the sidewalk. All them people we saw on our subway when Wurly was playin' his music so nicely. Yet even with all them people we passed, somehow, in less than twenty-four hours of bein' here when that picture was taken, we still managed to capture a familiar face."

Beatrice leaned around Tori's shoulder for a closer look. "You did? Who?"

Margaret Louise pointed toward the camera

screen a second time, her finger drawing their attention to a woman several feet left of Tori and Bobblehead Kenny. "That one right there."

"You know her?" Tori repeated as she squinted at the camera.

"*Know* her? No. But I've seen her before. We *all* have. At the Waldorf that mornin' when we were spyin' on Dixie."

Tori looked from Margaret Louise to the camera and then up at Beatrice. "Can you zoom this in so I can see her better?"

Beatrice took the camera, pressed a button twice, and then handed it back to Tori, a smile stretching her lips wide as she did. "Margaret Louise is right. We stole her plant, remember?"

"Stole her plant . . ." The words trailed from her lips as her thoughts traveled between the picture in front of her and the potted plant that had provided Tori and the rest of the crew a much-needed hiding place while checking on Dixie. For there, captured in the snap of Margaret Louise's picture-taking finger, was the steely-eyed woman who'd retreated to the safety of a second potted plant for a quieter and more unobstructed view of—

"You are so so *soooo* going to love me, Miss Victoria." Charles sashayed up to the chair with one arm linked around Leona's and the other holding a business card with writing on the back. Paris hopped along at their feet.

"I am?"

"You are." He took the camera from Tori's hand and replaced it with the business card. "Do you see that name scrawled on the back?"

Tori held it closer and tried to decipher the handwriting. All she could make out, though, was the first name and an address on West Seventy-second. "Caroline?"

Charles grinned. "That's right. Caroline Trotter."

She wanted to grab for the camera, to revisit the parade of thoughts that were just trying to line up when Charles and Leona strolled over arm in arm, but she couldn't. Not yet. Charles was doing them a favor. The least she could do was be polite. Looking again at the card, she recognized the letters in the last name now that it was spoken. "Caroline Trotter. Okay, yes, I see that. But who is she?"

"One of John's women," Leona drawled.

Tori's head snapped up, her focus now firmly on Charles and Leona. "One of John's women? Are you sure?"

Charles did a little dance without moving his feet. "I told you that you were going to love me, didn't I?" Without waiting for a response, he continued, his words coming at a rapid-fire speed. "Well, Caroline Trotter was in here with John sometime last week. They sat at that table right there"—he pointed a long, slender, recently manicured finger toward the very table where

118

Tori and Margaret Louise had been sitting not more than ten minutes earlier—"and he charmed her the way he charms—I mean, *charmed* all the ladies he brought in here. Normally, we never see them after that first meeting on account of the fact they start cooking and waiting on him from that moment on. But"—Charles stopped, took a deep breath, and went on—"Caroline left her scarf behind and called the store asking if it had been found. Vanessa—I call her *Vanny*—over there"—he pointed again, this time at the short, stocky girl behind the counter that had shown up to relieve Charles of his duties—"offered to bring it to Caroline on account of how upset the woman was."

"I'll never understand how someone can get all worked up over something so silly like leaving a scarf behind," Rose groused. "It's replaceable."

Charles held out his hands in much the way a crossing guard would, but with more flair. "Sugar, she wasn't upset about the scarf so much as she was John." Then, lowering his voice to a whisper, he darted his eyes from right to left. "Seems he did something that tipped his hand in the louse department."

Tori leaned forward. "What did he do?"

"Vanny didn't ask. She just offered to bring the scarf to Caroline the next time she was up that way, only she got sick." Charles raised Tori's lean hand with one of his own. "I have to tell you, Vanny had such *horrible* sniffles I thought I was going to die being around all those germs. It was completely and *totally* icky."

He shot a sideways glance in Leona's direction, and at her understanding nod, he moved on. "So I sent her home early that day. Needless to say, Vanny never got around to delivering Caroline's scarf."

"You really should breathe between words, son," Rose said, shaking her head in wonder. "Gives us old people a chance to catch up."

Charles giggled then winked dramatically at Leona. "Shall we show them, gorgeous?"

Leona perfected her already-perfect posture then pulled her arm from inside Charles's long enough to run a preening hand along the edges of her hair. "If you think we should," she teased. Then, reaching into her handbag, Leona extracted an expensive silk scarf and waved it around for all to see. "Charles and I think we should return this to Caroline *today,* don't you, dear?"

It was the break she'd been hoping for when Charles agreed to help. Suddenly, the time spent waiting for Charles's relief to show at the store was more than worth it, since it meant they already had a lead on one of the women John had scammed in recent weeks. She opened her mouth to voice her unequivocal agreement to the plan, but closed it as Charles took in the picture still magnified on the viewfinder of Beatrice's camera.

"Leona told me your time in Chicago made you sensitive to crime and its fallout, but . . . wow . . . you really *are* good, aren't you, Victoria? A real live Nancy Drew."

"Excuse me?"

Charles pointed at the same steely-eyed woman who'd claimed Tori's complete focus only moments earlier. "Here I am, all excited to hand you one of John's unsuspecting women via a horribly gaudy silk scarf and you've already found one of your own."

Tori looked from Charles to Leona and back again, before following their collective gaze to the camera once again. "Found one of my own?"

"Your own unsuspecting woman," Charles replied.

"You know that woman?"

"Know her? No. But I've seen her before. With a certain special someone . . ."

And then she knew.

The steely-eyed woman who'd been so irritated by their presence in the Waldorf that first morning had been there doing the exact same thing they had been doing. Only she hadn't been spying on Dixie the way Tori, Rose, Margaret Louise, Leona, Debbie, and Beatrice had been doing.

No, Ms. Steely Eye had been spying on Dixie's breakfast companion, John Dreyer.

"And now, thanks to this brilliant picture, she's

also been placed, for our viewing pleasure, at the scene of the crime," Charles summed up with a clap of his hands for emphasis. "Oooh, this is going to be so much fun I can hardly *stand* it."

Chapter 12

The disappointment was tangible across the board as the Sewing Circle Six Until They're Seven Again, aptly renamed by Charles himself, trailed their new friend and the gaudy scarf back onto West Seventy-second.

"We can try again later. Perhaps Caroline is out searching for something with a bit more *pop*. Of course, if she'd waited until *after* we met, I could have found her something in"—Charles snapped his finger in a triangular movement— "a red-hot flash." Then, stopping in the middle of the sidewalk just outside the Mayfair apartments, he beckoned for Tori and the rest of the ladies to gather around him. "This is *sooo* not a setback, friends. We can and we will track this woman down. So turn those frowns around and let's get a treat, shall we?"

Tori felt her ears perk at the mere notion of a much-needed sugar infusion, but shook it off as the image of Dixie in handcuffs resumed its spot in the forefront of her mind. "Charles, we can't.

Every moment we're out here, without answers, is another moment Dixie is sitting in that jail for a crime she didn't commit. We can't be stopping for a treat when we also need to track down Ms. Steely Eye."

"We can't?" Margaret Louise shouted over the roar of a garbage truck that was making its way slowly toward Central Park. "You sure 'bout that?"

Charles held up his hand like the perfect school crossing guard. Only, instead of stopping traffic, he stopped Tori from speaking. "Victoria. Surely you know that a well-timed treat—and a sinful one at that—is akin to putting supercharge gasoline in your car, yes?" He silenced himself long enough to exchange appreciative looks with Leona as a handsome man, dressed to the nines in his bellman attire, stepped out of a building across the street to help an arriving tenant. "Hmmm." Charles glanced down at the neon green Swatch on his wrist then back at Leona with a wink. "Same time, same place tomorrow, gorgeous?"

At Leona's nod, he continued, his focus straying back to Tori. "Anyway . . . where was I? Oh! Yes! Just because Caroline isn't available at this exact moment doesn't mean we can't move ahead with our sleuthing. Which means, it is time to hatch a plan. At CupKatery." Charles pivoted on the soles of his white faux leather booties and threw his hands in the air. "Margaret

Louise, love, CupKatery is a *total* must. Their cupcakes are to die for. Truly. Positively. Without. A. Doubt."

"Did you say cupcakes?" Margaret Louise asked in an elevated voice that no longer had anything to do with traffic noises. Then turning to Tori, she engaged her best sales tactic. "Now, Victoria. Charles is right. We need a little supercharge if we're goin' to keep wanderin' these streets on foot. Why, my dogs are barkin' already."

"Your dogs?"

"My feet, Victoria." Margaret Louise nudged her chin toward a beleaguered Rose while simultaneously pointing at Beatrice and Debbie with an elbow. "Everyone's feet. We need to make a plan for our investigatin'. You know that better than anyone else here, 'cept me, of course." Margaret Louise paused long enough to get Charles up to speed. "I'm the Ned to Victoria's Nancy back home when it comes to solvin' crime in Sweet Briar."

"Crime, I might add, we did not have before Victoria arrived from *Chicago*," Leona clarified.

Charles's eyes widened dramatically, prompting an exchange of wiggling fingers with Leona while Margaret Louise continued, "So why not do our plannin' over baked goods? Especially when I've been hearin' 'bout these New York City cupcake shops for years."

She wanted to protest, to argue a case for

heading over to John's street and asking random people where they might find Ms. Steely Eye, but she couldn't. Not without squashing Margaret Louise's excitement and pushing an obviously exhausted Rose into more walking than she could truly handle at that moment. Maybe a ten-minute break really would be best . . .

"Okay. Okay. But let's keep it short, okay? We've got work to do." She tucked Rose's hand safely inside her upper arm as they brought up the rear of the cupcake-quest. "You doing okay, Rose? Because if this is too much, I'm sure Debbie would be happy to ride back to the hotel with you."

Rose's slow gait ceased completely. "Victoria, do you realize how long I've known Dixie?"

Tori covered the elderly woman's bony hand with hers and patted it gently. "A long time."

"You're darn right, a long time. In fact, I've known Dixie more than twice as long as you've even been alive. Seeing her like that in the court-room this morning was awful. She no more belongs behind bars for killing that fool than that young man up there"—she pointed a trembling finger toward Charles, who was relishing his role as tour guide to Beatrice, Debbie, Leona, and Margaret Louise—"could kill a bug in my garden without screaming his head off. Yet there she is, alone in a cell, questioning everything about herself."

"I don't know how," Tori said, "but somehow, someway, we're going to get to the bottom of what happened to John, I promise." The second the last two words left her lips, she knew she'd probably made a mistake, but she didn't care. There was no way she was going to let Dixie waste away in that jail cell awaiting a trial that wasn't hers to have.

Rose blinked her misty eyes and resumed walking, her hand clutching Tori's upper arm firmly. "More than anything, I wanted to enjoy this trip with all of you. It may have taken eighty years to find the kind of friend group we have, but it was worth the wait."

Something about the way Rose was talking sent an actual shot of pain through Tori's body, and she rushed to head it off with her preferred scenario. "And we'll be together for a long time to come. For sewing meetings, barbecues, *my wedding,* and many, many more trips just like this one . . . minus the part about Dixie being arrested and tossed in jail, of course."

"This will be my last trip of this magnitude, Victoria."

This time it was Tori who stopped in the middle of the sidewalk. "No it won't."

"Victoria, I'm slowing down more and more with each passing day. I don't have the kind of years left that can accommodate many, many more trips, as you say."

The pain squeezed at her heart and brought tears to her eyes. "Please. I—I don't want to think like that. Not now. Not today. Not tomorrow. Not next year. Please—"

"Woo-hoo . . . ladies," Charles called out to them. "CupKatery is closing in half an hour. Chop! Chop!"

Rose untucked her hand long enough to guide a strand of hair behind Tori's ear with a soothing *tsk*. "Don't you fret, Victoria. I'm here now. Let's catch up with everyone and get one of these fancy-schmancy cupcakes Margaret Louise is hankering to try so badly. And while everyone else is supercharging with sugar, I'm going to bask in the sunshine of that young man up there . . ."

There was so much she wanted to say. So many things about Rose's influence in her life that she wanted to acknowledge. But not now. Not when the chance to make a new memory with the woman was right there at their fingertips.

Instead, she found the smile she needed and whispered a kiss across Rose's forehead. "Well? Shall we?"

"Indeed, we shall."

Ten minutes later, with Charles playing cheer-leader at their side, Tori managed to get Rose through the door of CupKatery and into the first available seat they could find.

"Don't bother sittin'," Margaret Louise mumbled in a rare display of disappointment. "In fact, you don't need to even pause in your steps in order to digest one of these—these cupcake imposters."

Charles looked up from the spot he'd helped secure for Rose and rested a hand over his heart. "Imposters? What on earth are you talking about, girlfriend?"

Margaret Louise looked from the glass cupcake case Debbie and Beatrice were fawning over to a perplexed Charles and back again, the sheer horror and disbelief on her face impossible to miss. "I've eaten *crumbs* that are bigger than those cupcakes!"

"But that way you can experiment with flavors without getting too full too fast," Charles protested.

"You can do that by stickin' your finger in a bowl and lickin' batter in my house. And I don't charge plumb near three dollars for a lick, neither!"

Charles reached out, patted Margaret Louise's vast shoulder, then winked back at Rose and Tori as he propelled her closer to the display case. "Let me make a few suggestions of cupcakes you need to try, sugarplum. Then, if you taste them and still think I'm crazy, I'll . . . I'll . . . I'll step right out that door and start singing a selection of your choice from either *The Sound of Music* or *The Phantom of the Opera* at the top of my lungs. Will that do?"

Margaret Louise tapped the tip of her index finger to her chin, leaned forward to study the many flavors available in bite-sized cupcake form, then met Charles's eye with a mischievous one of her own. "Make it a Kenny Rogers song for Beatrice and you're on."

Beatrice's head snapped and swiveled in one quick motion. "Oooh, Margaret Louise, thank you. I almost forgot. We just have to get a picture for Georgina and Melissa right here by the display case. We'll make it a group shot. Charles?"

Beatrice secured Bobblehead Kenny from her purse with one hand and handed the camera to Charles with the other. "Could you—"

"Of course I can find someone to take our picture," Charles gushed. Rising on his tiptoes, he turned to the customer seated at a nearby table. "Excuse me, ma'am? Would you mind taking a picture of my friends and me by the counter? We're putting together an album for our friends who couldn't be here today."

Rose dipped her head long enough to hide its amused shake then stood and shuffled her way over to the counter with Tori in her wake. "Looks like we'll have to give some thought to changing our name from the Sweet Briar Ladies Society Sewing Circle to something more inclusive when we get back home," Rose whispered.

"I was actually thinking that same thing," Charles replied. "Though, since I live so far away, maybe we could just add 'and Charles' at the end."

Ten minutes and several poses later, Bobblehead Kenny and the camera were back in Beatrice's purse and the six of them plus Charles were seated around a table, eating their way through CupKatery's vast assortment of pint-sized cup-cakes. As they munched and recharged, Margaret Louise kept a running commentary going on each and every flavor while Charles pointed everyone else's attention around the tiny shop by way of a series of photographs highlighting many of the sights and sounds of New York City.

"That, of course, is the Empire State Building." He swung his gaze back to the women seated around him. "Have you been to the top yet?"

At Leona's no, he rolled his eyes. "I am so going to correct that."

He pointed to the next photograph. "That's the famous Gapstow Bridge in Central Park. It's been the sight of countless marriage proposals over the years by men who prefer"—Charles paused and sighed—"true romance over staging some-thing so outlandish it might go viral before the woman even says yes."

He popped a s'more flavored cupcake into his mouth and chewed far more than the size demanded. When he was done, he made a face. "Last week, some barbarian in Wisconsin spelled out the words *Will you marry me?* in hot dogs. Can you imagine? If I had been that woman, I'd have reached across that table and used those very same hot dogs to write my response: *Oh, hell no*. Then I'd have slapped him."

"Try the pancake batter one next," Margaret Louise said, pointing Charles's focus back to the cupcake box. "It's my favorite so far."

"See? I told you." Charles wiggled his fingers at Leona's sister, then went back to describing the photographs around the shop, stopping as he reached the one on the back wall behind the register. "Will you look at that? My mother always said things happened in threes. Three great shoe purchases. Three pimples to cover. Three attractive men in the bookstore at the same time. You get the idea. And sure enough, she's right. There's our number three for today . . ."

Tori looked up from the cupcake flavor Margaret Louise was critiquing and followed the path of Charles's finger all the way to the framed photograph of a family standing beside a lake. "Do you know someone in that picture?"

"No. But John sure did."

Chapter 13

Despite the fact that they'd be closing in less than five minutes, the string of bells attached to CupKatery's front door jingled again and again as customer after customer came in to pick up a ten-pack, a twenty-pack, a thirty-pack, or even just a single, solitary cupcake. The people themselves came in all shapes and sizes, with most, if not all, on their way home from a long day of work.

No one lingered over the choices the way Tori and her friends had done. No, this last flurry of shoppers knew exactly what they wanted and wasted no time in their pursuit.

"Why, I still can't get over people payin' two bucks for a cupcake they can swallow whole," Margaret Louise said across the empty box still sitting on the table in front of them. "I reckon I could make a dozen full-sized cupcakes for not much more 'n that."

Flavor by flavor the cupcakes disappeared from the case as the second hand of the shop's clock closed in on five o'clock and Tori found her mental prayer for a moment or two of the shop-keeper's time growing louder and louder in her head.

Finally, at one minute to five, the break she'd

been waiting for presented itself along with a raised eyebrow directed at their table. "We'll be closing in just a moment." The young girl behind the counter flicked her dark ponytail back over her shoulder. "Is there anything else I can get you before I shut down the register for the evening?"

Tori approached the counter and the girl, whose name tag identified her as Gretchen, with a mixture of anticipation and trepidation. She wanted nothing more than the woman in the picture to be the key to Dixie's troubles, yet at the same time, she knew that would only mean worry and heartache for the smiling people standing around her in the photograph.

Still, Dixie was her top priority, and in order to get her released, Tori and the gang had to deliver John's true murderer to the police station's doorstep.

"I was wondering if you could tell me a little bit about that picture." With a slight rise of her chin, Tori guided the girl's gaze to the black lacquered frame that hung slightly off center on the back wall. "In particular about the woman in the middle."

"You mean Doug's mom?"

Tori took in the handsome, well-built man just beyond the young girl's outstretched finger and nodded. "If that woman in the center is his mom, then yes, I mean Doug's mom." She took a moment to study the rest of the photograph, which included a young woman with similar features to Doug and a tall blond man holding a baby Tori guessed to be about two years old. "What can you tell me about her? Is she Kate?"

Gretchen disappeared into what Tori assumed was the shop's kitchen and returned seconds later with a wet dishrag in her hand. Slapping it onto the counter, she began to clean off the finger- prints that had accumulated on the shiny silver surface over the past few hours, her words coming in starts and stops as she made her way through an invisible checklist of closing rituals. "There is no Kate in CupKatery. Everyone thinks there is, but there's not. It's just a cute name that sounds a lot better than CupDougery, you know?"

"Oh? This is Doug's shop?"

"Technically, it's half Doug's and half Diane's, but CupDougDiery isn't a whole lot better."

Again, Tori's gaze traveled back to the picture she'd been studying off and on since Charles first made the connection between John and the woman in the center. "Oh, I get it. Their mom picked a neutral name so as not to favor one sibling over the other, right?"

Gretchen shrugged. "I don't know. I've not really given it any thought."

"So what can you tell me about her?"

Flipping the dishrag over, Gretchen transitioned

her efforts to the now empty glass case save for three tie-dyed cupcakes that still remained. "You mean their mom, Clara?"

Tori nodded.

"You mean beside the fact she's dead?"

Charles's gasp just over her left shoulder provided the audio track for the one she tried to stifle between her teeth. "Oh, I'm sorry, I didn't know."

The girl shrugged. "I didn't know her all that well. Doug is really the one who we see in here all the time or, at least, the one we used to see in here all the time. The last few weeks he's been pretty hit or miss. Jillian . . . she's the assistant manager . . . says Doug is really having a hard time with his mom's death."

"It was recent then?"

"Two weeks ago."

Tori cast about for her next question and was grateful when Margaret Louise provided it with ease. "Bless her heart, had she been sick?"

"I think so but I don't really know for sure. I *do* know she'd been sad the last few times I saw her."

"I'm sorry to hear that," Tori said, regrouping. "Had something happened?"

"Something? No. Someone? Yes." Then, stopping just long enough to toss the rag into the kitchen, Gretchen opened up the back of the case, pulled out the tray of tie-dyed cupcakes, tossed them into the wastebasket in the corner, and then began stacking each of the empty trays atop her opposite arm. "Seems the guys my age aren't the only unfeeling jerks."

Splaying her hand to hold off the empathy she could sense oozing from Charles's pores, Tori dialed her voice down a notch in order to keep the girl talking. "Please tell me some man didn't kill Clara . . ."

"Nah, I'm pretty sure she'd been sick. But she was a real go-getter. You know, one of those live-life-to-the-fullest types. She was always traveling here, there, and everywhere, trying new places and new things. Doug was always getting calls from her about where she was and what she was doing, and he was always telling her to be careful." The girl reached inside the case for the last empty tray and chuckled as much to herself as Tori. "I always found it funny that he—as the kid—was telling her—the mom—to be careful. Total role reversal from the way things are in my house, I'll tell you. But he adored her, and I do mean *adored* her."

Margaret Louise smiled wide. "Sounds like my son, Jake. He loves me like that, too."

Gretchen shut the case, repositioned the stack of trays so she was holding them with both hands, and then set them on a wheeled cart against the back wall. "Is your son married?"

Reaching into her cavernous tote bag, Margaret

Louise removed her wallet and flipped open the picture section so it hung nearly to the floor. "He is. To Melissa. She's the apple of his eye just like she is mine. And see these beauties, right here? These are my grandbabies. All eight of 'em."

Charles clapped his hands and reached for the plastic sleeve. "Girlfriend, you haven't shown me these yet . . . oh. Oh. Oh! They are sooo precious, every last one of them."

"I wish Jillian were here right now," Gretchen said. "She's convinced the reason Doug hasn't married yet is because a guy who loves his mother to such an extreme will never think any other woman is good enough."

"Well, ain't that just the silliest thing I've ever heard." Margaret Louise waved off the comment then turned her attention and her face-splitting smile in the direction of Charles, who was still gushing over her grandbabies.

Tori, on the other hand, felt the invisible radar on top of her head beginning to ping. "So who was this person that hurt Clara?"

"Some local guy she met over the Internet." Gretchen shook her head. "Can you imagine a seventy-year-old woman looking for love on the Internet? Seems kinda funny to me, you know?"

"Old people get lonely, too," Rose interjected from her seat, not more than five feet away. "Having someone to talk to helps that."

"No, I get that. I just know that for every nice

guy one of my friends has met that way, the others have met ten times that many jerks. Something about a computer allows them to portray qualities that just aren't there in person."

"So Clara met a jerk, I take it?"

Gretchen got a second dishrag and headed toward the four tables that made up the shop's limited seating space. "I don't know the whole story. Just bits and pieces from stuff Jillian said when I asked why Clara looked so sad. Seems she really liked this guy and he gave every impression he liked her, too. But it wasn't really her so much as her money—and Clara had a lot."

Tori exchanged glances with a smug Charles, who'd stopped looking at pictures of Margaret Louise's grandbabies and was focused on the story Gretchen was telling. He placed a dramatic hand over his heart and sighed. "Please, Gretchen, tell me this techno-savvy scam artist didn't rob her blind . . ."

"He didn't. Clara figured out what was going on before it was too late. But by then, she'd kind of fallen for him."

"Oh, the poor dear. She must have been heartbroken."

Gretchen finished with the tables and headed back toward the counter. "She was. But she was also disappointed in herself for being such a fool. That's why she was so sad at the end."

Tori looked back at the picture and the man

who draped his arm around Clara with obvious affection and protectiveness, a question forming on her lips almost immediately. "How did Doug take that part?"

"You mean with the guy making her sad?"

At Tori's nod, Gretchen's eyes widened. "You've been to the Bronx Zoo, right?"

"No."

"The Central Park Zoo?"

"No. We're from South Carolina."

Charles's hand shot into the air then returned to his hip with flair. "Oh, we are sooo adding the Central Park Zoo to our list of must-do's while you're here. The sea lion feeding session at two o'clock simply can't be"—he snapped his fingers in his favorite triangle formation—"missed."

She heard Beatrice's voice, knew her reply included talk of Bobblehead Kenny and pictures, but she kept her focus on Gretchen and the question the girl had yet to answer. "And Doug?" she prompted in an effort to get them back on track.

"It doesn't matter whether you're looking at lions, bears, zebras, or sea lions. When one of their babies is being threatened, they go nuts." Gretchen dropped the dishrag onto the stack of trays and released a loud end-of-the-workday sigh. "Doug was angry that some guy tried to take advantage of his mother and made some noise about tracking him down. Clara, though, wanted it to be over and ordered him to let it go."

"But it had to eat at him that she was so saddened by what happened with this guy . . ."

"Jillian said it tore him up. Clara was a sweet lady. Always smiling, always happy." Gretchen took one final look at the picture and then wrapped her fingers around the handle of the wheeled cart. "None of us in the shop knew she was even dying, at her request. She wanted to hear laughter when she came in, not sadness. It's just too bad that someone who was so positive and so upbeat all the time had to leave this earth feeling sad and foolish because of someone else's doings."

Charles raked a hand through his red spiky hair and then wiggled his fingers at Gretchen in farewell. "Don't you fret too much, sister. Something tells me that Mama Lion had her say and then some."

Chapter 14

Tori really wasn't all that surprised at the dark circles, droopy lids, and incessant yawning that demanded room service's encore visit to Suite 451 that morning. She'd heard Rose's labored pacing as she'd tossed and turned throughout the night. She'd heard Debbie moving around the living room straightening things that didn't need to be straightened. And she'd even heard Leona—who missed her nightly beauty sleep for no one—

mumbling to Paris off and on as the darkness outside her window slowly surrendered to a new day.

They'd all tried to shelve the current crisis long enough to enjoy dinner and a quiet evening, but every time Dixie had come up in conversation, even on the fringes, the mood had soured.

One of them was hurting.

One of them was scared.

One of them was being railroaded for a crime she didn't commit.

And if nothing else about the Sweet Briar Ladies Society Sewing Circle was true, the fact that they stuck together like family was.

Sure, they fought. What family didn't?

Sure, they made mistakes and hurt one another's feelings on occasion. What family didn't? But when push came to shove, they had one another's backs.

"We've got to figure this out and we've got to figure this out faster than we are now," Rose said as she shifted her tired body just enough to allow Beatrice a spot on the floral love seat. "I couldn't sleep last night thinking about Dixie in that cell surrounded by people who really *have* committed crimes."

Heads nodded to Rose's left and right.

"Every time I'd slip off to sleep, I'd have me a different nightmare," Margaret Louise shared between yawns. "One had Dixie cryin' nonstop in some room I could never find, and the other was a sewin' meetin' back home . . . without Dixie bein' at it."

Beatrice offered her usual dash of optimism despite her own ashen complexion. "Maybe Dixie had something else to do that night."

"No, she was in jail. For good." All eyes in the room turned to Leona in accusing fashion. "What? I had the same dream."

"She did. I heard her tellin' Paris 'bout it 'round three a.m."

Debbie stared down into her still-steaming mug of coffee and released an exhausted sigh. "Rose is right. We've got to figure this out. Now."

Oh, how Tori wished it could be that easy. That they could just point the police in the direction of some random passerby on the street and have her be the killer. But sadly, it didn't work that way, regardless of how much they all wished otherwise.

"I say we make one of them lists we're always makin' when we're tryin' to figure out somethin' like this, Victoria." Margaret Louise swiped a notepad from the old-fashioned rolltop desk in the corner and settled with it, and a pen, on the edge of the floral ottoman at Rose's feet. "Now, let's see . . . we've got Doug—that's who I'm thinkin' is our main suspect, the never-home Caroline Trotter, and the one who found my sister to be annoyin'."

"I said we need to figure this out faster, Margaret Louise," Rose groused. "You start filling the list with people who find your sister annoying and it will take years."

Leona opened her mouth to retort but closed it as Tori rushed to head off the ensuing battle. "Margaret Louise? You're really leaning towards Doug?"

"So am I." Debbie set her mug on the end table to her right then pulled her dark blonde hair into a ponytail. "I think he had motive to want to do it and the kind of strength to make the push count."

Margaret Louise put two tally marks next to Doug's name on the notepad. "Someone hurtin' your mama like that right b'fore she went off to Jesus is just the kind of thing that could make a good boy snap."

Debbie nodded.

"Perhaps. But my money is on that Caroline Trotter woman." Leona pointed at the pad and waited for her sister to place a tally next to her guess, stroking her opposite hand down Paris's back as she did. "We must remember, hell hath no fury like a woman scorned."

Rose cleared her throat then shifted awkwardly from side to side atop her sofa cushion. "As much as I hate to say these words, I have to agree with Leona."

Waving off Debbie's slight gasp and Beatrice's wide eyes, Rose continued. "No woman wants to be hornswoggled. Particularly—I imagine—if they're from money."

Margaret Louise paused mid–tally mark and glanced up from the notepad. "We haven't met her yet. There's no way of knowin' she has money 'til we do."

Tori pushed off the armrest she'd claimed beside Rose and wandered around the room, her friends' opinions and theories looping their way through her thoughts. "I'm not an expert on New York City by any stretch of the imagination, but I'm thinking that apartment building she's living in isn't cheap."

"Neither was that scarf she left behind at Charles's bookstore."

Rose pinned Leona with a stare. "I thought you said that scarf was gaudy."

"Trust me, old goat, the wealthy might buy well, but they're not immune to your kind of taste."

"*My* kind of taste?" Rose pointed at Paris's jewel-studded collar. "I'm not the one who dresses my rabbit like a garden-variety hooker."

Debbie's second gasp was drowned out by Leona's red-faced sputtering. "Take—take that back, Rose! Take it back right now!"

"I think Paris looks beautiful," Beatrice whispered in a rare show of side-taking.

Debbie shot a pained look of disapproval in Rose's direction before reaching across the corner of the end table to pet Paris. "I do, too."

"That wasn't nice, Rose," Margaret Louise agreed. "And you know that."

"I know. I'm sorry." Rose stared down at her trembling hands, her voice garbled. "I'm sorry, Leona. That was uncalled for."

Seconds turned to minutes as Leona worked to control her breathing, the hurt and anger Rose's words had inspired in her making the silence in the room almost unbearable. But just before Tori could think of something to say to diffuse the situation, Leona stood, walked around the back of the love seat, and gently laid Paris atop the elderly woman's lap, her own voice choked with a rare burst of emotion. "I'm worried about Dixie, too, you old goat. So is Paris."

Tori felt the lump forming in the middle of her throat and knew, if she gave in to it, she'd be in trouble. Rose and Leona would have other moments. Dixie was, and needed to remain, the sole focus of their morning powwow. "I'm leaning toward Ms. Steely Eye from the potted plant at the Waldorf."

Margaret Louise swiped the back of her hand across her cheek then added one mark next to Ms. Steely Eye for Tori and another for the fast-nodding Beatrice on Rose's right. "Why you sayin' that, Beatrice?"

"She was in both places. First, at the fancy hotel, then later, on my camera, at the scene of the crime."

Tori nodded. "That's my thinking, too."

"But that could be a coincidence. We don't

know for certain that she was even looking at Dixie and John's table that morning." Debbie peeked into her coffee mug but opted not to drink any more. "I mean, I realize New York City is big, but even Charles said he sees familiar faces all the time."

"Charles lives here. He's had time to know people, recognize people. We've only been here a few days," Tori said as a counterpoint even though she knew Debbie was right. She of all people knew that just because something seemed a little odd didn't mean there was anything to it. Then again, she also knew that sometimes there was . . .

"When's Charles coming by again?" Beatrice asked, glancing at her watch. "Soon, yes?"

On cue, the hotel phone rang and Tori picked it up. "Hello?"

"Good morning, Victoria! Are my ladies well rested and ready to hit the ground running this morning?"

She paused in her answer to take in the faces of each of her friends.

Rose, still embarrassed by her attack on the rabbit now cuddled in her lap, suddenly looked ninety-five instead of nearing eighty-five. The unfamiliar surroundings, coupled with the stress of Dixie's predicament, were taking a heavy toll on her energy level.

Likewise, Debbie's normal go-go-go quality

exhibited a nervous energy Tori had never seen in the bakery shop owner. No, Debbie had life together twenty-four/seven, juggling her roles as business owner, mother, and wife with an ease that was mind-boggling. Toss in a problem or two along the way, and she was unfazed. Dixie's situation had changed that.

Beatrice, while the most rested looking of the crew, seemed even more subdued than normal and Tori knew why. Beatrice took solace in peace and quiet. It was as if the young woman needed those key ingredients in order to think, act, and function.

Leona was equal parts quiet and jumpy, like she wanted to bask in the glow of the city, yet had lost the heart to do so the moment Dixie was carted off to jail.

And then there was Margaret Louise—the nurturer, the caregiver—with her hands essentially tied where one of her oldest friends was concerned.

"As ready as we'll ever be, I guess," she finally uttered into the phone. Were they exhausted? Without a doubt. Were they ready to go home? Absolutely. But none of that mattered without Dixie by their side. "We even made a list of the suspects we think are most viable."

"Great minds, Victoria, great minds," Charles gushed in her ear. "I got out my pastel Sharpies this morning and made one, too. I'll bring it up now."

She gave him their room number then moved

about the sitting area, encouraging everyone to get their shoes, hats, purses, and whatever else they might need for a day of sleuthing in the Big Apple.

At Charles's melodic knock, Beatrice let him in, her shy greeting morphing into a frustrated exhale of words. "This bloke was at this con for a long time, right?"

Tori nodded along with everyone else.

"Which means people knew what he was up to, right?"

Again, everyone nodded, with Charles adding a triangular hand snap to Leona's impatient eye roll. "I smelled a rat my first week on the job when he came in with a second woman in as many days," Charles boasted. "Vanny did, too."

"So did his neighbor," Tori said, recalling the words of the woman standing next to her on John's street that fateful day. "In fact, to hear her talk, it was only a matter of time before one of the women he was always wronging came back and . . ."

Came back . . .

Came back . . .

"That's it!" she said before slapping a hand across her mouth out of respect for the guests staying in nearby rooms.

Charles clapped once, twice. "Don't say it, Victoria. I know exactly what you're thinking." He marched back to the door and flung it open, turning back to the Sewing Six with unbridled excitement. "Well? Shall we?"

Chapter 15

Tori didn't need to look at her hands to know what Beatrice shoved into them as the first of two cabs pulled up to the curb outside their hotel.

"I know you'll be quite busy these next few hours, but just in case a moment arises, I thought, perhaps you could take a picture or two for me." Beatrice stepped to the side to afford easier access to the backseat for Rose, then moved closer to the cab's open door as Debbie slipped into the middle. "We'll tell her you asked after her, and that you'll visit just as soon as you can." Then, with a nod to Margaret Louise and Leona, Beatrice got in the cab and waved. "We will see you at the zoo at two o'clock."

Tori didn't look at Margaret Louise and Leona as the cab pulled away. She didn't need to. The silence between them said everything that needed to be said.

The three of them wanted to visit with Dixie every bit as much as Rose, Beatrice, and Debbie. In fact, watching the cab drive away and knowing that was where they were going was crushing.

But just as Dixie needed a few hours of face time with people who loved and cared about her, she also needed someone to track down John's real killer so her spot in the downtown cell could be relinquished accordingly.

"We're gonna get 'im, Victoria."

"Or *her*," Leona corrected.

"You can bet your sweet petunias we're going to find the person who did this." Charles waved at the driver of the second cab then led the way to the vehicle with a half walk, half skip. "Who wants to ride shotgun?"

Margaret Louise's hands shook along with her head. "Not me. Why, I want as much paddin' between me and everything outside this cab as possible when we're zippin' and dartin' 'round all those cars and people."

Charles glanced at Leona and Tori then back at the cab. "How about I take the front seat and I can pretend I'm your tour guide!"

As their cab pulled away from the curb less than a minute later, Charles made good on his plan, guiding their collective gaze first to the right and then the left as they wound their way around illegally parked cars, waiting cabs, and a host of other interferences that neither fazed nor slowed their driver from his mission.

Tori felt Leona tense once or twice as their driver sped toward pedestrian-clogged intersections, but it was Margaret Louise's white knuckles—one set on the side door and the other poised to draw blood from Tori's jean-clad thigh—that told the complete story.

"It's going to be okay, Margaret Louise," she whispered after one too many gasps of her own involving baby carriages and the Daytona 500 driver who was apparently moonlighting as their cabbie. "Seriously. Pretend it's you driving."

"I don't drive nothin' like this, Victoria!"

She resisted the urge to laugh and instead did her best to sound soothing. "We're almost there."

"Actually, Victoria, we've still got a ways to go," Charles said, spinning around in his seat. "We've still got to get around Times Square and make our way past Columbus Circle before we're at John's old place." Then, with his telltale snap of excitement, he let loose a hair-raising laugh. "My friends and I call this part coming up here the pedestrian slalom."

The cab driver's eyes met Victoria's in the rearview mirror. "One point for old person, five points for crying kid, ten points for fast walkers. The cabbie with the highest points at the end of the night gets a free burger and fries."

Tori howled in pain as Margaret Louise's hand clenched down on her thigh even harder, drawing a laugh from the driver. "I am kidding. There is no free burger. Only fries. Big, thick fries . . . with lots of salt."

Charles giggled. "You're funny."

"Thank you." Then, stepping off the gas a hairbreadth, he met Tori's eye once again. "You look familiar to me."

"That's because she was on *Taped with Melly and Kenneth* a few days ago. So were Margaret Louise and Leona."

The driver nodded. "That's it. The southern ladies. You guys were a stitch."

Charles's eyes widened tenfold. "I know! Weren't they?"

Leona reached into her satchel and pulled out a nose-twitching Paris, positioning the bunny between her own body and the seat belt. "Are you a fan of the show"—Leona inquired, bobbing her head around Charles's shoulders to afford a better view of the driver's name and credentials listed on a placard strung around the rearview mirror—"Abram?"

"I've been trying to get on their rising talent segment for six months."

"As a—as a race car driver?" Margaret Louise stuttered.

"Nah, as a comic." He stopped at a light and tapped his fingers along the top of the steering wheel. "I'm going to make it one day. I know I am. But in the meantime, I do this." The light turned green and they continued on, the bright lights and hustle and bustle of Times Square now behind them as they traveled north. "West Sixty-eighth and Central Park West, correct?"

"That's right," Tori said, nodding.

"Gorgeous street. You got friends that live there?"

"More like answers." Charles guided their eyes to the left as the cab made its way around Columbus Circle and past the southwestern corner of Central Park.

Abram's eyebrows rose but he said nothing, his concentration returning to their rapidly approaching destination. When they approached Sixty-eighth Street, he glanced at Charles. "You want me to actually pull onto the street or let you off alongside the park?"

"The park!" Margaret Louise answered, her breath coming in fits and starts as she finally let it go. "We can walk across the street."

Again, Abram's eyes moved to the rearview mirror. "Are you retired, ma'am?"

"Who? Me?" Margaret Louise asked before matching his nod with one of her own.

"Harry has been looking a little hungry lately. I suppose some fries would help fatten him up."

Margaret Louise looked from Abram's reflection in the rearview mirror to Tori and back again, her confusion evident in everything from her raised brows to the squinty eyes they topped. "Harry? Who's Harry?"

"The cabbie behind me." He pulled to the right, stopping at the curb as Leona, Tori, and Charles laughed away Margaret Louise's horror. "It was a pleasure escorting you to your answers. May you find exactly what you're looking for."

Two minutes and twenty dollars later, they

waved farewell to Abram and made their way across Central Park West, Margaret Louise leading the way. "Hurry your feet now. The little red hand is blinkin'."

Leona slowly lifted her nose and sniffed. "Charles? Victoria? Do you smell French fries?"

Margaret Louise ran to the other side of the street then sank onto a set of wide stone church steps and pointed an accusing finger at her sister. "You ain't funny, Leona."

Leona made no pretense of trying to hold back her smugness. "Charles laughed. Victoria laughed."

"Well, I reckon you're the only ones."

It felt good to laugh, it really did, and for just that moment, Tori could almost see the fun they'd all envisioned when news of their contest win had arrived. Oh, the plans they'd had, the crazy food they'd wanted to try, the tourist sites they'd wanted to visit.

Yet in the blink of an eye, all of that had changed.

For Dixie more than any of them.

"I want to laugh like this again tomorrow or the day after tomorrow . . . but only if Dixie can be laughing, too," Tori said, peering down the street that, just three days earlier, had been closed off by crime scene tape on account of John having been pushed to his death from a third-floor balcony.

"We will, girlfriend, just you wait and see.

Super Charles and the Sewing Six are on the case!" Charles extended his hand to Margaret Louise and helped hoist her back onto her Keds. "We will not give up, we will not fail. Dixie Dunn is too good for jail."

"That she is," Leona said, pointing the way down the picturesque city street with its flowering trees and welcoming brownstone stoops. "Now, if I remember correctly, that balcony right there was John's."

Tori, Margaret Louise, and Charles followed the path cut by Leona's manicured finger to an empty balcony on the opposite side of the street, its wrought iron railing not much different from the ones on neighboring brownstones to its left and right. "What makes you think it's that one?" Tori asked.

"Because a very handsome, very sweet police officer pointed it out to me when we were talking that day, and I remember, just as I'm quite sure he remembers me." Leona straightened the hem of her spring blazer around her waist and then turned to Charles. "If he hadn't had to keep the crowd from sneaking under the tape, I'm quite certain he'd have taken me to dinner that night."

"Dinner?" Margaret Louise repeated.

"Yes, dinner. He was quite smitten with me. Everyone standing around us could see it."

"Now, Twin, I'm thinkin' them folks probably thought you were that officer's mama."

Leona stumbled back a step, then stopped, regrouped, and huffed her way across the street, mumbling something about jealous sisters under her breath.

"Oooh, drama!" Charles clapped a quick beat then leaned closer to Tori as Margaret Louise hightailed it after Leona. "I thought Rose was the one who gave Leona the business."

"Rose is notorious for keeping Leona's ego in check, but that doesn't mean Margaret Louise, Dixie, and Georgina don't poke at her as well." She watched the sisters reunite on the sidewalk outside John's brownstone and felt the smile making its way across her mouth. Life was never dull now that she had Margaret Louise and Leona as friends. "But really, it's all in fun. The reality is that Rose and Leona care about each other very much. We all do."

Charles placed his hand on his hip and looked pointedly at Tori's arm. When she took his hint and allowed him to escort her to the waiting duo, he expressed his pleasure with a slight hop that ceased nearly as quickly as it started. "Uh-oh. It's a buzzer building, ladies."

"A buzzer buildin'? What's that?"

"That means you can only get into the building if you're buzzed in by one of the tenants," Charles explained once they reached the brownstone's front door and the six distinct buttons next to six placards listing the last names of five of the residents. "Hmmm, they've already removed his name, see?" He pointed to the top button and the blank strip of white paper beneath the directory's Plexiglas coating.

Margaret Louise shrugged off Charles's concern with her usual sunny disposition. "I reckon we can just stand here and wait for someone to come out. Maybe it will be the one we're lookin' for."

"Or maybe we could take a guess on which apartment that neighbor lives in," Tori suggested, looking down the list and stopping on 2A. "That woman said she lived just below John, so if John was in 3A"—she moved her finger back up to the empty slot—"then it stands to reason that she lived in 2A, yes?"

Margaret Louise jabbed a playful elbow into Charles's side. "That's why Victoria is so good at solvin' things. She's real smart, ain't she?"

"It's basic deduction, Margaret Louise," Leona mused in boredom. "If I'd known she lived below John, I'd have come to the same conclusion." Then, without any conversation or planning, Leona reached out and pushed the button for 2A.

"Yes?"

"My name is Leona Elkin, and I'm here to speak with you about the two-timing weasel that lived above you until someone pushed him to his death on Monday afternoon."

Tori smacked the heel of her hand to her

forehead and groaned inwardly. Subtlety was certainly not one of Leona's strong suits.

"I've already given a statement to Officer Pollop. I have nothing else to say."

The occasional happy yip-yip of a dog, intermingled with bursts of canned laughter in the background, ceased.

"Well, so much for that angle." Leona turned toward the sidewalk, her stylish pumps making soft clicking sounds as she moved. "So where to now?"

Tori turned back to the buzzer. "No. We can't give up that easily. Dixie's freedom could be riding on this woman." She pressed the button again.

"Yes?"

"My name is Victoria Sinclair. We spoke briefly the afternoon Mr. Dreyer's body was found. We were standing side by side along the crime scene tape, and you said something that might be able to help a dear friend of mine out of a very bad place." She took a deep breath, sending up a mental prayer as she did. "Please, I won't take too much of your time. I promise."

The woman said nothing, the television program and yipping dog the only indication Tori wasn't talking to herself.

"Oh my goodness, that's a corgi I'm hearing, isn't it?" Charles gushed. "My grandmother had a corgi and she sounded just like that."

158

"Who are *you?*" the woman asked.

"I'm Charles—Victoria and Leona's friend. I work at McCormick's Books and Café. But if I had my say, I'd be walking corgis all day long in the park. They're just so very, very precious."

Margaret Louise's left eyebrow rose.

"Well . . . I suppose I can give you five minutes or so. But no more. *The Bold and the Beautiful* will be on shortly, and Ruffs and I don't want to miss it."

A loud buzzing sound granted them access to the brownstone, and Leona scurried back to the door just in time, a knowing smile creasing the edges of her eyes. "Charles, I'm impressed with your tactics."

Charles beamed brightly as if he'd been given a prestigious award. "Thank you, Leona."

Two minutes later, they were met on the staircase between the first and second floors by Ruffs the corgi and his owner, a woman Tori recognized instantly, even if it didn't go both ways.

"So which one of you is the one who claims we've met?"

Tori stepped forward. "I am. I'm Victoria. From Sweet Briar, South Carolina."

The woman let her gaze start at the top of Tori's head and slip slowly down to her toes. "Can't say that I remember you. We spoke?" Then, sweeping her gaze outward toward Leona and Margaret Louise, she stopped. "Wait. I remember you. You talk funny."

"I reckon I do." Margaret Louise leaned forward and stroked the back of the corgi's head. "So this is Ruffs?"

"At your service." At the sound of her name, Ruffs wagged her tail with gumption, seemingly diffusing any tension her owner brought to the staircase meeting almost immediately. "So what is it I said that had you buzzing my doorbell?"

Tori closed her eyes briefly, the woman's past words finding their way to her own mouth. "You said it was only a matter of time before one of those women wised up to John's ways and exacted revenge."

"And I was right, wasn't I?" The woman glanced down at her watch then back up at each of them. "John collected women the way I collect magnets. The difference was that I hang mine on the refrigerator and call it a day. John used those poor, pitiful women to line his wallet."

"How do you know this?" Tori asked quickly.

"Because he'd tell me about the women he was off to meet whenever I met him outside the building on the way back from walking Ruffs. He'd tell me their first name, where they lived, and invariably, their connection to money— whether it was an impressive job they'd retired from, a wealthy spouse who'd passed on, or in some cases, good breeding.

"In the beginning, I just thought he was simply a ladies' man, someone who enjoyed the company of women."

"What changed your mind about that?"

The woman met Victoria's gaze and held it as she spoke. "Because he never spoke about them with any real interest until that last day. Instead, he went on and on about the things they'd bought him and the various things he was poised to get from them. It made me very glad my dogs have always been enough for me."

"I take it you've seen some of his women along the way?"

"A few here, a few there. Mostly he met them away from here, which was probably by design." The woman patted her lower leg and Ruffs came running. "The third date usually took place here. A popcorn movie night complete with a showing of *Singing in the Rain*."

Leona rolled her eyes. "Tell me he didn't . . ."

"Oh, yes, he did. The ones that made it to that date always left his apartment with this starry-eyed look like he was just the cat's meow." The woman pointed over her shoulder to the door marked 2A. "I could hear the movie through the ducts in my apartment but couldn't ever hear what—if anything—John and his date discussed. Then when the movie was over and I heard his door open upstairs, I'd stand on the other side of my peephole and watch her come down the stairs with the same gaga expression on her face as the woman three days earlier.

"Within twenty-four hours, John would be showing off a new toy—an electronic gadget, a silk tie, Broadway tickets, money, you name it."

"Money?" Charles clarified. "They'd actually give him money?"

"From what I gather, he was"—the woman used her fingers to simulate air quotes—"short on rent from time to time and they were eager to help."

Charles made a funny face. "From time to time?"

"Pretty much each month from what I've heard around the building."

"Wow." Charles scrunched up his nose in disgust. "Where were these women's friends?"

"Your guess is as good as mine." The woman looked again at her watch but remained where she stood, the pull of her daytime soap opera appearing to lose its standing on her list of priorities. "Most of them seemed to disappear quietly. But others, like this one woman who cried outside the main door night after night for nearly a week, didn't go quite as quietly. I spoke with her one night and she seemed to know she'd been taken, but still couldn't wrap her head around the fact she was better off. Eventually, though, she gave up, but not before leaving a stuffed animal on the doorstep and a note saying she'd always remember John fondly and wishing him well in his future relationships."

"I don't even know her and I want to smack her," Leona whispered through clenched teeth before being silenced by Margaret Louise's wide hand.

"Did any of them ever get *mad* at him?" Tori asked.

"Sometimes, I suppose. But nothing like what happened the night before he was murdered."

Tori leaned forward in sync with Margaret Louise, Leona, and Charles. "What happened then?"

"I'd just finished preparing Ruffs's dinner when I heard the pounding. At first, I thought it was the maintenance man hammering a nail into one of my neighbors' walls. But it didn't stop. It just got louder and louder and louder." The woman slowly lowered herself to the closest step and sat down. "Then the yelling started. At first, it was just demands for John to open the door so they could talk. Then, when he didn't do it, the demands shifted to threats."

"Threats?" Tori and Charles echoed in unison, swapping glances with each other as they did. "What kind of threats?"

"Bodily ones." The woman placed Ruffs atop her lap and rested her chin between the dog's ears. "The man threatened to rip John limb from limb for—"

"It was *a man?*"

At the woman's nod, Tori begged her to continue.

"He kept saying John would regret his choice, then finally, he turned and bounded down the stairs and straight out of the building."

"Regret his choice?" Tori repeated.

"I'm just telling you what I heard. The deciphering part is up to you."

Tori looked at Margaret Louise, who looked at Charles and Leona and then back again. Leona was the first one to finally speak. "Did you happen to see him through your peephole when he passed?"

"I tried to. But his head was down when he went by."

"Did you catch his hair color? General size? Anything?" Tori inquired.

The woman pulled her head from atop the dog's long enough to shake it from side to side. "Other than that he wore a hat and seemed fairly tall, I really didn't see much. He moved fast and the hall was dim on account of a broken bulb that Alex, the maintenance man, finally got around to fixing just last night."

Tori did a mental run-through of everything the woman had shared thus far, Doug's face appearing in her thoughts almost instantly. One look at her friends told her they were thinking the same thing. "Did you happen to call the police that night?"

"I almost did, but then he was gone and that was it." The woman set the dog on the steps beside her body, grabbed hold of the wooden banister, and pulled herself back to her feet. "I did tell them about that night after John was pushed. But since they already had their killer, they didn't pay it any mind."

Already had their killer . . .

"Well they should have," Leona hissed through clenched teeth. "Because they've got the wrong person."

Chapter 16

For Tori, there was something about sitting on a park bench beneath a canopy of oak trees in the middle of the busiest city in the world that was almost surreal. It was like two different worlds— one quiet and peaceful and ripe with nature, and the other filled with concrete, skyscrapers, and people as far as the eye could see—had been tossed into one of Margaret Louise's blenders and mixed together to create a flawless culinary masterpiece.

"I see 'em, I see 'em!" Margaret Louise pushed off the bench and shot her hand into the air, waving it wildly from side to side, but to no avail.

Charles placed his hand on Margaret Louise's shoulder. "I've got this, sugar." He put two fingers into his mouth and blew, the whistle he created

165

causing more than a few dogs to turn in their direction. Sure enough, Beatrice looked up from whatever deep conversation she was having with Debbie and Rose and looked from side to side. "Woo-hoo! Southern Ladies . . . we're over here!"

Tori felt the knot of dread in her stomach tighten when the smiles she would have expected from their friends failed to make an appearance. Rising to her feet, she tried to muster one for them instead. "Boy, am I happy to see the three of you!" She took Rose's upper arm from Debbie and led her the last few steps to the bench. "How was your morning with Dixie?"

Rose slowly lowered herself to the hunter green–painted bench and exhaled. "Dixie is a wreck. She cried almost the whole time, and she's lost, what"—Rose looked to Debbie and Beatrice for corroboration of her guess—"a good pound or so already, wouldn't you agree?"

Debbie nodded. "Her face is pasty white and drawn in, like the weight of the world is on her."

"Because it is," Rose said before turning to meet Tori's worried eyes. "Victoria, she can't stay in there much longer. It's going to kill her."

It was hard to comfort someone when you didn't have a whole lot to offer, but still, she tried. Rose was failing enough on her own—the stress of what was happening to Dixie might be just enough to push her over the edge. "Rose, we're going to figure this out."

"That's what you keep saying, but I'm worried it won't happen." Rose twisted the ends of her sweater inside her hands then looked off into the distance, with nothing else to say.

Debbie moved in closer, wrapping an arm across Tori's shoulder as she did. "So tell us how things went on your end. Any luck finding Caroline Trotter?"

"No. We stopped by again on the way here but no such luck."

"But after what we learned from John's downstairs neighbor, tracking down Caroline is probably a waste of time," Charles gushed. "In fact, if you ask me, I think we can remove her name from the list entirely."

Beatrice stepped into the makeshift semicircle around Rose's bench, closing it off from any curious passersby. "We can?"

"John's neighbor told us about an incident the night before the murder. We think the man she recalls pounding on John's door could very well be the cupcake lady's son, Doug."

"He threatened to tear John limb from limb," Margaret Louise added triumphantly. "Which is just what I said this mornin', ain't it? A good boy could snap if someone hurt his mama."

Rose re-engaged eye contact, the faintest hint of hope removing some of the darkness from her features. "Is this true, Victoria? Did you get the break we've been waiting for?"

More than anything, she wanted to say yes, wanted to ease the worry from Rose and deliver concrete proof to the police that Dixie wasn't the one who'd murdered John Dreyer. But she couldn't.

Not yet anyway.

She felt Debbie's arm tighten around her shoulders as she searched for the best way to answer Rose's questions without completely annihilating the hope the woman so desperately needed just to hang on and stay positive. "What Charles and Margaret Louise said is true, Rose. A man did pound on John's apartment door the night before the murder. That man did threaten him, saying John would regret his choice. But whether or not that man was Doug remains to be seen. John's neighbor didn't get a clear look at his face, so we're just hypothesizing at this point."

"It certainly fits, though." Charles twisted his lips into a contemplative pout then allowed them to part as he opted to share a thought. "And if it does, Caroline Trotter is a moot point."

"We can't rule her out, Charles, even if we can determine the man John's neighbor heard was, in fact, Doug. To simply write her off is exactly what the cops did when the neighbor told them about this mystery man and they already had Dixie."

Charles gave Tori an admiring nod that included a glance in Margaret Louise's direction. "She really is good at this stuff, isn't she?"

"It's like I said to you earlier, our Victoria is a modern-day Nancy Drew."

Rose's shoulders caved inward, prompting Tori to disengage from Debbie and squat beside Rose. "Hey . . . Rose . . . it's going to be okay. Somehow, someway, this is going to work out. Dixie is innocent. You know that, I know that, everyone here knows that, and soon, the police will know it, too."

"I pray you're right, Victoria, I truly do," Rose whispered in a voice void of any emotion or strength.

Tori cocked her head upward and peered at her friends, the worry she saw in their eyes surely reflected in her own. But it was Charles who finally spoke, the singsong quality of his voice coupled with his bottomless supply of positive ideas providing the exact reprieve they needed at that moment.

"The six of you need to have a little fun. Something to lift your spirits and help that sunshine right there"—he pointed at the steady ray of light poking its way through the trees above them—"reach your insides, too."

"How are we supposed to have fun, young man, when our friend is sitting in a jail cell in a strange city for a crime she didn't commit?"

For a moment, Charles didn't answer. But just as Tori was beginning to worry that Rose had hurt his feelings, he reached forward, gently took Rose's hands, and tugged her to her feet, assuming walking-buddy duty with a link of his arm. "You let the sea lions have it for you and just go along for the ride the way I do when someone's had the audacity to paint my rainbow-colored world in warship gray and dirt brown."

Leona, Margaret Louise, Beatrice, Debbie, and Tori fell in step behind Rose and Charles as they made their way through the southern section of Central Park to the zoo. Once inside, they secured a spot on the top step that encircled the sea lion pool and waited—along with a trio of eager sea lions—for the arrival of the three trainers tasked with feeding the animals and showcasing their many abilities to the steadily growing crowd.

As they waited, Tori couldn't help but marvel at the way Charles had won over her friends, his ability to listen and relate making him and his many quirks more than a little endearing.

In a matter of minutes, he managed to make everyone feel special. With Leona, he swapped makeup tips as well as an occasional under-the-breath commentary about its poor application by several zoo goers. With Margaret Louise and Debbie, he shared kitchen success stories and a handful of laugh-worthy disaster tales. With Rose, he shared his list of favorite books, citing several that had given him the courage to be the person he was meant to be. With Beatrice, he hummed a few Kenny Rogers tunes.

Tori watched the various interactions, even smiled at a few of them, but she simply couldn't seem to find the modicum of peace her friends had managed to seize as they awaited the trainers.

Charles, of course, noticed, scooting his backside closer to Tori as Beatrice turned her attention to her camera and a Bobblehead Kenn–holding Margaret Louise.

"You're mighty quiet over here, Victoria," he said by way of a statement, rather than a question. "I know we can't celebrate Dixie's freedom just yet, but we've found some good leads."

She knew he was right, knew from past experience that the chips would invariably fall into place if they didn't give up, but still, she couldn't shake the nagging sensation that something about Doug wasn't adding up. Something she couldn't put a finger on herself, let alone explain to Charles or anyone else.

Instead, she lifted her left hand to shield the sun from her eyes and tried to find comfort in the sweetness of the sleek faces that kept bobbing out of the water in anticipation of the fish they seemed to know was near. "Did you know sea lions are Dixie's favorite zoo animal?"

"I do now."

She exhaled a blast of pent-up air from her lungs. "I guess I'm just worried about Dixie more than I want to let on. Rose needs to see me confident, even if I'm every bit as worried as she is."

A burst of barking rang up from the pool as three uniformed zoo trainers rounded the corner near the penguin house and made their way toward the pool, a large metal bucket in each one's hand.

Tori leaned forward just enough to see her friends, the momentary glee on their faces bringing a strange mixture of happiness and dread to her chest. Sure, she was glad they were having some much-needed fun even if she knew it would last only as long as the show, but Dixie should be there, too, smiling and enjoying the sweet innocence of her favorite water creatures.

Innocence . . .

She closed her eyes for a moment, only to open them when she felt Charles studying her rather than the sea lions like everyone else. "I'm sorry, Charles," she whispered through the lump that had formed in her throat. "I'm not trying to be a killjoy. But picturing Dixie in that jail cell is all I can think about right now."

The lump was followed by a misting in her eyes when his hand closed over hers and squeezed ever so gently. "A friend of a friend is on the force. I'll give him a ring once we're done here and ask him to look in on Dixie tonight. Maybe knowing she's got someone on the inside looking out for her in much the same way she has all of you rallying to her defense here on the outside will make things a little easier. For her . . . and for you."

Chapter 17

Despite the fun she'd ended up having at the sea lion show, and the reassurance Charles's offer had given her in terms of Dixie's well-being that night, nothing was able to quiet Tori's mind in quite the same way as hearing Milo's voice on the other end of the line. Although they were a good seven hundred miles apart from each other in a physical sense, there was something about his soothing voice that made him feel infinitely closer.

"I'm worried about you, baby," he said earnestly. "I can hear the exhaustion in your voice. Are you getting any sleep at all?"

She considered telling him the simple truth but knew that would only increase his worry. Besides, what was the point? There wasn't anything he could do to change the situation and, thus, her lack of sleep.

Instead, she took a deep breath and told him just enough to keep his radar from going off. "I'm trying to, Milo. But it's hard. Every time I drift off to sleep, I invariably wake up with thoughts of Dixie and the cell she's being forced to sleep in."

"I still can't believe the police actually think

Dixie killed this guy. I mean, do they not see she's in her seventies?"

"They do." Tori flopped onto the couch in the empty sitting room and stared up at the ceiling, the occasional snore from Margaret Louise the only discernible noise aside from her own quiet breathing. "But they don't care, Milo. Dixie had the other half of the scarf found at John's apartment and that's all they seem to care about."

"But she said she's never seen it before, right?"

"Right. But they say she's lying."

"They're wrong."

She closed her eyes and inhaled sharply, the certainty in his words a perfect match for the certainty in her heart. The problem, though, was how to spread that same level of conviction to the police. Oh, how she wished her say, and that of Margaret Louise, Leona, Beatrice, Debbie, and Rose, mattered.

Slowly, she opened her eyes and fixed her gaze on the window across from the couch, the one that provided a view of New York City in all its nighttime glory. It was a sight that had enthralled her their first night there, yet frightened her now, four days later. "That's why we're still here. We have to make them see that."

"Any luck on that yet? Any viable suspects?"

It was a valid question. Her answer, though, left much to be desired. "Maybe. I don't know."

"Maybe?"

"I mean, there are three people that have our attention right now, none of whom we've spoken to directly."

"Why not?"

"Well, Ms. Steely Eye doesn't have an official name yet. Just a picture."

Milo's laugh tickled her ear and brought a much-needed, albeit fleeting, smile to her lips. "Ms. Steely Eye?"

"If you'd seen her that first time like we did, you'd understand."

"You've seen her more than once?"

"Twice, actually, though we didn't realize the second instance until after the fact."

At his confusion, she did her best to explain. "We saw her the first time the morning of the murder. We'd gone to the Waldorf to spy on Dixie and John's breakfast date. But Ms. Steely Eye wasn't too keen on sharing the massive potted plant that was big enough to shield all of us at one time."

"Wait a minute. Are you saying she was spying on Dixie, too?"

She brought her fingertips to her right temple and began to knead at the dull pain just below the surface of her skin. Too much stress plus not enough sleep equaled a veritable cycle that showed no signs of breaking anytime soon. "At the time, I didn't connect the dots, but after . . . when Beatrice was scrolling through the pictures we'd taken so far, she came across one I took near the murder scene later that afternoon. Ms. Steely Eye was there looking, well, steely-eyed."

"Sounds like she's one to track down, that's for sure," Milo said. "And the next possibility?"

"His name is Doug. He's the son of the owner of a popular cupcake shop here in the city. His mother was one of John's cons from what we've been able to gather."

"And let me guess . . . Doug is the protective type?"

Tori thought back over everything Gretchen had said at the cupcake shop the previous day, her head nodding against the phone as she did. "Combine that with his anger over the effects that experience had on his mother's last days on this earth and, well, you can imagine why he's on our list. Especially when there's a possibility he may have been at John's apartment the night before the murder, threatening to rip John limb from limb for what he'd done."

A long, low whistle came from Milo's end of the line. "Wow."

"He's Margaret Louise and Debbie's top choice, while Ms. Steely Eye is mine and Beatrice's, simply because her appearance in both places seems way too impossible to be a coincidence."

"You said there's only three people on your list right now . . ."

"Right," she answered, dropping her hand to her lap.

"So does that mean that neither Rose nor Leona has an opinion at this time?"

"No, it means they're in agreement on the culpability of our third suspect, Caroline Trotter." She heard the sharp intake of air in her ear yet had little to no energy left to laugh. Besides, her head hurt too much. "Thanks to Charles, we've been able to confirm her as one of John's most recent women, and potentially a scorned one at that." She stopped, contemplated her own words for a moment, and then continued, the rambling quality of her voice audible even to her own ears. "We actually have an address for her thanks to a scarf she left behind."

"Does it match the piece found in Dixie's handbag?"

She sat up straight, intrigued by the question. "No . . ."

"I figured as much, but I had to ask. So why haven't you talked to her if you have her address?"

"She hasn't been at her place the few times we've stopped—"

The ring of the hotel phone caught her off guard and sent her scrambling for the bureau before it woke her friends. "One second, Milo, okay?" Then, lowering her cell phone to her hip, she reached for the hotel phone with her other hand. "Hello?"

"Victoria. I was hoping you'd pick up. I've got news. B-i-g news."

"Is it Dixie?" she asked, suddenly breathless. "Is she okay?"

"I spoke to my friend this evening and told him about this pile of hoo-ey that's being thrown on Dixie. He agreed to ask his friend, Al—the cop—to look in on her. Al called me a little while ago to tell me he spoke to Dixie and told her he was a friend of a friend of *mine* and that I'm a friend of *yours*."

"And?"

"He told her he'd look after her and that she's going to be okay."

Somehow, despite knowing they were just words with nothing to back them up yet, Tori still found a measure of comfort in knowing that someone was looking after Dixie from the inside. "Thank you, Charles. I can't tell you how much this helps."

"Well, there's more."

"Oh?"

"I stopped by Caroline Trotter's apartment again this evening. She still wasn't there."

"Surprise, surprise." She heard the bitterness in her voice and the increased pressure it brought to her already aching head.

"That's what I thought. So I asked some questions this time."

"What kind of questions? And to whom?"

"The night doorman is different than the day guy and this one is way, way, *way* cute—even Leona would approve." Charles took an audible breath then rushed on, "Caroline hasn't been seen since Tuesday morning!"

"Maybe she went on vacation."

"Nate—that's the doorman . . . wait. Did I mention he has the greatest dimples ever? Well, anyway, Nate said tenants always tell them when they're going to be away. But Caroline said nothing to him, Timothy the day guy, or anyone in the office."

She tried to see why Charles was so keyed up by this development but she came up empty. Things came up. It was part of life.

"And now, for the b-i-g news I mentioned earlier." Charles stopped, waited a moment or two, and then released a little squeal. "Caroline's daughter has been calling. Even she doesn't have any idea where her mother is."

"Okay . . ."

"Nate said she's fit to be tied that her mother may have taken up with another con man like"—a Charles-made drum roll sounded in her ear—*"John."*

Her jaw slacked open. "J-John?"

"That's what Nate said. He also said the daughter spent nearly ten minutes ranting and raving about how she'd tried to warn her mother but it didn't work."

"What does that mean?"

"I don't know but I bet we can find out . . ."

"Charles, you're amazing. I can't believe the way you're helping us like this. I can't even begin to tell you how much this means to me . . . to all of us." And it did. Being a stranger in a strange city was stressful enough. Being a stranger in a strange city while trying to clear your friend of murder charges was another thing entirely.

"Stick with me, sister. We'll get Dixie out of that nasty-smelling jail cell in no time," Charles promised before giving in to a long yawn. "We've got an author event at the bookstore tomorrow morning so I'll be tied up until about two. I'll give you a call once I'm clear and we can get out our magnifying glass and start looking for more clues, okay?"

"Sounds good, Charles. Thanks again." She placed the hotel phone down on its base and lifted her cell phone back to her ear. "Milo? Are you still there?"

"I am."

Quickly, she filled him in on her call with Charles, ending with the question now circulating in her thoughts. "Do you think Caroline heard about John and is off mourning his death?"

"Maybe. But maybe she already knew and decided to run."

Chapter 18

There was a part of Tori that felt guilty for taking a morning off from the Dixie investigation, but without a clear head or a game plan, she wasn't doing anyone any good anyway.

She'd considered taking first Margaret Louise, and then Leona, up on their offers to come along, but in the end, she knew she needed time alone—time to think, time to strategize, and time to stamp down the spurts of anger that had her tossing and turning through yet another sleepless night.

If Margaret Louise, Beatrice, and Rose had only stayed out of Dixie's business, the trip to New York would have been exactly what it was supposed to be. Instead, the fun and excitement they'd imagined had been ripped from beneath their feet, with Dixie paying the biggest price of all. And now, instead of being able to go home and put the finishing touches on her autumn wedding to Milo, she was trying to find a way to get Dixie out from under a tragedy of other people's making.

She'd been so close to taking Milo up on his offer to come to the city and help during his upcoming spring break, but eventually she'd declined. Adding one more person to the mix wasn't going to help, and really, all she wanted to do was go home.

A horn off to her left prompted her to glance up from the sidewalk passing beneath her feet and get her bearings. She'd passed the outer edge of Central Park a few blocks earlier, and now, as she stood still and looked around, she found that she actually recognized the intersection she was about to cross.

She'd been at that exact corner before . . .

Craning her head around the man in front of her, she allowed her gaze to continue down the street, stopping, as she suspected, at McCormick's Books & Café.

She hadn't set out to go there, hadn't planned on being anywhere near yet another tie to Dixie's mess, yet she wasn't surprised, either. Books had been her comfort in life for as long as she could remember. They'd gotten her through the occasional bad day at school as a child, they'd forged connections with people she never would have met otherwise, they'd been her saving grace after her great-grandmother had passed away, and they'd been the reason she'd moved to Sweet Briar, South Carolina, in the first place—a town where she'd met not only her future husband but also a stable of friends she could no longer imagine life without.

With her destination now in the conscious part

of her brain, Tori crossed at the light and hurried toward the bookstore and the throngs of older women pouring onto the sidewalk from its main entrance. The women seemed to be in groups—three here, four there. But all were talking a mile a minute, with some even engaging their hands as they spoke.

"He was wonderful," gushed one.

"He makes it all sound so simple . . . so possible," said another.

When Tori reached the door, she stepped to the side to allow more women to exit, her gaze catching on the poster just inside the plate glass window and the familiar face it sported.

Suddenly it all made sense. The demographic exiting the store, the elation and hope she saw on their faces, and even the now-remembered reason Charles had given on the phone the night before as to why he wouldn't be available for sleuthing until after 2 p.m.

Gavin Rollins had spent the morning at McCormick's talking about his blockbuster book to an audience of captivated older women—the title of his book alone serving as a magnet for all those who found themselves seeking love after sixty-five. And judging by the volume of books leaving through the door, the event had been a success for the store.

She stepped inside and allowed her eyes a moment to adjust to the break in sunlight that had warmed the back of her head throughout much of her walk and blinded her each time she turned to look over her shoulder. Sure enough, as the bright spots of daylight receded, she was able to make out the temporary seating area the shop's workers had set aside for the author's visit, a handful of women still lingering behind as they watched Gavin sign the last few books for their friends.

"Oooh, Victoria, I didn't know you were coming."

Turning, she met Charles's raised eyebrow with an easy shrug. "I didn't know I was coming, either, until I got here." She waved her hand toward the mostly empty chairs and the display case to Gavin's right. "It sure looks like your event was a success."

"Was. It. Ev-er." Charles grabbed the metal chair closest to him and folded it quickly. "I'm shocked that old register we have didn't catch fire with how hard it's been working."

She couldn't help but smile. In this day and age, when people seemed to be flocking toward electronic versions of everything, seeing hard-cover books flying off the shelves at such a rapid rate was encouraging if not downright exciting. "That's good, real good."

"You bet your cute little jazz pants it is." Charles paused with his hand on the next chair and nodded approvingly at Tori's choice of attire for the day. "You are looking oh so good, Miss Victoria. We might just have to take a picture and send it to that handsome man of yours everyone is always talking about." Then flipping his hand forward along with the chair, he made a little face. "Which brings me to two questions. First . . . when am I going to get to meet this Milo Wentworth? And second . . . where is everyone?"

Setting her purse on the floor by her feet, Tori began folding chairs and adding them to Charles's stack, the chance to do something with her hands a welcome reprieve for her brain, even if it only lasted a minute or two. "You'll have to come to Sweet Briar one day. You can meet Milo then."

Charles stopped folding chairs long enough to do a little hop-skip move. "And come to a sewing circle meeting! If you let me borrow your kitchen when I come, I can whip up my famous New York–style cheesecake for everyone!"

"It's a date."

Satisfied, he returned to his chair-folding task and his second question. "And the ladies? Where are they this afternoon? They would have enjoyed Gavin Rollins's talk."

"They're at the hotel. They needed a day off, and so did I."

Again, Charles stopped folding. "Is everything okay? I mean, besides the obvious?"

She allowed her gaze to travel back to Gavin

and the last woman in line for his signature and felt her shoulders slump almost instantly. "This trip was supposed to be so different, you know? We were supposed to sightsee. We were supposed to laugh. We were supposed to eat in the kinds of places Sweet Briar will never have. We were supposed to revel in our one and only stint on a real television program. And instead we have this."

Charles transferred his last folded chair to the pile, took Tori's from her, and then led her to a pair of seats not far from Gavin and the women who'd obviously been lingering for photo opportunities. "Sit, Victoria."

When she did as she was told, he took her hand and squeezed it gently. "We made it to the zoo yesterday, didn't we? That was sightseeing!"

She swallowed.

"We laughed when the sea lion danced to Beatrice's ring tone, right?"

She looked down at his hand atop hers and nodded.

"I took you to CupKatery for the yummiest cupcakes this side of the Mississippi, didn't I?" He pulled his hand from hers and braced it against his thigh. "And as for the television show, I would imagine Leona will find a way to work all of you into her show come fall."

Ahhh yes.

Leona's cable TV program, *Leona's Closet*. The

one with the ten-minute segment entitled, *Who Dresses You Anyway?*

"I'm not sure we want to be on Leona's show," she mused in an effort to lighten the mood she'd singlehandedly brought down. "But I know what you're saying, Charles, and you're right. There *have* been some good moments on this trip. Even some funny ones. But it's just that . . ."

Her words trailed from her mouth, only to be picked up and given voice by Charles. "You wanted Dixie to be part of it all, too."

She swallowed harder this time, her nod barely perceptible even to herself.

"Well, Charles, it looks like I'm all done here."

Tori looked up to find Gavin standing mere inches from their seats, his eyes widening as they met hers. "Hey . . . I know you. You're Victoria, from the show the other day."

Rising to her feet, she offered her hand to Gavin, smiling warmly as he took it and added a smile of his own. "I am. It looks like you had quite the turnout here today, Gavin."

"And then some, I'd say." He released her hand. "I thought you ladies were heading back to your little southern town a couple of days ago."

"We were."

It was all she could manage to say at the moment, on account of the lump that had formed in her throat at the notion of going home.

"You needed a bigger bite of the Apple, eh?"

She considered telling him the truth, but knew if she did, she'd no longer be able to ward off the tears that threatened to drown everything in sight. Instead, she went with the best noncommittal response she could give. "Yeah, I guess you could say something like that."

"I see." He motioned toward the empty book display and the sign that served as the only remaining indication he'd been there at all. "Well, Charles, we sold through the entire stock."

She took in the empty shelves then turned back to the author. "Gavin, can I ask you a question?"

He nodded. "Sure, shoot."

"Do you think those guys you write about in that section Kenneth talked about on the show will ever realize that what they're doing is wrong and move on to something else?"

"You mean the cons?"

At her slow nod, he shook his head, grimacing as he did. "I wish I could say I do, but I can't. Greed isn't going anywhere, anytime soon. And because of that, guys like I write about aren't going anywhere, either."

"How can you stand writing about them?" Charles interjected in his usual boisterous way. "I mean, isn't that kind of like giving them validation?"

"I see it more as giving my readers a blueprint for exactly the kind of man they need to avoid as they're moving through their silver years looking for love. Forewarned is forearmed, as my mother always said." Gavin brushed a hand down the front of his navy trousers and sighed. "By talking about these guys, I'm able to open up my readers' eyes before they fall prey in their quest for love."

"Have you heard from readers who avoided these types of situations because of your book?" she asked.

"Have I ever," he said, smiling broadly. "Those are my favorite letters, quite frankly, because I know that I saved that particular person from heartbreak, and possibly financial ruin, too."

"Seeing as how that's such a popular section in your book, will you put one like it in the second book?" Charles rose to his feet and began folding and stacking chairs once again.

"How could I not when that's the part that everyone seems to want to talk about? Though maybe I'll also touch on the ways these con artists affect a woman's self-confidence, too. Can you imagine how heartbreaking some of *those* stories will be?"

She felt Charles studying her and knew what he was thinking. Dixie could write that section all by herself.

Assuming she wasn't confined to jail for the rest of her life . . .

Forcing her thoughts from the slippery slope they were in danger of going over, Tori took the conversation in a different direction, one that kept yet another round of tears at bay. "If you go out on tour with that next book, you should try to come down to Sweet Briar. We'd love to have you at the library."

Charles snorted. "Something tells me those southern ladies, while quaint and well mannered, could probably teach Gavin's duped readers a thing or two about comeuppance at the end of a shotgun."

"I imagine they could," Gavin said between laughs. "Maybe that can be a section in the third book—'Tried and True Tips for Getting Even.' "

Chapter 19

Tori stepped inside the now familiar cupcake shop and sniffed, the tantalizing aromas of chocolate, peanut butter, mint, and cinnamon overpowering all others in their silent, yet magnetic pull toward the front counter. Her stomach gurgled as her feet heeded the invitation.

"Welcome to CupKatery. What size box would you like?" A woman of about thirty, clad in a pretty white-and-pink apron, pointed at the back-lit sign above her head. "Our twenty-five count is the best value."

Tori glanced toward the case, her eyes instantly gravitating toward the flavors she'd tried with her friends only days earlier. "Um, yeah, sure . . . okay, the twenty-five count will be fine."

That decided, the woman moved toward the glass case and waited.

So, too, did Tori.

Finally, the woman shifted the empty box to her left hand and shot a pointed look in Tori's direction. "Which cupcakes do you want in the box?"

"Oh, I have to fill it now, don't I?" Tori shook off the fog that had settled around her thoughts the moment she walked inside the shop and forced herself to focus. Once the cupcakes were selected, the questions that had propelled her to stop there in the first place could commence. "I'll take five each of the pancake batter, the s'more, the peanut butter cup, the cookies and cream, and . . . wow, I'm at a loss now."

The woman pointed to the middle rack. "The maple chip is our flavor of the month. It's very good."

"Then let's finish up the box with those."

Nodding, the woman filled the box with the specified cupcakes then rang up the purchase with a practiced hand. "That'll be thirty-five dollars and forty-two cents please."

She took a moment to count out her change, mentally praying all the while that the store would remain empty. When she had what she needed coin-wise, she carefully placed it in the woman's hand and nudged her chin toward the kitchen. "My friends and I stopped by here the other day. Gretchen took good care of us."

"I'm glad to hear—"

The string of bells above the shop's front door rang, touching off a flurry of apron straightening and over-the-top eye contact from the woman. "Thanks so much for stopping by CupKatery. I hope you love your selections."

"I'm sure I will." She glanced over her shoulder to see who was responsible for the clerk's obvious nervousness and felt her own mouth go dry. There, standing in the doorway, looking around the tiny eating area, was the same dark-haired man from the picture on the wall behind the counter—the man who'd draped his arm so protectively across his mother's shoulders and who, according to Gretchen, had been furious at the notion that some man had broken his mother's heart just weeks before her death.

Barely missing a beat, Tori turned back to the counter and smiled. "You know what? I think I'd like to sample one of those maple chip cupcakes now . . . and maybe one of the pancake batter ones, too."

"For here or to go?"

"For here!" She cringed inwardly at the too-eager lilt to her voice and was grateful when the woman didn't seem to notice. A moment later, after her money had been exchanged for the bite-sized cupcakes, Tori wandered over to the very same table she'd shared with Rose two days earlier, her ears perked and waiting.

Doug didn't disappoint.

"Jillian. How's it going so far today?"

"It's going well." Jillian grabbed a cloth from somewhere just outside of Tori's field of vision and began wiping the already-clean counter. "How are things at the Connecticut store?"

"Pretty good. I had to go over a few kitchen expectations with the bakers but, other than that, not bad." Doug took in the dining area then crossed to a table on the opposite side of the counter from Tori. Within seconds, all chairs were pushed under the tables in uniform precision.

"I was just about to do that," Jillian offered weakly.

"I got it." He crossed to Tori's side of the shop, exchanged a brief smile with her, then stopped at a neighboring table to remove a newspaper that had been left on one of the chairs. "So did I miss anything exciting while I was up there this past week?"

Jillian shrugged. "Not really. Gretchen and I did fine holding down the fort."

Tori saw him nod, peer down at the paper, look back up at Jillian, and then jerk his focus back down to his hands. "Well, I'll be damned! Did you see this, Jillian? This is the piece of garbage who hurt my mom . . ."

Jillian cleared her throat in between nervous glances in Tori's direction. "Um, boss?"

Oblivious to his employee's efforts to remind him of Tori's presence, Doug continued, his words providing the reason for the ever-widening smile on his face. "Some woman pushed him off his balcony on Monday afternoon."

"Boss—"

"Wow. Too bad I was at the Danbury location, eh? I could have helped."

"Boss!"

Doug looked up, a strange expression on his face. "What?"

Jillian tilted her head toward Tori, widening her eyes as she did.

"Oh. Yeah. Sorry about that." He tucked the paper under his arm and shrugged a smile in Tori's direction. "Don't mind me. I guess I just got carried away there for a moment at the notion that a truly awful human being got what was coming to him."

She considered a simple nod in response, even heard the voices in her head telling her that was best, but in the end, she gave in to the desire to engage him in conversation. "What happened?" she asked, pointing at the paper.

Any initial hesitation he showed about answering fell to the side as he followed the path of her finger back to the newspaper in the crook of his arm. "Well, let's just say there's a woman charged with murder who really should be given an award." He glanced back up at Jillian and laughed. "Think the NYPD would let us bring her a carton or two of cupcakes to say thank you?"

If Jillian answered, Tori didn't hear her over the sudden roar in her ears. For Doug, John's murder represented an end to a problem. For Dixie, it was merely the start. No amount of cupcakes could ever make that right.

A phone just on the other side of the swinging kitchen door rang and Jillian stepped inside to answer it, her voice audible through the opening left by a well-placed foot. "CupKatery, how can I help—oh, hey, Russ . . . yes, he's here . . . hang on, I'll put him on." Then, holding the phone outward, she addressed her boss once again. "It's Russ. He says he needs to talk to you about a delivery or something at the other store."

Doug looked from the phone to the paper before depositing the latter on a nearby table and heading behind the counter and into the kitchen to take the former.

"Hey, Russ, what's up?" The door swung closed behind Doug, taking the rest of his conversation with him as Jillian finished wiping the counter. When she was done, she reached down to an area Tori couldn't see and pulled out a pink-and-blue-checked scarf that she casually draped around her neck. "Gretchen had the opening shift today, which meant I got to sleep in," she said to

Tori. "But even with a noon alarm, I still didn't get up in time. So I've been dressing in spurts since I got here. Just before you arrived, I managed to get some mascara on my lashes."

Tori laughed. "I've had those days. Though no matter what holes I find in my day to rectify the situation, I never seem to pull it together as well as you have." She collected her napkin and walked it to the trash can that sat just inside the tiny dining area. "I love that scarf by the way. It's very pretty."

"Thanks! I got it yesterday from one of the side-walk vendors. He sold it to me for ten bucks, can you believe it?" After a quick check over her shoulder, Jillian whipped open a tube of lip gloss and applied it to her lips with two quick strokes. "I like it even better than the one my cat tore up last week, and I paid twenty bucks for that one."

"That's good—"

"Jillian? Could you come in here for a second?"

The assistant manager dropped the tube of lip gloss back into her apron pocket. "Is there anything else I can get you before I talk to my boss?"

Tori started to shake her head then stopped as her gaze fell on the paper Doug had left behind. She retrieved it from the table and held it out for Jillian to see. "Would you mind if I took this with me? It's a nice day. Maybe I could read it in the park."

"Sure. Go ahead. It's almost four o'clock. Most people have already read the morning paper by now and there's another copy in the rack by the door if they haven't." Jillian put her hand to the kitchen door but kept her focus on Tori. "Have a great rest of your day, okay?"

And then the assistant manager was gone, her apron-tied back disappearing behind the kitchen door as it swung shut in her wake.

Tori looked down at the paper and the masthead she'd only seen during the opening segments of a few late-night talk shows. It had been a whim to ask to keep it and one she didn't fully understand, but if nothing else, it would be one less proclamation of Dixie's guilt out in the wild.

Slowly, she made her way out of the shop, her feet choosing the direction she turned with absolutely no input from her brain. Around her, buses and cars traveled south on Columbus Avenue toward a particular destination. Strangers passed her on the sidewalk, some walking in the opposite direction, some matching or shadowing her steps for a block or two before breaking off to enter an apartment, a store, a restaurant, or a subway station. Yet Tori kept going, her mind as jumbled as it was when she'd left the hotel that morning in search of fresh air.

There was so much to think about, so much to process, but she was at a loss for where to start.

Doug had been away during John's murder.

That fact alone removed him from the short list of suspects Tori and the others had drafted. Caroline Trotter hadn't been seen in days, the timing of her disappearance suspect but nothing they were capable of following up on their own. Ms. Steely Eye was still a player, of course, but without a name, she'd be like finding a needle in a haystack.

And then there was the nagging feeling that Tori was missing something—something big. Twice over the past two days something had tickled at her subconscious, only to recede into no-man's-land before she could give it its due. She'd hoped her walk would clear her head, maybe point her in the next direction she needed to go, but it hadn't.

Sure, she'd enjoyed her time at the bookstore with Charles and Gavin. In many ways their book-related chatter had been a momentary dalliance with normalcy. And the cupcakes she'd just had had been a nice reprieve, too. But in the end, they'd both been nothing more than a temporary detour from a road she had to travel one way or another.

Dixie was still in jail. For a crime she didn't commit.

And all Tori and her friends had to go on was a ripped scarf that had been planted in Dixie's purse . . .

"A ripped scarf . . ." The words drifted from

her lips as she stopped midway down the block, the familiar tickle sensation in her thoughts bringing her up short.

But before she could grab and examine anything closely, her cell phone rang. Reaching into her purse with her free hand, she pulled out the device and held it to her ear. "Hello?"

"Victoria? It's Charles." She stepped closer to the building and covered her open ear in an effort to drown out the street sounds. "I think I know what you need more than anything right now."

She heard the exhaustion in her laugh and allowed it to send her shoulders sinking back against the brick exterior of a sandwich shop. "What I need, Charles, is for Dixie to be released from jail so we can all go back home together."

A beat of silence was followed by Charles's still-cheery voice. "Let me rephrase. I think I know what you need more than anything *next* to having Dixie free."

"A hug from Milo?"

"I would if I could, darlin', but since I don't know Milo, try again."

"A full night's sleep?"

"You're ruining my excitement, Victoria. You do realize this, don't you?"

She glanced to her right, spied a bench roughly ten yards from where she stood, and made a beeline in that direction. "I'm sorry, Charles. I'm not trying to be a killjoy, I'm really not. I'm just stressed is all." Then, after taking a moment to catch her breath, she filled him in on Doug's whereabouts at the time of John's murder. When she was done, she took yet another deep breath, releasing it slowly along with her summation of her outing to CupKatery. "So now we're down a suspect from our already too-short list."

"Well, then maybe time with Dixie will unearth a replacement name."

She sucked in her breath, earning her a strange look from a couple who strolled by her bench, hand in hand. "Did you just say time with Dixie?"

"Remember Al? The cop friend of my friend?"

Tori nodded then realized her mistake and said, "Yes."

"He said we can have some face-to-face time with her this afternoon if we can get down there before five."

"Face-to-face time?"

"Face-to-face . . . as in no glass. Just the three of us in a room with Al or one of his buddies watching."

She felt the lump as it rose up her throat, its final choice of resting spots making it difficult to breathe, let alone speak. But she had to speak if for no other reason than to thank him.

"I don't know what we did to deserve you, Charles, but I am beyond grateful."

"Just invite me to the wedding and we'll call it even, sugar."

Chapter 20

Tori slid the mini-cupcake-topped napkin across the table, blinking back tears as she did. Somehow, despite knowing the seriousness of Dixie's predicament, she'd been able to insert an image of the woman she knew into surroundings she could only imagine. Yet within moments of arriving at the jail, she realized she'd been right about only one.

And it wasn't Dixie.

The Dixie Dunn whom Tori knew was a force all her own. Hovering somewhere around the five-foot-three mark, the woman was solid through and through. Her white hair and age spot–adorned skin might lull a person into believing she was slowing down, but her sharp tongue and fear-inducing glares set the record straight in about two seconds flat.

The Dixie Dunn sitting across from them at that very moment was but a shell of the original. The solid take-no-prisoners stance she usually wore like a badge of honor was gone, in its place a hunched-at-the-shoulders posture that was as foreign to the woman as the defeat that robbed her hazel eyes of anything resembling fight or even life.

"Try this, Dixie," she rasped. "It's peanut butter cup and it's from the cutest little cupcake shop on Columbus Avenue between Seventy-second and—"

"I know where it is . . ." Dixie's words petered off as her head sank forward and she began to cry, the back-and-forth motion of her shoulders ratcheting up Tori's sense of helplessness a hundredfold.

Charles retrieved the cupcake box from his lap and held it out for Dixie to see. "There are other flavors if you prefer—pancake batter, maple chip, s'more, and cookies and cream . . ."

Slowly, Dixie looked up and stared at Charles through tear-soaked eyes. "Who are you?"

"I'm Charles."

When Dixie's stare refused to yield, Tori filled in the gaps. "Charles is helping to get you out of here."

The quiver of Dixie's bottom lip unleashed yet another pair of tears down her pale cheeks. "But he doesn't even know me."

Charles scooted his chair closer to Dixie and took her hand, releasing it slowly as the guard assigned to watch over them stepped forward. "No touching please."

Charles held the cupcake box out to the guard. "Would you like a cupcake?"

"No."

"I won't tell."

The guard's gaze dropped to the box, prompting him to lick his lips ever so slightly. "Where'd you get those?"

"CupKatery," Tori answered.

"You got pancake batter in there?"

Charles pointed to the row of cupcakes that were second from the left then added his most enticing smile. "They want you as much as you want them."

A momentary hesitation fell to the pull of temptation, and the guard reached into the box and extracted two cupcakes. As he ate, Charles patted Dixie's hand. "You're right, we haven't met before now, but from what I saw on *Taped with Melly and Kenneth* the other day, we share a love of books. And as soon as we get you out of"— he waved his hand toward the colorless cinder-block walls that surrounded them, his upper lip curling in the process—"this dank, musty, *awful* place, I suspect we'll find we have even more things in common, too."

"I'm not getting out," Dixie whispered.

"Don't say that, Dixie!" Tori rose to her feet. "The person who should be here is the person who killed John. That's not *you*."

"They've certainly done a good job making everyone believe it's me."

She spun around but kept her mouth closed as Charles took up the fight. "That's not true, Dixie. Victoria, here, knows you didn't do it. Rose,

Margaret Louise, Debbie, Beatrice, and Leona know you didn't do it. And so do I."

A flash of something resembling the Dixie whom Tori knew and loved skittered across the woman's face, only to disappear just as quickly behind the one fact none of them could get around. Yet. "The police think I did, and in this case, that's all that really matters, isn't it?"

The guard gestured toward the box and his favorite row that now contained two less occupants. "Mind if I have another?"

Charles handed the box to him and then turned back to Dixie. "I knew John."

Dixie's face crumpled under the weight of more tears. "You—you knew John?"

He nodded. "I know how he was with women like you. I know the way he worked your hearts."

Dixie pulled her hand from underneath Charles's. "What are you talking about?"

Warning bells sounded in Tori's head, but not in enough time to thwart Charles from alluding to the part of the John story that Dixie still didn't know. "If I'd known what he was doing, I would have found a way to warn them and you. But I didn't."

"What he was doing?" Dixie echoed. "What are you talking about?"

Charles drew back, his eyes wide with shock. "Padding his bank account and accumulating assets off women like you."

"Women like me?"

Tori stepped behind Charles and gripped his shoulder with a well-placed hand. "What Charles is trying to say is that John wronged some people . . . one of whom obviously felt the need to settle the score once and for all."

She was aware of Charles's head turning to afford an uninhibited view of Tori's face, but she refused to make eye contact, choosing instead to keep her focus on Dixie. "All we need to do is figure out who that person is and hand him or her over to the police in your place."

"But who would want to hurt such a sweet and giving man?" Dixie implored.

Charles coughed loudly, stopping only after the second smack Tori delivered to the back of his head.

"With any luck, we'll have that answer sooner rather than later." Tori reclaimed the empty seat next to Charles and gestured toward Dixie's cupcake once again. "Please, Dixie. Eat. I know it's not exactly healthy, but it's something. You need to keep up your strength."

She held her breath as Dixie reached for the cupcake and took one nibble and then another before laying it on the napkin once again. "I've been trying to figure out how a piece of scarf from the crime scene ended up in my purse, but I keep coming up empty."

"There's only one explanation that makes any

sense," Charles finally said after a sheepish peek in Tori's direction. "It was planted there by the true killer."

"But I didn't go anywhere after I found out," Dixie said around a third bite of her cupcake. "I cried myself to sleep in my hotel room and woke to find that police officer at my door."

Tori allowed her eyes to flutter closed at the memory, the wish for a rewind button in life more than a little overpowering. Short of that, though, all they had were the facts—even if they were proving impossible to comprehend, let alone explain. "Then there's only one other explanation that works."

Dixie looked up expectantly and waited, the notion that was so obvious in Tori's mind noticeably absent from hers.

"That piece of scarf was planted in your purse before John was pushed."

Dixie's mouth gaped, then closed, then gaped again. "P-planted? By whom?"

Charles waved his hand in the air. "By someone who had John's murder planned and saw you as a viable scapegoat."

"But who had access to my purse?"

And just like that, the thought that had tickled at Tori's subconscious over the past several days stopped its game of hide and seek and demanded her full attention.

Who had access to Dixie's purse, indeed . . .

She reached into her own purse and pulled out the sheet of hotel paper she'd been carrying around for days, its wrinkled appearance a testament to how many times she'd folded and unfolded it in the hopes of finding the truth she coveted. This time, however, the names on the list were visible in a completely different light.

For Ms. Steely Eye and Caroline Trotter to remain on the list, they would have had to have contact with Dixie prior to John's fall. But short of Dixie's breakfast with John, the seventy-something hadn't been anywhere that Tori and the rest of the sewing circle members hadn't been as well.

Charles's chin grazed Tori's arm as he consulted the list and then addressed Dixie. "Did you meet a woman named Caroline, by any chance?"

"No."

Tori rubbed at her temples in an attempt to ward off the dull pain she felt building. "Did you meet *any* women when you were at breakfast with John that first morning?"

"No."

"Did you pass any women who seemed to *know* John when you were heading out of the restaurant?" Charles interjected.

Dixie started to shake her head and then stopped. "There was one woman who tried to grab his arm as we stepped onto the sidewalk, but he said he didn't know her and we left shortly after that in a cab."

"Onto the sidewalk where?" Tori asked.

"Outside the Waldorf."

Outside the Waldorf . . .

Charles's finger tapped the paper, leading her focus to the top name on the list—Ms. Steely Eye. "This is the one you saw while you were there, right, Victoria?"

"One you saw where?" Dixie repeated woodenly.

Charles swung his crossed leg back and forth, his answer coming easily and without any shred of the guilt Tori felt creeping across her own face. "At the restaurant. While standing behind the potted plant."

Dixie turned her now fiery eyes on Tori. "Why were you standing behind a potted plant at the Waldorf?"

Tori swallowed once, twice. "Um . . . Margaret Louise wanted to see you on your date."

"You and Margaret Louise were spying on me from behind a potted plant?"

"Beatrice, Debbie, Rose, and Leona were there, too," Charles happily reported before retrieving the cupcake box from the police officer and liberating a maple chip cupcake for himself. "Thank heavens those potted plants were big, right?"

The fear-inducing glare was back.

And it was trained squarely on Tori.

"You watched me on my date with John?"

"Only for a few minutes," she admitted through a mouth that was suddenly dry. "We just wanted to see you being happy."

"They weren't the only ones, either." Charles snapped his fingers toward Tori's purse. "Show her Beatrice's camera. Let's see if she remembers Ms. Steely Eye from that morning."

Grateful for any opportunity to remove herself from the path of Dixie's mental dagger throws, Tori reached into her purse, pulled out Beatrice's camera, located the desired picture on the display screen, and set it in the middle of the table. "Have you ever seen this woman?"

She felt Dixie's icy stare as it left her face in favor of the camera now positioned halfway between them on the simple metal table, the subsequent gasp of air from the woman's throat sending a welcome chill down her spine.

"That's her," Dixie mused. "The one who grabbed John's arm as we were stepping outside to catch a cab across town."

Charles sat up straight, shoulders back. "Are you sure?"

"Yes."

"Did she approach you?" Tori asked.

"Not at that time, no. But I did recognize her from the bathroom earlier. We washed our hands next to each other."

Tori felt an infusion of adrenaline course through her body. "Where was your purse?"

Dixie's brows scrunched in thought. "On the counter. Between us."

"Did you step away from it at any point?"

"I dried my hands, of course, but I don't see what any of this has to do with anything."

"It may answer the question as to how that ripped scarf was planted in your purse." A face-lighting smile crept across Charles's face just before he grabbed Dixie's hand and gave it a good squeeze. "We're going to get you out of here, Dixie, I can feel it in my bones."

"But how can a woman John didn't know plant something in my purse for a crime that hadn't yet happened?"

"She couldn't."

Dixie dropped her head into her hands and groaned. "You're talking in circles."

"She couldn't if she didn't know him, but we're fairly confident she did."

Dixie lifted her head and pinned Tori with eyes that were bewildered yet tired. "I don't understand."

Slowly, she pulled the camera back across the table and shut it off, Ms. Steely Eye disappearing from the screen, but not from Tori's thoughts. She remained silent for a moment as she returned the equipment to its case then slipped it back into her purse, the love and loyalty she felt for Dixie

210

making her choose her next set of words carefully. "I know that in the grand scheme of things, we haven't known each other as long as you've known Rose or Margaret Louise or any of the others in the circle. But in the time that I *have* known you, Dixie, I've always admired your ability to land on your feet. You did it after the library board retired you in preparation for my arrival in Sweet Briar, you did it when you dusted off that hurt and stepped in for Nina when she went out on maternity leave and I was on my own at the library, and you did it again just a few months ago when Nina came back and there wasn't money left in the budget to even keep you on in a part-time capacity. I mean, look at you, Dixie. Look at what you did. In a span of a few short weeks following that heartbreak, you landed a volunteer position with Home Fare, helped solve a murder, and managed to secure a paid position for yourself as the organization's volunteer coordinator. Who does that at *thirty-five,* let alone *seventy-five?*"

Dixie sat up proudly, widening her gaze to include an obviously impressed Charles. But after a second or two in the spotlight, her shoulders slumped once again. "I don't see how any of that has to do with"—she spread her hands wide—"this."

"You believed in yourself, Dixie. You believed in what you had to offer people inside and outside the library. And when one door closed, you found another to open." She reached across the table and nudged Dixie's chin upward until their eyes met. "I believe in you, too, Dixie. I know you didn't do this. We *all* know you didn't do this. And you, more than anyone else, have taught me that rolling over in the face of defeat is not an option."

"I—I taught you that?" Dixie asked in a voice choked with emotion.

"You did. And it's why I refuse to roll over and accept this as your fate." She stood up once again, reached into the box, and extracted another cupcake for Dixie's now-empty napkin. "You mark my words, Dixie, I'll have us all back in Sweet Briar before you know it."

Chapter 21

Tori trailed behind Charles as they made their way north from the jail, the speed with which her thoughts were processing failing to translate to her feet.

"I think someone's gone and gotten herself all pooped out," Charles declared. He stepped to the edge of the sidewalk and allowed a throng of tourists and businesspeople to pass while he waited for Tori to catch up.

"Who?"

"You, silly." He rolled his eyes, but any attempt at frustration was quickly offset by the smile that lifted his mouth. "I think Miss Rose would have passed you a few times over by now."

When she didn't respond, his smile gave way to concern. "Hey. You okay, Victoria?"

She wanted to say yes, to acknowledge the lift she'd gotten from spending a little time with Dixie, but she couldn't. So much of what she'd done over the past few days had been a complete and utter waste.

Ahhh yes, square one, a place she hated to be yet seemed to frequent often . . .

"I'm tired, Charles," she finally admitted, the words tasting a little bitter on her tongue. "Maybe even a little defeated."

He studied her closely for a moment or two and then hooked his arm through hers, leading her across the street and into a small pocket park with a handful of benches and only a smattering of people actually using them.

"Here. Sit." He fairly shoved her onto the first empty bench they found and then plopped down beside her with a happy enough sigh. "I have to tell you, Victoria, I couldn't get out of that room fast enough."

"Oh?"

His eyes widened just before he waved his hands side to side. "Don't get me wrong, I'm so so *sooo* glad I finally got to meet Dixie in person. And I think we managed to cheer her up at least a little, wouldn't you say? But taking natural light out of my day for even thirty minutes is like fitting Judy Garland with Crocs instead of ruby slippers. It just doesn't work."

Something resembling a laugh made its way up her throat but stopped just shy of the stage. Instead, she set the day's paper on the empty space between them and took in the leafy tree above their heads.

Seconds turned to minutes as they sat there, side by side, with Tori staring at leaves and Charles staring at her. Finally he spoke, her lack of anything resembling conversation thus far no match for his exuberant personality. "We're going to get her out, you know."

"I'm not so sure about that anymore, Charles."

There. She'd said it.

"Don't say that, Victoria."

Slowly, she turned and lowered her head until her focus was entirely on Charles. "Don't you see how much time we've wasted tracking down people who couldn't possibly be John's killer?"

"No."

"C'mon, Charles. I knew about the ripped scarf in Dixie's purse. I knew it linked her to the scene of the crime. And in talking it out with everyone back at the hotel, I even knew it had to have been planted there *before* John was actually pushed to his death." She allowed herself a chance to pause, the laugh that had died short of her lips only moments earlier now exploding with a self-mocking, almost maniacal sound. "Yet never did I make the connection that Dixie would have had to have crossed paths with the person in order for it to be planted in the first place."

"Cut yourself some slack, sugar. Do you know how many times I had to resemble a blowfish before I realized I was allergic to strawberries? Or how many times I got my lanyard stuck in the register drawer—while it was still around my neck, mind you—before I learned to step back half an inch after making change at the store?" He snapped his fingers in his triangle formation then concluded it with a dramatic lean forward. "Too many."

She chuckled in spite of her dour mood, although the lighthearted effects were over all too soon. "But those mistakes weren't a big deal."

"You say that only because it wasn't *your* face that grew twenty sizes in a span of ten minutes and it isn't *you* who is still mocked by their co-workers on a daily basis *three years* later."

"I'm sorry, Charles. I don't mean to make light of what you said. I'm just feeling pretty stupid about all the brain power I spent thinking the guy from the cupcake store and Caroline Trotter were actually legitimate suspects in John's death." She lurched forward on the bench and caught her head inside her hands. "Ugh. Ugh. Ugh!"

"And they're not suspects now because why?"

She dropped her right hand and tilted her head to afford a view of her companion. "Because Doug never came in contact with Dixie. And we have no reason to think Caroline did, either. All we've got is Ms. Steely Eye . . . who doesn't have a name or anything else that will help us track her down."

"What makes you think she couldn't have come in contact with Doug?"

"Because she wasn't with us when you took us to CupKatery that first time. She was already in jail because John was already dead, remember?" She heard the frustration in her voice and knew it was aimed at herself every bit as much as it was Charles. "That, coupled with the fact he was visiting another one of the shop's locations in Connecticut when John was killed, makes his inclusion on our list an act of futility if not out-and-out stupidity."

Charles squared his back with the bench and crossed his legs at the knees before shaking his head so hard she swore the leaves above their head rustled in response. "Oh no it doesn't."

"How do you figure that?"

"Well, first"—he held up the index finger of his left hand—"there's your notion that Dixie didn't cross paths with Doug."

216

She felt her left brow arch. "Because they didn't. She and John only had one date—for breakfast at the Waldorf."

"It may have started with breakfast, Victoria, but that doesn't mean it stopped there."

She grabbed the next digit on his hand as he began to raise it and held it down. "No. Not yet. The limo picked us up to go to the studio that day at one o'clock."

"So? When did she meet John?"

Tori thought back to the day that had started so magically and tried to remember. "I don't know, nine, I think."

"When did the spying begin?"

"Nine-thirtyish. Maybe ten."

"And end?"

She pulled her hand from Charles's and let it fall back to her thigh. "I don't know, Charles. We were there for fifteen minutes maybe?"

He smiled triumphantly. "Which means they were out of there by ten thirty at the latest. That left them two hours to go across town. More than enough time to become acquainted with CupKatery's many flavors."

"Across town? Who said they went across town?"

"*Dixie* did, that's who."

Pivoting on her backside, Tori hiked her upper leg onto the folded newspaper between them. "No she didn't."

"Don't you remember what she said when John

bumped into Steely Eye on the street outside the hotel but didn't seem to know her?"

"No . . ."

"She said they were hailing a cab across town. From the Waldorf, your hotel would be *down-town,* not *across* town."

Tori stared at Charles as he continued calling attention to details she'd completely missed in her jailhouse funk. "And when you started to tell her where CupKatery was, she cut you off, saying she already knew."

"She did?" she asked around a hard swallow.

"You betcha."

The excitement she felt building dissipated just as quickly as she moved on to the second reason Doug couldn't be involved. "None of this matters when you consider the fact that this guy wasn't even in the state when John died."

It was Charles's turn to laugh. "You haven't looked at a map recently, have you, Victoria?"

"A map?"

He reached into his back pocket and whipped out a handheld device. Then as she watched, he hit a few buttons, made a few faces, and then held the colorful screen across the space between them. "Connecticut is a relatively small state, as you can see. No matter where in the state you might be, you're no more than two hours from the city."

"He was in Danbury."

"Even better. That's an hour. An hour and ten minutes, tops."

She looked from Charles to the screen and back again, the meaning behind his words hitting her square between the eyes. "So even if he was visiting another location, he could be back here in little to no time . . ."

"To borrow one of my favorite catchphrases from Margaret Louise, you're darn tootin' he could."

"But it was a *woman's* scarf that was in Dixie's purse," she mused as much for clarification as a point of contention. "We can't forget that."

"If Doug did it, it was out of revenge . . . for his mother. Maybe it was *her* scarf."

She shook her head in amazement, the man's hypothesizing not only keeping Doug on the list but possibly even moving him to the top. "Wow. You're good, Charles. Real good."

Charles postured and preened under the praise then addressed yet another of Tori's earlier worries. "And as for Caroline Trotter, we don't know whether Dixie came in contact with her or not. Maybe she did, maybe she didn't. But in the event she *did,* the timing of Caroline's disappearance off the face of the earth certainly calls for a little added investigation."

Just like that, all mental chastising ceased.

Charles was right. Scratching anyone off their already too-short list was far too premature.

"I wish I'd had some time with Dixie when she got back from her date. But we had to leave for the show less than fifteen minutes later and things were a little harried to say the least. Maybe if they hadn't been, and we'd had time to talk, I'd know more about where she and John went after breakfast . . ." She let her foot drop back to the ground and retrieved the paper from the bench. Tucking it under her arm, she stood and offered her free hand to Charles. "C'mon, it's been a long day. I think we need to call it quits for now or the crew will be sending out a search party the likes of which this city has never seen."

Charles took her hand and allowed her to pull him to his feet. "I'll walk you back to your hotel, but you have to promise me you're going to find a way to relax until we pull out our magnifying glasses again in the morning."

"I'm sure I'll be talking to Milo before I go to sleep—that'll help a little."

He draped a casual arm across her shoulders and they started walking, the occasional blaring horns and airbrakes of passing busses doing little to drown out his displeasure. "While I'm certain a phone call with your man might make you smile for the ten minutes you're talking, sugar, I'm talking about the kind of relaxation that gets inside your soul."

Stopping, he turned to face her. "It's the only way you're truly going to be able to help Dixie."

She followed what he was saying but couldn't make it fit with her current reality. "I get what you're saying, Charles, I really do. But it's hard to find that when everything around you is strange—the room, the building, the city, the people."

"Then focus on the thing that can lift your spirits and get you back on your feet no matter where you are."

And then she knew.

It didn't matter if she was in Sweet Briar, South Carolina, or New York City. It didn't matter if she was sitting in her armchair at home or on the edge of a bed in a fancy hotel room. When she held a needle and thread in her hands—and surrounded herself with her closest friends—peace and a clear head were hers for the taking.

Chapter 22

It was as it had been since she was eight years old and her great-grandmother had handed her a needle and a spool of thread of her own for the very first time. Something about making a shirt or hemming a pair of pants or creating soft-sided menu items for a child's pretend store or restaurant was like no other therapy she could imagine—except perhaps reading.

But while books provided a way to escape chaotic moments in life, sewing helped Tori deal with them by clearing her head and allowing her to think with an open mind—two things she desperately needed if she was going to be successful in freeing Dixie.

The events of the past few days had made it next to impossible for Tori, Rose, Margaret Louise, and the rest of the sewing circle to work on the zipper flower pins Georgina was counting on as welcome gifts for next month's First Annual Mother's Day Picnic on the Green. They'd packed the necessary supplies for the sewing portion of the pins in one suitcase when they left for the city, but it had remained mostly closed since their arrival, their group time thus far focused on trying to figure out who killed John rather than converting zippers into floral masterpieces. It was a decision that had proven to be a mistake, if the restless atmosphere and short-fused tempers she'd returned to thirty minutes earlier had been any indication.

Now, as some hands guided scissors through zippers while others sewed, the sense of normalcy they'd all been craving was theirs for the taking. And it felt good, real good.

Tori looked up from the flower base she was forming and took a moment to study each of her friends as they worked.

Margaret Louise smiled broadly as she whipped

her threaded needle in and out of the zipper pieces to form a petal . . .

Beatrice cut a piece of felt to form the flower base for the pin taking shape beneath her capable hands . . .

Debbie leaned over Rose's frail shoulder, watching as the most skilled seamstress of the group talked her through the lone sample . . .

Tori shifted in her seat to afford a better view of Leona, a smile igniting across her face as she did. For even though Leona's hands held a travel magazine instead of a needle and thread, being around the others as they sewed seemed to hold a therapeutic benefit for the self-proclaimed beauty queen as well.

"Boy, this feels good, doesn't it?" she asked no one in particular as she returned her visual focus to her own flower pin. "Like maybe everything isn't so bad after all, you know?"

"Dixie is still in jail," Rose groused as she set the sample back down on the coffee table and moved on to another pin.

"I know that, Rose, and I haven't forgotten that fact for a minute." Tori gazed down at the petal in her lap and found that she was pleased with her first attempt. "But something about sitting here, working on a project together like we would if we were back home, gives me hope that we're going to figure this out soon."

"The trip wasn't all bad," Margaret Louise

reminded them in her usual cheery way. "We did get to be on *Taped with Melly and Kenneth* . . . and ride 'round in one of them fancy limousines."

Beatrice jumped on the positive-thinking bandwagon with both feet. "And watch the Central Park zookeepers play with the sea lions!"

"Don't forget those cupcakes yesterday." Debbie worked her petals to form a perfect flower and held it up for all to see while she revisited CupKatery with her words. "They've made me want to get into the kitchen as soon as we get home and experiment with a few cupcake flavor variations of my own for the bakery."

Rose stilled her scissors-holding hand above the next zipper and looked up. "I just wish Dixie could have some memories from this trip, too, the way it was supposed to be."

"She had herself a hoot when we were tapin' the show." Margaret Louise leaned forward across the coffee table and took a closer look at Rose's sample. "And even if it ended badly, I know she felt like a princess on her breakfast date accordin' to that smile she had while she was eatin' and chattin' with John."

Tori waved her needle above her petal. "Which reminds me of something I wanted to ask all of you."

Five sets of eyes turned in her direction, waiting.

"I was so busy getting ready for the taping that

day that I never got to hear all the details of Dixie's date with John. And then, after the show, I headed out with Margaret Louise and Leona almost immediately, only to discover John had been murdered." She looked from Rose to Beatrice to Debbie to Margaret Louise before landing on Leona. "Did she tell any of you about everything they did?"

Five heads began to shake simultaneously with Beatrice adding a little commentary in her British accent. "I guess we were all so bloody excited about the show that we didn't ask more than whether she had a good time. And then, after the taping, while the three of you were at the crime scene, Dixie was off getting her hair done for a dinner date that never happened."

"Why are you asking?" Debbie inquired. "Does it really matter?"

She shrugged. "I'm not sure. Maybe. Maybe not."

She held the phone to her ear even after her nightly call with Milo was over, the memory of his voice, coupled with the good that had come from an evening of sewing, slowly falling prey to a reality she could no longer keep at bay.

Dixie was still in jail.

And until they found John's real killer, she might very well remain there until a trial could get under way.

Turning her head toward the snoring on the other side of the room, Tori couldn't help but marvel at the way Margaret Louise seemed to be able to compartmentalize her life. It wasn't that the grandmother of eight never had any worries, because she did. But somehow Leona's twin sister was able to deal with them in a way that didn't impact her sleeping, her eating, or her mood overall.

It was a way of living that Tori needed to learn. Someday, anyway.

She looked back toward the ceiling and exhaled a burst of air through pursed lips. Nope, someday wasn't *that* day . . .

Snapping her phone closed, she set it on the nightstand between the two beds and swung her legs over the side of the mattress. She'd done the stare-at-the-ceiling thing the past four nights, and she knew firsthand that it didn't entice sleep to her doorstep. In fact, all it really did was make her head hurt.

With one last glance at the sleeping mound that was Margaret Louise, Tori inched her feet into her slippers and padded into the empty sitting area. She could make a few more zipper pins if she wanted . . . or watch a late-night movie on the flat screen . . . or even read a few chapters in Rose's prized copy of Gavin Rollins's book . . .

But no matter how many options she entertained, the one least likely to invite sleep was the

226

one she couldn't seem to dismiss. Especially since the shaft of light spilling out from beneath the appropriate door called to her like a beacon in a storm.

"Rose?" she whispered against the door. "Rose? Are you still awake?"

A grunt and groan followed by a distinct shuffling sound yielded the result Tori sought, even if the face that accompanied it looked more than a little grumpy. "Good heavens, Victoria, don't you ever go to sleep?"

She stepped into the room and closed the door behind her, yawning and nodding as she did. "I could ask you the same thing, you know."

"I'm old. I have bladder issues. What's your excuse?"

"Margaret Louise snores."

Rose shuffled slowly across the room then lowered herself onto her bed. "So you want to sleep in Dixie's bed?"

It would have been so much easier just to nod, to climb under the neatly placed sheets and revel in the chance to sleep in silence, but to do so wouldn't be entirely honest. Especially since the notion of sleeping in Dixie's bed hadn't crossed her mind until that moment.

"I guess . . . maybe." She stepped toward the empty bed then stopped. "No. That's Dixie's."

"She's not using it."

"I know. But she should be."

A rush of silence gave way to the sound of Rose's hand patting the edge of her own bed. "Come. Sit here beside me for a moment."

Dutifully, she did as she was told, the tightening of her throat making it difficult to speak.

"I may be old, but I'm not dumb." Rose nestled her head against her stack of pillows and reached for Tori's hand. "I'm worried about her, too, Victoria."

"She seemed so defeated when I saw her today."

"Can you blame her?"

"No, of course not, Rose. But this whole trip was supposed to be special—a real once-in-a-lifetime, dream-come-true kind of thing."

"Life plays tricks sometimes, Victoria. Cruel tricks."

Something about the elderly woman's voice sent a chill through Tori's body. "Rose? Are you doing okay?"

"Like you, I wanted this trip to be special. Something I could draw on for strength and happy memories at the end."

She froze in place. "End? What end?"

Rose released Tori's hand and gestured down at her sheet-covered form. "Victoria, you're a bright young woman. You know I'm starting to run down."

"No, you're not. You're just tired is all." She blinked back the tears that burned the corners of her eyes and pushed off the bed as a way to keep them at bay. "We're all tired, Rose. Being away from home like this, with the stress of everything going on, is exhausting."

She felt Rose watching her as she paced between the beds but refused to meet her eyes. If she did, she ran the risk of sobbing uncontrollably.

"It's more than the stress of Dixie. It's my age . . . my body . . . my everything. My clock is running down."

"Then we'll wind it back up again as soon as we get this Dixie nonsense taken care of, Rose."

"How do you propose we'll wind it back up?"

She risked a peek at her friend. "With rest."

"I can rest when I'm dead!"

"But you have to rest. You have to take it easy. The doctors have told you this over and over."

Rose beckoned Tori back to her side, a shaky smile playing at the corners of her thinning lips. "Which brings me back to one of life's cruel tricks. When you're young and have all the time in the world, you don't need to rest. When you're old and your time is limited, you don't want to waste any of the time you have left resting . . . but you have to."

For a moment, she was by her great-grandmother's bedside, looking down at the woman who had taught her so much about life— the importance of honor, the joy of hard work, the simple pleasure of loved ones. And just like she'd been back then, she wasn't ready to say good-bye.

"Is there something you haven't told me, Rose?"

"You mean like whether I'm sick or something?"

She worked to steady her breath. "Yes."

"Other than the arthritis, I'm fine. I just know my body is telling me I don't have a lot of years left."

Tori's sigh of relief echoed around the room. "Well, tell your body it has a wedding to attend in a few months, and a dress to button up for the bride, and an honorary grandchild to hold when that day comes, and a garden to help me plant, and—"

"I get it. I get it." Rose's laugh was weak, yet no less beautiful, and it warmed Tori's heart just to hear it. "I want to be there for all those things, too, Victoria. More than you can imagine."

She leaned forward along the edge of the bed and whispered a kiss across the woman's head as a single, defiant tear made its way down her cheek. "Oh, trust me, Rose, I don't have to imagine. For either one of us."

Rose reached up, wiped the tear from Tori's face, and then slowly closed her eyes. "I know you were upset with yourself earlier for not having time to hear about Dixie's date before everything turned sour, but maybe some of those things over there will fill in the blanks."

She straightened up, her gaze following the path indicated by Rose's finger. "Things? What things?"

"Over there, on the dresser."

Rising to her feet, Tori made her way around the foot of Dixie's bed to the dresser on the opposite side of the room.

"It looks like they went to the zoo, just like we did."

"The zoo?" And then she saw it. A souvenir picture of Dixie and John in a tiny Central Park Zoo frame shored up Rose's words.

"I haven't seen Dixie look that happy since Franklin was alive."

Somewhere in her head, she knew Rose was talking, maybe even registered some of what was being said, but the bulk of her attention was on the photograph. Dixie's smile was breathtaking, but so was John's. For as smitten as Dixie obviously was with him, he seemed to share that same intense feeling for Dixie.

"I don't care what Leona says, Victoria. Maybe he was a con man. Maybe he took advantage of women on a daily basis in the hopes of living large off someone else's money. But Dixie was different. She reached him on a different level."

She plucked the frame from the dresser and pulled it close as Rose continued, the elderly woman's assessment of the photograph a near perfect match of Tori's. "You can see it in his eyes. No one can fake that."

A mixture of relief and dread welled up inside her and she set the frame back down, her gaze coming to rest on a familiar logo peeking out at her from underneath the simple gold earrings she'd leant Dixie for the date. "Rose? Is this your napkin over here?"

"Napkin? What napkin?"

She swallowed. "From CupKatery."

Chapter 23

They were all having tea when Tori finally emerged the next morning from the room she shared with Margaret Louise.

"My sister kept you up all night with her insufferable snoring again, didn't she?" Leona drawled from her spot on the window seat overlooking the city.

Margaret Louise's shoulders slumped next to Debbie, prompting Tori to set the record straight. "Um . . . no. I slept. A little."

"For what? Twenty minutes?" Leona tapped Paris's nose with her French-tipped index finger and made a silly face. "Victoria is just determined to resemble a raccoon, isn't she, my sweet precious baby?"

She considered defending herself and her inability to sleep in light of everything going on, but she let it go. To argue would only get Leona's back up, and that would be detrimental to the plan she'd concocted as dawn crept across Margaret Louise's bed and onto Tori's side of the room.

"Would you like a spot of tea?" Beatrice asked while rising from the couch and heading toward the room service cart and the pot it held. "It's still hot enough for a cup."

"No, thank you. I think I'll grab some juice down in the lobby as we're heading up to the bookstore."

Leona groaned. "The bookstore? Again?"

"I realized we never showed the picture of Ms. Steely Eye to any of Charles's co-workers. Maybe one of them can put a name to the face he recognized." Tori dropped onto the love seat beside Rose and gently shook the edge of the newspaper the woman held. "Anything good?"

Rose shrugged. "Seems a murder story only holds front page appeal in this city for a limited time, unlike in Sweet Briar, where it still finds its way in six months later."

"No mention of John?"

"Not today." Then with a quick fold of the paper in her hand, Rose exchanged it for another at her side. "Even in the paper you brought in with you last night, they never said how he died.

233

They just mention Dixie's name in relation to John's and give details of her arraignment."

"I guess there's no reason to keep saying he was pushed." Debbie set her empty teacup on the coffee table and stretched her long slender arms over her head. "Murder is murder, whether it's a push from a balcony or—"

"Wait a minute," Tori protested. "It says he was pushed from his balcony on the front page."

"No, it doesn't." Rose turned the paper toward Tori and pointed at the opening paragraph of an article positioned below the fold. "It just says Dixie was arraigned and that she will be assigned a public defender for her murder trial."

Murder trial . . .

Shaking her head, Tori liberated the paper from Rose's lap and searched the entire front page for the details Doug had read aloud while standing in the middle of his cupcake shop the previous afternoon.

But there was nothing.

No mention of a push.

No mention of a balcony.

"How on earth?" she rasped even as the answer filled her thoughts with the kind of clarity that left little room for doubt.

Doug had known about John's murder long before he picked up the paper, yet he'd pretended otherwise. Of that, she was absolutely certain.

The only question that mattered now was *why* . . .

● ● ●

It was just shy of noon when they walked through the door of McCormick's Books & Café, Beatrice's camera clutched tightly in Tori's hand.

Rose released her death grip on her shoulder-mounted purse and scanned the store. "Is Charles working today?"

"Not today. It's his day off."

When she noted the collective shoulder sag around her, she couldn't help but laugh through the headache that had accompanied her onto the subway and refused to be left behind when they disembarked and made their way along the park-bordered sidewalk. "He's really managed to wrap everyone around his finger, hasn't he?"

"A wondrous fellow, he is," Beatrice said by way of agreement.

Rose nodded. "It's like he swallowed a ray of sunshine, and every time he opens his mouth, he shares a little bit of his take."

The compliments continued with Debbie, Margaret Louise, and then Leona chiming in, but Tori didn't hear their words. No, her own thoughts were off and running on the many ways the stranger-turned-invaluable-friend exemplified an expression she'd heard often throughout her life.

"You never know when the next person you meet may change your very essence for the better." The words were no sooner past her lips than the misty-eyed smile that always attended thoughts of her late great-grandmother sprang into action, earning her a quick embrace from Rose.

"Your great-grandmother might as well have been talking to me when you first came to Sweet Briar, Victoria," Rose mused. "Because I know you've certainly changed me for the better."

Leona stopped stroking Paris and drew back, her eyes wide behind her stylish glasses. "From where I'm standing, Rose Winters, you're as rotten now as you've always been."

"That's just because I don't like you, Leona. Never have, never will."

Beatrice's gasp was echoed by first Debbie and then Margaret Louise before being waved off by Leona herself. "Jealous women rarely do, Rose."

"Jealous? Good Lord, what do I have to be jealous about where you're concerned?"

"To paraphrase Elizabeth Barrett Browning if I may . . . let me count the ways." Leona stopped, indulged in a noteworthy smirk, and then continued in her most cultured voice. "My unparalleled beauty, my magnetic personality, my keen intuitive business sense, my runway-worthy eye for fashion, my ability to turn heads regardless of age, my—"

"Amazing ego? Unbelievable imagination?" Rose supplied.

Instantly, Leona's plump lips and diminutive fists tightened in preparation for battle, drawing a hush from the group, as well as a handful of nearby rubbernecking book browsers. "Take that back, you old goat, or I'll . . . I'll petition the court to regain custody of Paris's baby, Patches, on the grounds his adopted mama is evil incarnate! And I'll win!"

Rose's eyes narrowed to near slits just as Beatrice stepped forward, waving Bobblehead Kenny in forced surrender. "Now, Leona, Rose. We mustn't say such things. Dixie needs us to be strong and to work together."

Tori stepped forward, linked her left arm with Rose's and her right arm with Leona's, and clucked softly beneath her breath. "Beatrice is right. Every moment we stand here arguing is another moment Dixie must spend in that jail cell."

For a second she thought Rose was going to argue, the need to challenge Leona's custody threat with a biting zinger written across every nuance of her lined face, but in the end, the eighty-something woman merely exhaled the fight from her pint-sized body and pulled the flaps of her cotton sweater more tightly against her body. "I'm sorry. I don't know what came over me."

"The same thing that comes over you virtually every minute of every day," Leona sulked.

"Shut up, Twin!" Margaret Louise extricated

her sister from Tori's grasp and marched her over to the café, glancing back at Tori as she did. "We'll be over here, enjoyin' one of them fancy frothy drinks when you're done askin' 'bout that picture, Victoria."

She mouthed a thank-you at her friend, deposited Rose with Debbie in the reading nook on the opposite side of the store from the café, and then made her way up to the counter and the stocky brunette with the tiny gold stud in her left nostril. "Vanny?"

The girl, whom Tori estimated to be in her early twenties, looked up from the pages of an unjacketed hardcover novel propped behind the register and shook off her initial dazed expression. "Oh. Yeah. Sorry about that. I know I'm not supposed to be reading between customers but, well, I like books. Especially ones that are so good I forget where I am while I'm reading them . . . though, my boss probably wouldn't approve."

"Nor would the folks at my library who are just trying to get my attention long enough to answer a routine question," Tori said by way of agreement.

Vanny stopped chewing her gum then transferred it to a resting spot on the right side of her mouth. "You're a librarian?"

"I am."

"I thought about going that route, but college wasn't really my thing."

"A bookstore works." She pointed to the book in Vanny's hand. "So it's good then, huh?"

"It's better than I expected, especially considering I'm not exactly the target demographic. But I'm supposed to read it, so I am."

She felt her left brow arch. "Supposed to read it?"

Vanny worked her gum briefly before answering. "We run a few book clubs outta the store every month. One's based on mystery titles, the other on women's stuff—fiction, self-help, that sorta thing. At first I was bummed when my boss gave the mystery one to Charles, but so far the books the women's group has been reading have been pretty good."

"So which one is that?" she asked, pointing at the book again.

"*Finding Love After Sixty-Five* by Gavin Rollins." Vanny turned the book for Tori to see, laughing as she did. "The group wanted to read it to coincide, as close as possible, with his visit here to the store. It was a natural choice considering most of the women in that club are retired except me. So I figured I'd read it and maybe pass on some helpful insights to my grandmother when I visit her this summer, maybe even take a few mental notes for when I hit that age myself. But surprise surprise, I'm actually learning things I can use now, at twenty-five."

"Oh?"

"Sixty-five-year-old women aren't the only ones who come across jerks in the dating department."

"Don't I know it," Tori mumbled as an image of her late ex-fiancé emerging from a coat closet with one of her best friends filtered through her thoughts before being pushed to the side by the present. Lifting her left hand into the air, she wiggled her ring finger ever so slightly. "But I'm here to tell you that there are some gems out there, too. Amazing ones, as a matter of fact."

Vanny worked her gum again, this time with an almost ferocious burst that lasted close to a minute. "I'll have to trust you on that one. In the meantime, I'll keep reading . . . and taking copious notes in the hope I can save myself some grief out there."

She nodded, the young woman's words bringing her back to the reason she was there in the first place. "I was hoping maybe I could show you a picture on my camera and see if you can tell me anything more about a woman that is in the background of one of my shots. Charles said he's seen her in here before but can't place her with any specific details or even be sure he's seen her recently or back when he first started here."

"You know Charles?"

Again, she nodded.

"Wait. You're one of those southern sewing

circle ladies he's been yakking about this past week?"

Her third nod accompanied a smile. "Yup, that would be me and"—she glanced over her shoulder long enough to point out Rose and Debbie in the reading nook, Beatrice perusing the children's section, and Margaret Louise looking on as Leona flirted with the handsome teenaged barista behind the café counter—"them. In the flesh."

Vanny nudged her chin in the direction of her enamored and well-built co-worker and laughed. "I'm guessing that one's Leona, yes?"

She considered asking how Vanny knew, but opted to bypass the rhetorical question in favor of her previous one. "So? Would you mind looking at a picture real quick and telling me if you know the woman in it?"

"Yeah. Sure. I'll take a look." Vanny tucked a bookmark into her place, closed her book, and then eyed the camera in Tori's hand. "But I have to tell you, if Charles can't place her, I'm not sure I can. He's the detail person around here."

"Oh, he can place her. He knows she's a customer here for sure. He just thought maybe you'd have more details that could be helpful." She turned on the camera and scrolled through Beatrice's visual diary of their trip to New York City. When she reached the picture taken near the crime scene, she focused the image on Ms. Steely Eye and handed it to Vanny, the urge to cross her fingers overwhelming. "Do you know anything about her? Who she is? Where she lives—"

"Sure, I know her. That's Barbara Letts. She's in the same book club as me."

Tori felt the relief as it coursed through her body and failed to thwart the squeal before it emerged from her mouth. When she composed herself, she glanced back over her shoulder one more time to find five sets of eyes trained in her direction. "Do you know how I can find her?"

Vanny handed the camera back across the counter then retrieved her book and held it up for Tori to see. "I sure do. She'll be here tomorrow night. For book club."

Chapter 24

Even without the slumped shoulders and snail's pace at which they traveled the sidewalks, Tori could tell the quest to free Dixie was taking its toll once again. The normally good-natured banter that was as much a part of the group as their shared love of sewing had taken on an edgy quality. No longer was it just Rose and Leona snapping at each other over every little thing.

Suddenly, Debbie and Margaret Louise weren't being quite so respectful of each other's food-related opinions, and Beatrice was showing less tolerance for even the slightest eye roll at the mention of putting Bobblehead Kenny in an impromptu picture.

"I'm thinkin' we're 'bout to have some bloodshed 'round here soon, Victoria." Margaret Louise huffed and puffed her way to the front of the pack. "Now don't get me wrong, I want Dixie out of that jail as much as anyone, but there ain't gonna be anyone left to free her if we kill one another first."

She peeked over her shoulder at her fellow sewing sisters and noted the sorry state of each and every one.

First, there was Debbie, who spent more time looking at her phone than anything else, the longer-than-expected separation from Colby and the kids dampening her usually unstoppable reservoir of energy.

Next came Beatrice, the quiet, even-keeled British nanny who currently seemed to be channeling her charges' mood when a favorite cookie had been promised and then denied.

Then, and possibly most alarming, came Leona and Rose, side by side, the silence between them enough to add a few exclamation points to Margaret Louise's words.

"We're only a block away from our next piece of information and it would be silly to turn back now. But maybe, when we're done, we could do something touristy for a few hours. Just to regroup."

"We could go to the Statue of Liberty. Or maybe the Empire State Building," Margaret Louise said by way of agreement. "I've always thought Lady Liberty was mighty purty and real majestic standin' 'longside the water with her torch."

"We could take a vote . . ."

Margaret Louise stopped, took a few quick breaths, then continued to keep pace with Tori. "Think maybe we could take that vote when my twin is goin' to the restroom or maybe winkin' and blinkin' at some doorman or somethin'?"

Tori froze mid-step, Margaret Louise taking full advantage of the momentary pause to wipe her brow with the backside of her hand. "Woo-wee, you're a fast walker, Victoria."

"Margaret Louise, you're a genius!"

The grandmother of eight's round face spread still wider as she gave in to a smile she simply couldn't hold back. "I am?"

"You most certainly are." Tori spun around to face Leona as the rest of the group caught up, Margaret Louise's words still ringing in her ears. "I know how we're finally going to get some honest-to-goodness information on Caroline Trotter."

When no one responded, she followed up her gaze with an outstretched finger. "Operation Leona is now in effect."

All eyes turned.

"You mean we finally get to dispose of her on the side of the road the way I've been asking to do since we got here?" Rose groused, earning an unexpected laugh from Beatrice.

Before Leona could mount a verbal defense, Tori reached for the woman's arm and drew her closer to the front of the makeshift line. "The first time we stopped by Caroline's apartment, the doorman on duty seemed to be rather smitten with you, Leona, didn't he?"

"He was male, wasn't he?"

"And you found him attractive as well, didn't you?" she asked by way of an answer to a rhetorical question.

Leona hesitated a moment, tapping her French-tipped finger to her chin as she did. "That was the doorman with the blue pin-striping rather than the red worn in our hotel, yes?"

Heads nodded around them, prompting a slow smile from Leona in return. "Well then, I most certainly did. Timothy paid much more attention to me than he did your questions, that's for sure."

"Hence the need to employ Operation Leona."

Margaret Louise bounced up on the toes of her Keds and clapped her hands. "Why, Victoria, you just might be on to somethin'."

"If I am, it's only on account of your winking and blinking comment a few minutes ago." Tori took a moment to arrange the information they needed in some semblance of order, then shared it aloud with her friends. "Obviously, we want to know how we can reach Caroline. Short of that, anything you can find out as far as when, specifically, she disappeared and who might be looking for her would be helpful, too."

"Maybe some basic tidbits about her would help us, too," Debbie suggested with a renewed sense of energy. "Maybe the doorman would be able to tell us if he ever saw John and Caroline together. Maybe the first meeting Charles witnessed at the bookstore never went beyond that . . . or maybe it did."

She considered Debbie's words and realized they held merit. A lot of merit.

"Think he'll talk to her if we go in as a group? Or should some of us veer off and let Leona work her mag—her . . . whatever it is."

Leona's chin jutted into the air. "I won't do anything until you finish that sentence, you old goat."

"Finish what sentence?" Rose echoed via a death-glare-initiated eye roll.

"Let me work my *what?*"

"Your evilness?"

"No."

"Your phoniness?"

"No."

"Then I have no answer."

Leona handed Paris off to her sister, crossed

her arms, and waited. "I'm not budging from this spot until you say what you stopped yourself from saying."

Rose threw up her hands and turned with a slow shuffle. "On the sidewalk, along the side of the road—not much difference in the end. Either way, we'll still be rid of you once and for all."

"And then Dixie's death inside a jail cell will be on *your* neck, you old goat, not mine."

For a moment, Tori thought Rose was going to keep walking, the determined set to the elderly woman's shoulders impossible to miss, despite the ill-fitting sweater that hung off her frail frame. But finally, she turned, defeat evident in her bifocal-enhanced eyes. "Okay, okay. You win. Work your *magic,* Leona."

"What was that, Rose? I couldn't quite hear you."

"Oh, put a sock in it, Twin!" Margaret Louise placed a warning hand on her sister's shoulder and gave her a nudge forward. "If we all heard her, Leona, I'm quite sure you heard her, too."

Leona let her protest die on her lips as she took in the exasperated faces around her. "Okay. Okay. I heard the old goat."

Rose used her hand to stop the wagons from circling then shook a warning finger at Leona. "Remember, you're flirting to help Dixie, not add to whatever lifelong tally sheet you're keeping."

• • •

There was no denying the doors that opened to Leona with a mere blink of her false eyelashes or the perfectly timed cross of her ankles. It was as much a certainty in her life as breathing was for everyone else. The only thing that didn't make sense was why Tori hadn't thought to employ her friend's considerable prowess sooner.

"So you haven't seen Caroline since early Tuesday morning?" Leona fairly purred through intentionally puckered lips that only served to make Timothy's Adam's apple bob more noticeably with each swallow. "I guess that must mean she's off somewhere on a fabulous vacation to the beach. Mmmm, I envy her, don't you, Timothy?"

Tori fought her jaw's urge to slack open as the doorman came around from behind his station in the marbled lobby in order to stand closer to Leona. "I bet you're a vision in a swimsuit, Leona."

"You're too kind." Leona touched her fingertips to the base of her throat and fluttered her lashes a few times. "So you think that's where she's gone? To the beach?"

Timothy's gaze traveled slowly down Leona's front, stopping momentarily on her shapely legs. "Uh, I . . . huh? What?"

"Caroline. Do you think she's at the beach?" Leona repeated.

Reluctantly, the doorman switched his immediate focus to the front door and the pair of tenants that entered and passed en route to their apartment. When they were safely inside the elevator, he addressed the stunning and seemingly ageless woman standing next to Tori. "No one knows where she is."

Leona gasped an appropriate gasp. "You mean she disappeared?"

"Pretty much. She didn't put a hold on her mail. She didn't ask us to turn the security on in her apartment when she left. And she didn't tell her annoying offspring, either. Which means we're dealing with a whole lot of annoying as a result."

Tori felt her antennae rise and was grateful when Leona's did the same. "Annoying offspring?"

Timothy nodded once, twice, adding a snort where a third might have been. "That's putting it nicer than my co-workers would, but I was raised to be a gentleman."

"I can see that." Leona let her hand drift to the doorman's arm, where it lingered for just enough time to earn her another, more deliberate swallow. "What can you tell me about Caroline's child? Is she worried sick about her mother?"

The snort returned. "Or her mother's money . . ."

Tori felt Leona's eyes flit to the side of her face and did her best to refrain from responding either by word or movement for fear Timothy would clam up. Leona's trance-inducing abilities were in full effect. Tori was darned if she was going to do anything to mess that up.

Still, she was thrilled when Leona's next question was nearly verbatim to the one on the tip of her own tongue. "Is Caroline wealthy?"

"She lives in a three-bedroom on the top floor. Place is worth close to four mill from what the other guys say."

"She lives alone?" Leona asked.

Timothy nodded.

"So her daughter is grown then?"

He nodded again. "She's probably thirty, maybe thirty-five like us."

This time, she had no control over her jaw.

Us?

As in him and . . . Leona?

Leona, of course, took the statement in stride, as if being viewed as a thirty-five-year-old were something that happened to her every day.

"And you get the sense that this young woman is more interested in her mother's money than she is in her mother?" Leona posed.

"I mean, who wouldn't be when you're that close to having it all yourself?" Timothy looked left then right before lowering his voice to a near whisper. "My boss, and even Nate, the night guy, thinks she's just real protective of her mother, but the rest of the guys and I think she's gotta be counting the days until she can sell the apartment, collect the cash, and head back to whatever Asian country she was adopted from as a little kid."

Tori exchanged looks with Leona and hoped their next question would match.

"Is there a father?"

It wasn't the direction she was going in her head, but it wasn't half bad, either, so she cocked her head and waited for the answer.

"Nope. From what I've been able to gather over the last two years I've been working here, Caroline adopted Susie when she was around two. Seeing as how she was from family money herself, she was able to lavish Susie with the kind of attention few kids get. Sent her to one of the fancy private elementary schools downtown, sent her to another for high school, paid the way for her to go to Harvard, and then set her up with an apartment a couple blocks north when she dropped out. The boss says she's got some upstart web design company of her own going, but considering how often she stops by here to check on her mother and meddle in her life, I can't imagine she's doing all that much."

"She meddles in her mother's life? In what way?"

"Every time Ms. Trotter had a date, Susie was here to see them off. Like she was the mother instead of the daughter."

"Did Caroline go on a lot of dates?"

"Not really. But if you saw the way Susie inspected them, you'd understand why. And for whatever reason, Ms. Trotter seemed to let her get away with it." He crossed to the door to let in a tenant then resumed his spot beside Leona. "Kinda sad that the one time she finally made up her own mind about a guy, he had to meet his demise the way he did."

It took everything in her power not to speak, but Leona held the course fine all on her own. "His demise?"

"Poor guy was pushed from a balcony not too far from here."

"How awful!"

"Wouldn't have happened in this building, I can tell you that much. No one gets through this lobby without going through me first." Timothy waved the subject aside with both a hand and an explanation. "What's done is done. They've got someone behind bars, that's all that matters."

She recognized the restraint Leona showed where mention of Dixie was concerned and knew it matched her own. Now was not the time to reveal who they were and why they were there asking after Caroline Trotter.

"Susie must be beside herself with worry about her mother," Leona offered, steering the conversation back a few beats.

Timothy shrugged. "Or she wants it to look that way so no one starts pointing fingers at her when her mother finally turns up at the bottom of the river."

Leona sucked in her breath. "At the bottom of the river?"

"Yeah. Kurt, the maintenance guy, and I like to sit around and figure out what makes rich folks tick. Anyway, that's what we came up with when Ms. Trotter didn't come home—someone, most likely her daughter, killed her for her money." The words were no sooner out in the open than Timothy's face began to redden. "Oh. Hey. Let's pretend I didn't say that, okay?"

Unable to keep her mouth shut any longer, Tori heard herself speaking before she even realized what was happening. "But you did."

Startled, he pulled his gaze from Leona and fixed a far less seductive version on Tori. "Excuse me?"

Leona moved her hand upward on Timothy's arm, moaning ever so softly at the feel of the muscles beneath his shirtsleeve. "Mmmm, you spend a lot of time in the gym, don't you?"

He looked from Tori to his arm and back again, Leona's magic obviously starting to pale against the reality of his job. "Yeah, but I really shouldn't say anything else. I could lose my job."

Leona stepped closer to Timothy, angling him in such a way as to remove Tori from his field of vision. "My lips are sealed . . . except with you, Timothy."

But it was no use. The spell was broken. If he'd been ready to share more information before Tori piped up, that was no longer the case.

"Look, I really can't say anything more. Ms. Trotter has a lot of clout in this place, and by extension, so does Susie. If either one of them got wind I was talking about them like this, they'd have my job."

Tori knew her disappointment was palpable. She could feel it as certainly as she could Leona's. But the window had closed. She'd seen to that all on her own with her inability to keep quiet.

After a few beats of uncomfortable silence, Leona sashayed her way over to the counter and made a dramatic show of leaning over the top in search of a piece of paper and a pen. When she'd commandeered both, she jotted down her cell phone number and handed it to Timothy, her free hand closing around his in the process. "If you change your mind and want to talk, give me a call. Just don't make me wait too long, okay?"

Chapter 25

They stepped onto the subway and settled in for the thirty-plus-block ride south to their destination, Rose's head sinking onto Tori's shoulder the second the doors swooshed to a close.

"Are you okay, Rose?" she inquired over the unending swirl of self-recriminations still parading around in her head. "Do you want me to take you back to the hotel?"

"No. I just want to rest my eyes for a minute."

"I'll take her back and see that she gets some sleep." Leona slid onto the bench seat beside Rose.

Margaret Louise followed suit, her loud, boisterous voice drawing more than a few looks in their direction. "I know what you're doin', Twin. It's as plain as the nose on my face."

Leona's right elbow disappeared into Margaret Louise's side, drawing a yelp in the process. "I'm just lookin' out for Rose is all. Like any friend would do."

"But we're not friends," Rose mumbled without opening her eyes.

"Rose Winters, that's not nice!"

"But it's true—"

"Would you lookee there . . ." Margaret Louise pointed toward the door at the front end of their subway car, a broad smile making its way across her face as she did. "It's Wurly! And his magical ukulele!" The grandmother of eight stood and started waving her hands wildly from side to side. "Woo-hoo, Wurly! It's me . . . Margaret Louise. Your southern-fried friend!"

She felt Rose and Leona sinking into the seat beside her as riders to their left and right stared at them in shock. But it was too late. Wurly had spotted them and heeded the invitation that was most likely a rarity in his world.

"Hello there, southern-fried friend of mine." Wurly tipped his ball hat at Margaret Louise.

"Wait! Wait! I know what that means now." Margaret Louise reached into her tote bag, pulled out a five-dollar bill, and pushed it into the hat, which was now back on his head. "You play a real nice ukulele, Wurly."

The subway musician plucked the money from the space between his hair and his hat and stuffed it in his pocket. "What can I play for you today, friend?"

"How 'bout 'Sweet Caroline'? Rose, over there"—Margaret Louise leaned across her sister to tap Rose, earning herself a wary eye from both—"loves that song, don't you, Rose?"

Wurly shook his head. "Can't do it. This is New York, not Boston. And I don't want to get shot."

The subway hurtled through the underground labyrinth, then screeched to a stop near Rockefeller Center. Riders exited and entered while Margaret Louise scratched her head. "Hmmm. Then how 'bout 'New York, New York'? I've always liked that line 'bout people ridin' in a hole in the ground . . . just like we are now."

"Don't know that one."

"You don't know that one?" Margaret Louise

echoed in shock, only to have Beatrice throw out a request.

"How about a Kenny—"

"No!" Rose and Leona said in unison.

"But—"

"No!"

"You southern ladies sure are a handful, aren't you?" Without waiting for an answer, he began gently plucking at his ukulele. "So where are you off to today?"

"The Empire State Buildin'."

"Going all the way to the top of the observation tower, eh?"

Leona blanched.

"We sure are. All the way to the tippy, tippy top." Margaret Louise returned her sister's earlier elbow. "Ain't that right, Twin?"

"Oh, shut up!"

Wurly laughed then reached into his pocket, extracted a slightly crumbled business card, and handed it to Margaret Louise, jerking his head toward the door as the subway came to yet another stop. "This is your stop, ladies. I'll play you off . . ."

The first few notes of Rose's favorite song disappeared along with the subway as they stepped onto the platform and Margaret Louise looked at the card in her hand. "Oh, would you lookee here, Victoria, Wurly does weddin's!"

She laughed over Rose and Leona's groan.

"We've already got a deposit on the band, Margaret Louise, but I'll keep him in mind in the event that falls through."

Then, turning her attention to the wall-mounted map and the route they needed to travel to reach their final destination, Tori left Margaret Louise to study the rest of Wurly's card alone. She was about two blocks into the mental journey when she was yanked back to the here and now.

"Well, wouldn't you know, Leona's winkin' and blinkin' sure can help our investigatin', can't it?"

When she didn't respond, Margaret Louise continued, " 'Cause if you hadn't shared what she learned while the rest of us were sittin' in the park, I would have looked right past this."

She looked from the map to Margaret Louise and waited, the woman's words making little sense for all of about two seconds.

"Caroline Trotter's daughter *does* run a web design company. It's called Trotter Web Design, and she designed Wurly's page for him."

If the way Leona white-knuckled her way through the elevator ride to the observation deck of the Empire State Building hadn't been enough of a clue to her feelings about heights, the fact that she refused to go near the Plexiglas walls that afforded its world-renowned view of the Big Apple sealed the deal.

"How did I not know you were afraid of heights?" Tori whispered in Leona's ear.

"I'm not afraid of heights, dear."

She felt the laugh building but did her best to hold it back. "You're not?"

"Of course not, dear. I'm above such things. You know this."

"Then how do you explain the death grip you had on my arm in the elevator just now?"

Leona's stab at confusion was almost Oscar-worthy. Almost. "Death grip? What death grip?"

Pushing the sleeve of her white blouse upward, Tori gestured toward the red mark on her fore-arm—a mark that still bore the distinctive shape of at least three fingers. "Um, perhaps this one?"

The flinch was lightning fast, but still, Tori caught it before it disappeared behind yet another stellar acting performance. "You're deficient on iron, dear, that's all."

She let her sleeve slip back down her arm and then gestured toward their friends, who were oohing and ahhing at the view of Manhattan looking north. "Okay, then why are you hovering back here instead of up there with everyone else?"

"I don't want to crowd them. I'm very generous that way."

"Well, then your generosity has paid off." She gestured toward an elderly man now walking away from the clear walls. "There's a wide-open spot right next to your sister."

"No, I'll wait. You take it."

"Victoria, it ain't no use," Margaret Louise said. "There are times when the big dog just won't hunt."

"Excuse me?"

"You can't make chicken salad out of chicken feathers."

She looked to Leona for help in deciphering Margaret Louise's crazy expressions but got nothing but a sheepish shrug in return.

"It means there ain't no way you're goin' to get my sister over by this wall. Not unless the same view can be seen from the first floor."

She let that fact take root in her head then pushed it into the land of impossibilities. "You can't be afraid of heights, Leona. I mean, didn't you spend time at the top of the Eiffel Tower when you were in Paris?"

Margaret Louise laughed. "That would imply my twin was actually in *that* Paris."

Leona's eyes narrowed to near slits just before she smacked her sister. "I'm warning you, keep your mouth closed, Margaret Louise."

"No, no, no . . . you don't get to leave me out of this one, ladies." Tori looked from Leona to Margaret Louise and back again. "What Paris was Leona in?"

"The one in Kentucky."

Suddenly, all the evil glares Leona had shot in Beatrice's direction whenever Paris was brought up made perfect sense. Leona hadn't been there. At least not the one in France anyway.

She opened her mouth to give Leona some much-needed ribbing but closed it when she saw the hurt and humiliation on her friend's ghostly white face. Sometimes having the last laugh wasn't always worth it . . .

"So you're really afraid of heights," she finally asked.

Leona's chin jutted upward in a show of defiance, only to sink back down at the realization that her long-held secret in regards to Paris was safe, at least with Tori. Seconds ticked by before the woman finally spoke, but when she did, it was apparent things were back to status quo.

"Does having me confirm my one flaw really mean that much to you, dear?"

She considered protesting the singular number but let it go when she saw the pain Leona's weakness added to an already awkward moment. Instead, she wrapped her left arm around her friend's shoulder and pulled her close. "Would it help if I walked *with* you? Maybe step by step until you simply can't go any further?"

Before Leona could answer, the elevator off to their right opened and five naval officers in dress whites spilled onto the observation deck and made their way over to the glass wall where Rose, Beatrice, and Debbie were setting up for a picture with Bobblehead Kenny.

The tallest of the officers placed a respectful hand on Margaret Louise's shoulder and offered to take the picture, earning him four wide-mouthed smiles in the process. "Well, aren't you a nice young man? You remind me of my son, Jake. He thought 'bout joinin' the Navy but he met Melissa and decided to be a husband and a daddy instead."

"I hope to be both those things myself one day, ma'am." The sailor tipped his head at Margaret Louise then took a step back to frame the picture, adding more with each fellow officer Beatrice and Debbie waved into the picture. "Is that everyone?"

"Not quite. You're missing Victoria and me." Leona ran a grooming hand down the sides of her soft gray hair and strutted across the deck and into the welcoming arm of the most attractive officer in the group.

"Don't look now, Twin, you're eighty-six floors above the Big Apple."

With a dramatic bat of her eyelashes, Leona glanced over her shoulder to the glass wall at their backs, shrugged, and then flashed an alluring smile at the man behind the camera.

"Well, don't that just put pepper in my gumbo," Margaret Louise proclaimed as the shutter snapped once, twice.

Chapter 26

She could feel Leona watching her as she hoisted her legs onto the couch and pulled them close to her body, but what exactly her friend was thinking was anyone's guess. If similar looks in the past were any indication, Tori had forgotten a vital makeup tip or committed an unforgivable fashion faux paus. But considering it was ten o'clock at night and even Leona wasn't wearing makeup, she went with the latter.

"My pajamas aren't really that bad, are they?" She clipped her pen to the notepad she'd been feverishly writing in for the past thirty minutes and stretched her arms above her head. "I mean, the pink top matches the stripe in the pants perfectly."

Leona peered at Tori above her glasses but said nothing, her hand stroking its way down Paris's back again and again.

She dropped her hands to the bottom of her shirt and tugged it down beyond the waistband of her pants. "It's not too short, Leona."

"Did I say anything, dear?"

"With words? No. With your eyes? Yes."

"Will the many ways in which you misunderstand me ever cease?" Leona released an exasperated sigh loud enough to stir Paris in her sleep. "Sometimes I don't know why I bother being a part of this group. No one appreciates me and the many things I have to offer."

The guilt that Leona was a master at serving up on a silver platter attached itself to Tori's heart and made her squirm. "I'm sorry, Leona. I guess I just saw you looking at me the way you were and figured I'd dropped the ball on something."

"I was simply wondering if you miss him."

"Miss him?" she repeated. "You mean Milo?"

"Is there another man in your life, dear?"

Milo.

It had only been a week since she'd last seen him, but it felt like both yesterday and years all at the same time. She said as much to Leona.

"Help me understand what you mean by that," Leona replied.

She took a moment to compose her thoughts into some semblance of order, the emotion they triggered making her both happy and sad at the same time. "I guess it feels like just yesterday because he's so vivid in my mind all the time. I can be walking down the street thinking about something and hear his laugh as clearly as if he's right there beside me. I know him so well that I know the things he likes and doesn't like and can picture his reactions, his expressions, et cetera. And when I hear his voice at night before I go to sleep, it's like he's here. With me."

Leona's eyes never left her face as she

continued, her thoughts switching to the part that hurt—the part that made it feel like it had been years since she'd last seen Milo. "But because he's such a part of me, it feels like something is missing when he's not there. It's almost as if the sun is a little duller, the joy in my day a little less special, my presence in this world a little less important."

"Then why did you tell him not to come here for his spring break?"

Why indeed.

It was a question she'd asked herself every night after they hung up the phone and she'd turned down his offer yet again.

She did her best to explain and hoped saying it aloud would convince her she was making the right decision. "I guess it's because I've worked really hard the past few weeks to focus our time together on the happy things coming our way—the wedding, the honeymoon, and starting our life together. Here, all of that is shoved in a corner while we try to get Dixie out of this mess. I don't want him to see or feel that, you know?"

"But he talks about it on the phone with you, doesn't he?" Leona slowly lifted her hand and smiled down at her sleeping rabbit. "And if he's offering to come, it's so he can help."

"I know that. I just want to concentrate on figuring out who really did this to John and getting everyone home . . . together."

"And if we can't?"

She felt the knot of dread in her stomach and pushed it away with her words. "We can. I'm sure we can."

"I hope you're right, Victoria, I really do."

"We've got some good stuff to go on," she said, glancing back down at her notepad. "There's the fact that Doug faked his surprise about John's death when—based on what was in the actual article—he obviously already knew. Then we have your top choice, Caroline Trotter, who not only has a confirmed connection with John, thanks to Charles, but it's now been reconfirmed by Timothy, who went so far as to say she really seemed to be smitten with him. And then, last but not least, is Ms. Steely Eye—aka Barbara Letts—who *we* can place around John *twice* on the day he died."

Leona gently shifted Paris into the cozy space between her hip and the chair and folded her hands neatly in her lap. "But you don't know Doug . . . Caroline has disappeared into thin air . . . and Steely Eye is one of a half-dozen members in a book club. You can't accuse someone you don't know of murder, and you can't prove someone did it if you can't find them."

There was a measure of truth in Leona's words, but only a measure. After all, if she'd learned nothing from the slew of murders she'd been roped into solving over the past two years, when it came to finding out information, where there was a will, there was a way. The written fruits of her solo brainstorming session simply outlined some of the steps she needed to take come morning.

"I can treat John's neighbor to coffee and a treat at CupKatery and see if Doug is the same man she remembers seeing through her peephole the night before the murder."

"Assuming Doug is there, of course."

It was a potential snafu she'd already considered. "I'll call beforehand to confirm."

"And Caroline's disappearance? How are you going to work around that, dear?"

"I'm going to arrange a meeting with her daughter. See what she can tell me."

Leona drifted forward ever so slightly in her chair, uncrossing and recrossing her ankles as she did. "Have you considered the fact that perhaps you should add her name to your list as well?"

"Whose name?"

"The daughter's."

She looked from her list to Leona and back again. "For getting rid of Caroline the way Timothy implied? No. I think he's just a doorman with way too much time on his hands."

"I tend to agree with that assessment but maybe we need to look at other possibilities. Like maybe Caroline simply disappeared to grieve John's death out of shock, and maybe she disappeared to grieve her *daughter's hand* in that death."

She heard the thump as her own legs dropped to the floor. "Wait. You think *Susie* could've killed John?"

"If there's even a shred of truth to the picture Timothy created of her, then why not? People have killed for far less than the kind of money Caroline apparently had."

She hated to admit it to herself, but she hadn't even considered that possibility. "But the offspring of two very different women? Are we stretching too far?"

"Different motives for different kids. Doug's is easy. His beloved mom was duped. But Susie's is easy, too. If things between John and Caroline developed, there may have been less money later on, when Caroline was gone."

She unhooked the pen and added Susie's name to the list then drew an arrow to the same course of action she'd planned for Caroline. Only this time, instead of trying to learn as much about the missing woman as she could while pretending to have an interest in setting up a web page, she'd be soaking up everything she could on Susie, too.

When she was done writing, she looked up to find Leona still studying her over the top rim of her glasses. "Now what?"

Leona offered the faintest hint of a shrug then

gestured toward the pad of paper in Tori's lap. "And Ms. Steely Eye?"

"I'm going to get to see her tomorrow night, at Vanny's book club."

"Are you going to sit down next to her and ask her, point blank, why she was at the Waldorf during Dixie's breakfast and by John's apartment later that afternoon?"

"I'm not planning on being that blunt."

"Oh?"

She pushed the notepad from her lap and replaced it instead with Rose's copy of *Finding Love After Sixty-Five*, her finger slowly tracing the letters of the title from left to right. "No, I plan on reading as much of this book as I can tonight so I fit in as naturally as possible with the group."

"Because you look like you're sixty-five, of course," Leona mumbled beneath her breath. "With an engagement ring on your finger . . ."

"I'll figure it out, Leona." She heard the exasperation in her voice and rushed to soften it. Talking to Leona, after all, had already helped more than she could have imagined. An occasional snide comment was simply par for the course and helped keep her grounded at a time when differentiating up from down wasn't necessarily easy.

That said, she was more than a little relieved when Leona plucked Paris from the corner of the chair and rose to her feet, the call of her nightly beauty sleep winning out over any further digs, disguised or otherwise. "Reading some of that book probably isn't such a bad idea, dear, but not if it's at the expense of your good-night call to Milo."

Tori dropped her gaze to the silver link watch on her left wrist and noted the time. She was already ten minutes late for her promised call . . .

"It won't be, Leona. I miss him much too much to go even one night without hearing his voice."

Leona marched toward the room she shared with an already sleeping Beatrice and Debbie, but stopped just shy of the closed door. "Before we head home to Sweet Briar, dear, you and I are going shopping."

"For?"

"Suitable bedroom attire."

Maybe it was her talk with Leona, maybe it was the simple fact that a trip that was supposed to be three days had stretched into a full week, with no sign of ending anytime soon, but whatever the reason, the sound of Milo's voice in her ear was more upsetting than it was encouraging.

She missed him. Terribly.

But was that a reason to make him give up his much-needed week-long break from teaching to traipse across New York City in a haphazard hunt for a killer?

"You sound kinda blue, baby. You okay?"

She took a deep breath and let it release along with the urge to change her mind and ask him to come to the city. His being there wouldn't change anything. Dixie would still be in jail, and the hunt for the real murderer would still claim her days. No, she needed the promise of normalcy that was Milo to be the ultimate carrot that guided her through her days until they could be together again.

"Yeah, I'm okay. Just tired, I guess." She filled him in on their day—bringing him up to speed on Ms. Steely Eye's proper name and the addition of Susie Trotter to the list of possible suspects, before finishing up with Leona's true travel history and the discovery of, and the miraculous end to, the woman's lifelong fear of heights.

"Kentucky, eh?" Milo's laugh chased the sadness from her bones and made her smile. "And the fear of heights? Wow. I'm shocked Margaret Louise never thought to use a man in curing her sister's phobia all these years. It seems like such a no-brainer now, doesn't it?"

"But that would almost imply Leona is an easy puzzle to solve."

"When you've only got four pieces in your puzzle, you're not all that difficult," he joked. "There's the unwavering-love-for-men-in-uniform piece, the belief-she's-thirty-years-younger-than-she-eally-is piece, the never-leave-your-house-looking-like-anything-less-than-a-runway-model piece, and the I-like-to-run-Victoria-Sinclair's-life piece. How hard is that?"

She smacked her hand over the laugh that threatened to wake the masses. "Wait. Wait. Don't forget the I-pretend-I-hate-Rose-but-I-really-don't piece . . . Oh! Oh! And the my-precious-Paris-is-the-most-beautiful-creature-on-the-face-of-the-planet-next-to-me piece!"

His speech grew raspy, sexy even. "Those are the best two pieces, aren't they?"

"They are?"

"If they make you sound as adorable as they just did, then yeah, they are."

She felt her face warm just before the sadness tightened its grip on her heart once again. "I miss you, Milo."

"I miss you, too, Tori."

Her breath hitched at the intensity in his voice, and she allowed it to nurture the smile she hoped would chase the mist from her eyes. "I'm going to figure this out and get back home to you just as soon as possible. I promise you that."

Chapter 27

Even the clock-confirmed realization that Charles would be knocking on their hotel door in a little less than four hours wasn't enough to make Tori set Gavin Rollins's book down in favor of the sleep her body knew she needed. The author's extensive research plus the short first-hand accounts sprinkled throughout the book had proven to be nothing short of fascinating, and more than a little difficult to put down.

Finding the right guy in young adulthood was hard, but finding him later in life sounded nearly impossible—a fact she'd never really considered until Gavin laid it out in a way that made perfect, if not heartbreaking, sense.

So much of a couple's foundation came from the history they created together via a home, children, traditions, the simple passage of time, and the shared memories born from those years. They were the very things she liked to envision when she looked ahead to the years that would take her to her fiftieth anniversary with Milo.

But for those later-in-life couples, the foundation was tougher to create. What constituted holiday traditions for one rarely matched those of the other person. Their families could blend if they were lucky, but they didn't share the same memories, upbringing, or even the same goals. And the house? That, too, was more about his and hers—his favorite chair, her favorite china—than furniture and items found and collected together.

The older couples who seemed to be most successful were those who were marrying for the first time. Those who had walked down the aisle once before seemed to have a fifty-fifty chance of survival.

That is, assuming they even got through the dating phase at all.

She finished the current chapter and paused, the sound of Margaret Louise's snoring on the other side of the bedroom door convincing her it wouldn't do any harm to read just one more . . . Besides, an hour or two of sleep were better than none, right?

Turning the page, she felt her stomach lurch as her gaze fell on the heading of the next section:

Protecting One's Heart
from a Wolf in Sheep's Clothing

If you ask the average sixty-something to name a handful of skills they'd once mastered yet no longer possess, you can probably guess some of their answers.

Understanding an algebraic equation.

Reading music.

Typing.

Riding a bike.

But what rarely finds its way onto the list is one that belongs there just as surely as the rest—dating.

By now you're probably scratching your head and wondering why this book about finding love after sixty-five has suddenly taken a turn toward the depressing, but like every other worthwhile how-to manual you'll come across in life, warnings have their place, too.

The words blurred on the page, prompting Tori to rub her eyes. She knew the smart thing to do was go to bed and try to make the best out of the three hours that stood between her and another day of real-life Clue, but it was hard. Somehow, despite a topic that had little to nothing to do with her, she was hooked.

The thinking part of her brain chalked up her fascination with the book to two things: the excuse it gave her to talk to Barbara Letts, the mystery woman formerly known as Ms. Steely Eye, and her own insatiable need to know what came next.

The feeling part of her brain knew it was much more.

Four of her dearest friends fell into the book's target demographic, making its tips and anecdotes more relatable in some way. Especially when she knew two of the four still carried interest in the notion of dating.

Granted, Leona needed no help from Tori or a book when it came to getting a date. The woman's calendar was full virtually every night. But just because Leona ate on someone else's dime five or six nights a week didn't mean her heart wasn't still potentially at risk.

And even if the self-proclaimed dating pro managed to keep things casual for the rest of her life, Dixie was a different story. Or could be, if Tori got her out of jail and she ever decided to give dating a whirl again.

Dixie.

She closed her eyes and considered the image of the uptight mad-at-the-world woman Tori had met just over two years earlier against the image of the same woman who'd shimmered like the brightest star as she sat across a breakfast table from a man she was now charged with murdering.

The first Dixie never smiled.

The new Dixie couldn't stop.

The first Dixie blamed everyone for everything.

The new Dixie had come to realize the power of a positive attitude.

The first Dixie believed her life wasn't worth living without her beloved position as head librarian of the Sweet Briar Public Library.

The new Dixie was eagerly opening doors she'd been too busy to open during her forty-year career.

The transformation had been slow, of course, but that hadn't made it any less awe-inspiring to witness. In fact, in some ways, it had made it more magical because each change had been inspired by something—volunteering, friendship, and even a well-timed hug and word of encouragement.

Yet in the blink of an eye, it had all changed, ripped out from under Dixie's feet with absolutely no warning at all.

Or had there been . . .

Whoever said pictures don't lie obviously walked this earth long before the dawn of Internet dating sites and the quest to find the perfect mate with a single self-portrait. Suddenly, a snapshot's ability to tell the truth has been manipulated to be twenty pounds slimmer, fifteen years younger, or even a million dollars richer.

It's a tactic that works for a while, when the only contact is e-mail. But when the ultimate goal is finding a mate, the face-to-face meeting is the real moment of truth.

Twenty pounds heavier than the picture you posted?

I'll know the second you walk in.

Fifteen years older than you airbrushed yourself to look?

I'll know the second you walk in.

Borrowed the clothes you wore from your

next-door neighbor because you're really living on a fixed income?

I'll know that within the first five minutes of our get-to-know-each-other meeting when you no longer have someone coaching you on what to say and how to say it.

I suppose, if I was desperate, I could overlook the weight and the age. But if I'm looking for something in particular, and you don't have it, I'm out the door and back on my computer before you've even finished wiping away the tears.

Sound cold? Maybe. But I prefer to say I'm honest.

I want something different for the latter years of my life.

I want to travel.

I want to buy expensive clothes.

I want to be the guy everyone wants to know—the one with the gorgeous house, the gigantic boat, and the private parties in exotic locales.

So I keep scrolling through the pictures and setting up those all-important first meetings.

My ticket is out there. Somewhere.

And she's desperate . . .

Just like I want her to be.

She reached the bottom of the page only to realize the sudden pain in her jaw stemmed from the clenching and unclenching of her teeth. It sickened her to think people could be so cold, so uncaring.

How someone could prey on a lonely woman in such a calculating manner was outside her realm of understanding.

But it was the world they lived in, just as Gavin said. It was a world where the anonymity of the Internet could disguise a monster long enough for someone's heart to be broken.

Or in Dixie's case, for their life to be ruined.

She fought the fatigue that pulled at her lids and read on . . .

The apprehension in their eyes when they walk into my chosen meeting spot is every bit as real as the shoes they painstakingly selected or the skirt they ironed a second and third time. I've seen it a million times.

I've also seen the apprehension disappear behind an answered smile and a flush of pleasure at the slow, appreciative once-over I've mastered on the countless women I will never tell you about.

I compliment your eyes, your hair, your chin . . . whatever feature you've tried to play up in the hopes I'll notice. Because by noticing, you become more comfortable.

I insist on buying your coffee and delivering it to your hands along with a single carnation I cleverly thought to buy five minutes before our meeting. That seemingly personal gesture makes you feel special.

I lean across the table as if I'm enthralled with every word you utter, asking questions along the way to encourage more detail. You think I'm attentive, but I'm simply gathering clues that will tell me whether you're my golden ticket or yet another waste of time.

If I choose to see you again, I will find a way to benefit.

Maybe our leisurely stroll down Fifth Avenue will net me a new suit. Maybe I'll become chummy with your personal driver and have little need for public transportation in the future. Maybe you'll help pay my rent when I'm "unable to do so because I'm taking care of my poor sick mother in Idaho."

It doesn't matter what I get from you or how long it lasts, though, because there's another lonely and desperate woman just around the next corner.

The blurring of Tori's vision was back, only this time, instead of fatigue, it was caused by rage.

Where was the sense of right and wrong?

Where was the desire to do good rather than evil?

Where was the respect for one another?

She turned the page again, her eyes narrowing in on yet another painful passage.

You caught me today.

Caught me red-handed as we walked past your apartment.

At first I tried to play it off, to introduce you to my latest target in such a way neither of you would be the wiser, but it didn't work.

I'd like to say the near eardrum-shattering tirade that ensued taught me a valuable lesson, but it didn't.

I am a con man, and lonely, rich women are my con.

She tried to keep reading but couldn't. Even in anger, her eyes had simply become too heavy to do much of anything except sleep.

Reluctantly, she closed the book and set it on the coffee table, the time denoted on the clock giving her little more than two hours of shut-eye before yet another round of sleuthing commenced.

Chapter 28

It was a few minutes after ten when Tori finally stumbled out of her room to find Charles holding court from the armchair in the center of the sitting area while Rose, Margaret Louise, Debbie, and

Beatrice lavished him with attention. She knew it was Charles, not because she could see his face—she couldn't, it was pitched downward and covered from full view by her friends—but because the tips of his spiked hair now matched the purple jacket slung over the back of his chair.

Stifling a yawn, Tori stopped beside the coffee table and swept her hand toward the piles of zippers, felt, and pin backs that graced its surface. "What's going on in here?"

Charles poked through the opening between Debbie and Beatrice and smiled triumphantly. "My gals are teaching me how to make a zipper flower pin for Mayor Georgina's Mother's Day Picnic. And look . . . I'm getting the hang of it!"

Tori accepted the pin he held out for inspection and turned it over carefully, the stitch work around the staggered petals impressive. "Wow, Charles, you're a natural."

The circle disbanded temporarily as the focus that had been so diligently trained on Charles's every stitch moved to Tori.

"He might be the quickest learner I've ever seen," Margaret Louise boasted. "All we've had to do is talk him through each step so far, ain't that right, Rose?"

Rose nodded in time with Beatrice and Debbie. "It's as if he's been sewing his whole life."

Charles reclaimed his pin and examined it himself, a small furrow forming between his brows as he did. "Wait. Do you see this stitch here?" He held his work in progress up for Rose to see then shifted his body away from the table lamp to afford the elderly woman the best light possible. "It looks slightly bigger than the one on either side, doesn't it?"

Rose held the pin closer to the light then declared it perfect as Tori's gaze fell on the pile of roughly fifteen or so completed pins. "Are those the ones we did the other night?"

"No, those are the ones from just this morning." Beatrice took a seat on the left side of the floral couch and retrieved her own pin-in-progress from the table. "We've been so preoccupied that we're rather behind on the number we told Georgina we'd get done."

Debbie sank onto the cushion beside Beatrice. "Having this unexpected hour this morning certainly helps."

Tori felt another yawn on the horizon and bit it back as best she could. "Yeah, about that . . . I'm sorry I overslept."

"When you stay up reading until six thirty in the morning, you can't really call waking up at ten oversleeping," Leona said as she breezed into the room in a soft pink fitted suit. When she reached the wall mirror over the sideboard table, she stopped and inserted a teardrop pearl earring into each ear. "Nor can you expect your average over-the-counter concealer to mask those ugly black circles under your eyes, dear."

"Black circles?" Charles dropped his needle and thread onto his lap, then spun his designer fanny pack around to the front, his hand poised to unzip before it came to a stop. "I have just the thing!"

Leona turned from the mirror. "You have something that will cover *those?*" she parroted, pointing at Tori the way one might point at a particularly bad sighting of roadkill.

"You bet your gorgeous brown eyes I do, sugar." He reached into his pack and extracted a small round container of skin-colored goo. "My old roommate, Michael Anthony, used this stuff all the time when he was dancing on Broadway. He smuggled this jar of skin perfection out for me before he left on tour."

Leona plucked it from Charles's outstretched hand and beckoned Tori over to the mirror.

"Leona, I really don't need that right—"

"Oh?" She felt Leona's hands on her shoulders, saw the room go by in a blur as she was spun around to face her friends. "Ladies? Charles? Does Victoria need a little assistance this morning?"

Five heads nodded as one.

"Now hold still." Leona uncapped the container, brushed her fingertips across the surface of the goo, and then transferred it to the skin just under Tori's eyes. When she was done, she stepped back in utter shock. "Charles, dear, this stuff is amazing! It makes Victoria look—look . . . *decent.*"

"You sound as if that's never been done before," Tori mumbled before liberating the container from Leona's hand and capping it tightly.

"I refuse to respond to that for fear I'll be stoned where I stand." Leona straightened her already perfect posture and turned Tori toward the mirror. "So instead, I'll let the mirror answer for me."

She looked at her image when the motion stopped and felt the instant slack of her jaw. "Whoa."

Charles leapt to his feet just beyond Tori's reflection but she barely noticed. All she could truly focus on was the flawless shading below her eyes.

"I said it was skin perfection, didn't I?"

"Charles, you are a veritable genius," Leona purred between dramatic bats of her false lashes. "You must know, of course, that I want one of those to bring home to Sweet Briar . . ."

Rose gasped, only to have her dramatics drowned out by a body-shaking cough. "Are you saying you get black circles, Leona?"

"Of course not, you old goat. But if Charles gives it to Victoria, it will get dropped into a drawer in her bathroom, never to be seen or heard from again."

Tori considered protesting Leona's erroneous insinuation but let it go when the reflection of the clock caught her attention. "We can't do this anymore. It's"—she turned to look at the clock to verify the translation her brain had conjured from the backward numbers—"almost ten thirty and we've got to decide which suspect we're going to approach first."

Charles's porcelain skin took on a hint of crimson. "Would I be overstepping if I told you I've already got everything in place?"

Tori froze en route to her room. "You've got everything in place? What does that mean?"

"Meetings. With two of our suspects—one old, one new."

She felt five sets of eyes turn in her direction as she tried to make sense of Charles's words. Still, she came up short. "I don't know what you're talking about."

Charles perched on the closest armrest he could find and took a deep breath. "Leona called me last night before she fell asleep and told me about Susie Trotter. She also told me about the web design company she's got."

"I'm the one who found out the name." Margaret Louise shifted just enough to allow her chest to puff with pride. "There I was, standin' next to that empty subway track and lookin' at Wurly's fancy business card when I spotted the name of the company doin' his website." She leaned across the open space between the couch and Charles's chosen perch and tapped him on the back. "Wurly is gonna be Victoria's backup in case the band she hired for her weddin' reception gets sick or somethin'. Ain't that right, Victoria?"

Something inside her told her not to nod, but she did it anyway in order to get back to the part of the conversation that mattered. "Go on, Charles . . ."

He reached around, gave Margaret Louise's hand a quick squeeze, then continued on, any hesitation in his voice quickly disappearing. "Since it sounds as if Susie could have as much motive to kill John as her mother, it makes sense we sit her down and have a chat. So I e-mailed her through her website after I got off the phone with Leona and arranged a meeting for all of us at eleven thirty."

"All of us?" she echoed.

"Well, maybe it should just be you and me at the table so as not to overwhelm her . . . but everyone else can be nearby, at a different table."

"We meetin' her at McCormick's?" Margaret Louise inquired while Beatrice and Debbie began to gather up the pin-making supplies in preparation for the group's pending departure for the day.

"No. CupKatery." Charles shifted backward on the armrest and let his feet dangle over the side.

"That way, when Doug comes in a little before one, we'll be ready to speak to him, too."

"Wait. How do you know Doug is coming in at one?"

"I took a chance they start baking first thing in the morning and called to ask." Charles slipped off the armrest and walked over to his original chair. With a quick hand, he removed his jacket to reveal Caroline Trotter's scarf. "I had the perfect reason to contact Susie and arrange a place to meet. Doug's place being what it is provides the perfect locale, don't you think?"

Tori knew she was staring and knew her friends were staring back at her, but she was at a loss for what to say. Sure, Margaret Louise had been a worthy investigative assistant over the past two years, with Leona and Dixie pinch-hitting a time or two, as well. But in most of those instances, they'd been following directions or taking advantage of dumb luck.

Charles, however, had taken initiative and figured out what needed to be done all on his own.

While she read. And eventually, slept.

Charles's fingers snapped in their three-pronged formation, only this time with a little more humility and a lot less sass. "Don't I just feel like the Neanderthal who thinks it's funny to share my personal sounds in the middle of a crowded elevator . . ."

"Dixie does that," Margaret Louise interjected. "But only when she's been eatin' too many beans."

Beatrice rushed to Charles's defense. "He was just trying to be helpful, Victoria. That's all—"

"No, I get that." She closed the gap between her original stopping place and Charles's position beside the chair, the awe she felt at his efforts serving as her body's propeller. "Charles . . . you are amazing. Absolutely, positively amazing."

"Sugar, tell me something I don't already know."

Chapter 29

They were sitting at a handful of tables when Susie walked in, her identity easy to pick out amid the near constant parade of customers on account of the rapt attention she gave the dining area as opposed to the cupcake display.

"I think that's her," Tori whispered, prompting Charles to rise to his feet and offer a friendly wave to the pencil-thin woman.

"Susie?"

Caroline Trotter's daughter answered by pushing a strand of silky black hair from her face and picking her way between the eclectic assortment of tables to reach the one Charles shared with Tori. When she arrived, she extended her hand and the confirmation he sought. "Yes, I'm Susie. You must be Charles."

"The one and the only as my good friend, Victoria, here will confirm."

Susie nodded at Tori in greeting then got straight to the point of their meeting. "I appreciate you taking the time to get my mother's scarf back to her . . ." Susie broke eye contact as she scanned the area in front of and around Charles. "You did bring it, didn't you?"

He nodded then gestured toward the empty chair between him and Tori. "Why don't you sit for a moment and I'll dig it out of my bag. It's been in there since Victoria and I first tried to bring it to your mom last week."

Tori watched the woman's face for any sort of reaction, but if there was anything to note, it was merely a flash of sadness. Reaching across the table, she rested a gentle hand atop Susie's forearm. "We stopped by her apartment building a couple of times, actually, in the hope we'd finally catch her home, but no such luck. No one has seen her in days. I hope everything is okay?"

She hadn't meant to be so direct as to ask after Susie's mother so soon, but sometimes direct was best. Time would tell if she'd made the right call.

"The doorman *told* you my mother hadn't been seen in days?"

"Yes."

Susie smacked her fist down on the table, surprising Charles out of his intentionally protracted search for Caroline's scarf. "You would think with the money my mother pays in fees and tips to live in that building, the staff would be more discreet."

Charles's mouth formed a little *o* just before he abandoned his search for the scarf in favor of the conversation taking place across the table. "He didn't just *volunteer* that she was gone. I told him she was expecting the scarf but that I was late getting it to her. He simply said she wasn't there. When subsequent stops yielded the same answer, I inquired more."

The fight left Susie's demeanor and she exhaled slowly. "That's encouraging to hear, although I'm not as much of a fan of that crew as my mother appears to be."

"Oh?" Tori prompted in an effort to keep the woman talking.

"My mother is a rather wealthy woman, as I'm sure you can guess from having seen her apartment building and its proximity to the park." At their collective nod, the woman continued, her chin finding its way onto tented fingers. "It's a world I've never been terribly comfortable living in on account of the insincere people it seems to attract."

"Don't you just want to *slap* those types?" Charles mused to no one in particular.

"I saw it in my classmates in my private schools and again in college. The people who were raised with money, like I was, took it all for granted. And the people who weren't seemed to want to be my friend in the hopes I might send some leftovers in their direction. Funny thing is, I always wished I could."

She felt Charles's eyes dart in her direction and hoped Susie didn't notice. Everything they were hearing sounded sincere, yet it flew in the face of everything Timothy had said and insinuated no more than twenty-four hours earlier.

"It's why I dropped out of college, much to my mother's dismay. I'd had enough of my pretentious classmates and I'd had more than enough of those people who loved to judge me for what I had rather than what I was. That's why I like my web design business. Most of the time, people never see my face. We just communicate via e-mail where I can be the me I am, rather than the me people assume I must be."

Tori couldn't help but laugh, earning her an odd look from Charles in the process. Susie, on the other hand, looked mildly offended. She rushed to explain before Susie's attention returned to the scarf Charles had yet to produce. "I've always found the written word to be a great way to express my true feelings, too . . . but last night, in a book I was reading, the author said e-mail is often a way for people to lie about themselves."

"I guess for some it might be . . ." Susie's words disappeared briefly only to rush back in on the wings of a memory. "Come to think of it, that author is probably right more than anyone realizes. Sadly, those falsehoods people put out into the universe about themselves can hurt far more people that just themselves. Like my mother, for instance."

Tori sat up tall, her motion mirrored by Charles and the five bodies strategically placed at tables to their left and right. "Your mother?"

"I guess my mother was starting to see some of the positive things that came with my choices in life—the genuine friends who like me for me, the give and take I've established with them in the process, and the satisfaction I get from making things happen on my own. So unbeknownst to me, she decided to try it herself—to establish a relationship with someone who didn't know her net worth."

"And?" She silently cursed the eager tone to her voice and was grateful when Susie didn't seem to notice.

"Sadly, she was led astray by someone she met online . . . someone who pretended to care about her. But it was just a trap to lure her in. Once they met and he discovered she had money, he knew all the right moves to get her to part with a little here and a little there. It was painful to have to point out to her what his true motivations so obviously were, especially when he'd done such a good job of convincing her he was a decent guy."

"But she figured it out? With your help?" Tori asked.

Susie's gaze lingered somewhere just over Tori's head, the haziness to her eyes making it obvious she was picturing a different place, a different moment than the one housing her physical body. "It wasn't easy. And at times, I felt as if I was the one breaking her heart rather than this guy . . . but eventually, she had to see it for what it was, whether she wanted to or not. It had simply become too obvious."

Charles sucked in his breath. "I hope she gave him a big what-for!"

"Trotter women don't handle trials like that, Charles. Me, I'm a karma girl. I believe the universe will always have the last say. My mother, on the other hand, reaches for her violin and plays music until she feels better. Or at least, that's what she did before this creep made her doubt everything about the person underneath the wealth and privilege."

"And after?" Tori prodded.

"She ran off to the Hamptons." Susie dropped her hands to the table and shook her head sadly. "Alone."

"Wait. You know where she is?" Charles asked, dumbfounded.

"As of thirty minutes ago, when the caretaker at

my mother's summer home called, yes." Susie pushed back her chair and stood. "I guess if I'd stepped outside myself and thought of the situation from my mother's perspective instead of my own, I'd have known where she went. But the thought that she'd actually mourn such a conniving creature was so far out of my realm of understanding that the Hampton house never entered my thoughts."

Tori shot a questioning look at first Charles, and then each of her friends, the look of shock on their respective faces confirming what she thought she'd heard. "Did you say *mourn?*"

Susie nodded. "You have to understand my mother finally wised up to this man's ways little more than a week ago, and it was with much reservation. Then, that night, as I was finishing up a client's webpage, I clicked on a link for the local news and saw the initial story about his death. It was too late at that moment to call Mom, but I let her know what had happened first thing the next morning. In hindsight, I should have asked her what she was feeling instead of going on and on about karma. Maybe if I had, she wouldn't have had to seek solace in an empty beach house instead of in the arms of her insensitive daughter."

Tori was virtually certain she could have heard a pin drop the moment Susie walked out of

CupKatery with Caroline's scarf in one hand and two of their four suspects wiped from their list with a wave of the other.

"I suppose we should have put more stock in the fact that Caroline disappeared the morning *after* John's fateful push," Rose mused to no one in particular, earning herself a raised cup of coffee and a hearty "Amen" from Leona in return.

More silence followed before Margaret Louise took charge. "So we went sniffin' in the wrong hole for a bit. It happens."

"So what do we do now?" Beatrice said between glances at the cupcake case and the flavor of the day that had been vetoed by the group when they first arrived.

"We move on to the next person." Charles pulled a sparkly purple cell phone from the pocket of his purple denim jacket and checked the time. "Who, according to my early morning phone call, should be arriving in about ten minutes."

Leona pushed her now-empty coffee cup into the center of the table and rose to her feet. "And John's neighbor?"

"In about twenty-five." He returned his phone to his jacket then crumbled his napkin and tossed it into the empty cupcake box on the center of Beatrice and Debbie's table. "I timed it that way to make sure Doug was really here when she arrived."

Beatrice's face brightened. "Can we get another round of cupcakes while we wait? I'm still rather peckish."

"Good heavens, if I eat another treat, I'm going to explode." Rose struggled to her feet then gestured toward the door. "I need to go for a walk. Who's with me?"

Reluctantly, Beatrice followed suit, along with Debbie, Leona, and even Charles.

"Charles?" Tori asked. "Don't you want to stay and see what happens with Doug?"

"I think Margaret Louise should get this one," Charles said over top of Rose's head. "You two have been at this Nancy Drew thing together for a while now. Maybe our luck will change if the correct duo is in place."

She opened her mouth to protest but closed it when she felt Margaret Louise's elbow in her side. "That's what I like 'bout you, Charles. You don't wear no blinders."

"Thank you, Margaret Louise." Charles nodded quickly at Tori then pushed open the door and waited for Beatrice, Leona, Debbie, and Rose to exit onto the street. "Good luck. Call me when you've nailed the sucker."

A feeling of unease washed over Tori as her friends disappeared from view. She knew she needed to be strong, knew she needed to continue the fight, but suddenly the mountain that had seemed merely overwhelming for the past week appeared completely insurmountable at that very moment.

The elimination of Caroline and Susie Trotter from the list of suspects left them with just two. If Doug and Ms. Steely Eye fell off the list, too, they'd have to start from square one all over again.

"Margaret Louise," she whispered. "I'm scared."

"I know that and you know that, but ain't nobody else who needs to know that," Margaret Louise replied as she settled into the chair vacated by Charles. "In fact, my daddy once said, if you're outnumbered, it's best to keep your mouth shut. Keeps 'em from tearin' your butt up like a tater field that's just been plowed."

Tori managed to laugh through the fear, the sound and its momentary reprieve from stress proving to be exactly what she needed at that moment. Maybe they would have to start at square one come morning. Then again, maybe they wouldn't.

Time would tell.

After they talked to Doug . . .

Margaret Louise reached across the tabletop and squeezed Tori's hand in much the way she had at similar moments in the past. It was a gesture Tori found immensely comforting, even as the words that accompanied it set her thoughts running. "You gonna be ready with your sleuthin' questions when he walks through that door?"

"You bet I am."

Chapter 30

Tori was struggling with the order in which to ask her list of questions when Margaret Louise pulled a small black spiral notebook from her cavernous tote bag and smacked it down on the middle of the table.

"You don't need to try 'n keep all those questions in your head, Victoria. That's what notebooks are for." Leona's twin sister reached into her bag a second time for a pen and handed it to Tori. "I've been watchin' them detective shows on TV for a long time, and I finally went out and found the kind of notebook they use for all their interrogatin'."

"Did you get one of those swinging lights, too?"

Margaret Louise made a face. "Quit your teasin' now, you hear? Writin' things down isn't always a bad idea. Keeps you from forgettin' things when your grandbabies start yappin' their jaws all at the same time." At the mention of her son's offspring, the woman's wide shoulders pitched inward along with a heavy sigh. "I miss my grandbabies, Victoria. I miss 'em somethin' fierce."

Tori reached past the notebook and tapped the table in front of her friend. "I know you do, Margaret Louise. I miss seeing them, too. But that's why we're here, waiting to confront Doug."

"You really think he did it?" Margaret Louise asked.

"I can't be sure, but there's an awful lot of things pointing in his direction."

"Like?"

She took advantage of the question to take stock of what she knew thus far. "Well, first up, his mom was one of John's victims. And unlike Caroline, who will get past the hurt and humiliation in due time, his mother is dead, and her final days far sadder than they should have been thanks to John."

Margaret Louise nodded emphatically. "My Jake would be none too happy if someone treated me like that. Why, I reckon he'd be spittin' mad."

"Exactly." Tori pulled the notebook and pen closer to her spot and flipped the cover open, her hand instinctively grabbing for the pen. "We've also got the possibility that Doug was outside John's door the night before the murder, threatening him."

"Which we'll know for certain once his neighbor arrives . . ."

"Maybe." She sketched a small door while continuing her verbal run-through of everything they knew so far. "But she only caught a glimpse of him through her peephole as he went running by. There's no guarantee that quick blur will be enough for a positive identification. If it was even him at all . . ."

"Don't know why he'd have lied 'bout that article in the paper you told us 'bout if he wasn't guilty." Margaret Louise dug another pen from her bag and used it to add a peephole to Tori's door. When she was done, she leaned back in her chair and crossed her arms just below her bosom. "I think we got 'im, Victoria. I think we got 'im good."

Any and all caution she wanted to offer over getting too excited was thwarted by the swoosh of the kitchen door as it swung open behind the counter and the same dark, curly-haired man they'd been waiting to see finally stepped into the room.

"He's here!" Margaret Louise whispered in her not-so-good-at-whispering voice.

She started to *shhh* away the warning, but it was too late—Doug's head snapped in their direction, followed by a look of casual recognition and then a much-needed moment to recover thanks to the string of bells above the front door tasked with announcing customers.

"Did you see the way he looked at you, Victoria?" Margaret Louise gushed. "I think he recognized you. Either that or he's taken by just how pretty you are."

"I'm thinking he probably just recognized me," she whispered back, only to pop up from her chair as his deliberate approach removed any conjecture that remained.

"I take it your return means CupKatery is a hit with at least one southerner?" Doug offered his hand and smiled broadly when it was accepted.

"Actually it's a hit with two if you count my friend here." Tori nudged her chin toward the still-seated Margaret Louise. "Six if you count the four who just left to take a walk."

"Don't forget Dixie," Margaret Louise reminded. "Charles said she liked them cupcakes you brought her in jail the other day."

Uh-oh.

Doug stepped back a half step, only to reclaim it just as quickly. "Did you say *Dixie?*"

Somewhere in the back of her head she knew there were probably a half-dozen or so ways she could play the question, but every one of them escaped her at that exact moment. Instead, she nodded while Margaret Louise filled in the blanks.

"Dixie Dunn. She's our friend from Sweet Briar. She came here with the rest of us to be on *Taped with Melly and Kenneth*. Only she got herself arrested for pushin' a man to his death."

A storm cloud whipped across Doug's face just before it erupted through his mouth. "John Dreyer was no man. He was a lying, cheating sack of—" He stopped mid-sentence, held his hands outward, and doubled his earlier step backward. "No, I won't finish that sentence. Not in front of ladies anyway."

"Your mama would be proud to hear that, just like any mama would be." Margaret Louise settled her back against her chair and reached into her tote once again, this time retrieving a pocket-sized leatherbound album that Tori recognized immediately. "It's not easy in this day and age to raise a boy into a man, but it can be done. My Jake is proof of that, too."

With a flick of her plump wrist, Margaret Louise opened the album to the first page and the picture of her only child and the father of her eight grandchildren. "This is Jake."

Doug made himself look, despite the tension that still had him clenching and unclenching his fists at his side.

"That's your mama over there on the wall behind the register, ain't it?"

Tori wanted nothing more than to place her hand over her friend's mouth but knew such an effort would be futile. When Margaret Louise got on the subject of mothers, there was no derailing that train.

He didn't need to follow the path of Margaret Louise's finger. Instead, he just nodded, the angry set to his jaw relaxing ever so slightly.

"She looks like she was a mighty special person. Real happy."

The tightness was back, accompanied by a

noticeable darkening of his eyes. "She was until she met that lying, cheating sack of—" Again, he stopped, but this time with even more noticeable reluctance.

A series of clucking sounds emerged from between Margaret Louise's lips. "He hurt her, didn't he?"

"Worse. He made her doubt herself."

Suddenly, all thoughts of forcibly shutting Margaret Louise's mouth fell away as the reality of what was happening in front of her became crystal clear.

Doug was talking.

That was all that mattered.

"That's not how she lived her life. She lived it with a smile and with hope. She was an optimist in the truest sense of the word. Yet because of him, that smile had been tested, that hope shaken." He lowered himself onto a neighboring chair and stared up at the ceiling. "That had no business being a part of her final weeks on this earth. No business at all."

"You're right, it didn't." It was Tori's first real contribution to the conversation at that point, but it was time. Somehow, someway, she had to start asking the questions that needed to be asked. "But I imagine knowing he got his in the end has to give you at least some measure of comfort, yes?"

"Heck yeah, it does." He brought his gaze down to hers in time for her to see the smile now creeping its way across his mouth. "How could it not?"

"Well, when it's your friend who's being framed for his murder, there is no comfort to be had."

"Framed?" he echoed, his expression unreadable.

"That's what they call it when evidence of a crime is planted on your person even though you weren't anywhere near the scene of the crime."

He exhaled through pursed lips, shrugging as he did. "I imagine that could be a tactic to try and get your friend released."

A familiar face appeared outside the window then made its way toward the front door, the woman's arrival emboldening her in a way she'd yet to find until that moment. "Maybe a better tactic would be to find the real murderer instead."

"Real murderer . . ." The echo died on his lips as he looked toward the door and the customer its bell announced. Instantly, the color drained from his face as John's neighbor lifted her hand in a wave at Tori, only to drop it to her side as her gaze fell on Doug.

"It's him, ain't it?" Margaret Louise shouted across the shop. "He's the one who went runnin' by your door the night before John was pushed, ain't he?"

Moving in an almost trancelike state, John's neighbor crossed the narrow entry foyer in their direction, her mouth moving a full minute before any words actually emerged. "You were the one.

The one I saw across the street that day. Does it still haunt you like it haunts me?"

Tori shot a sideways glance at Margaret Louise and saw the same confusion she now felt. "Across the street? I thought you saw him through your peephole as he went running by."

John's neighbor shook her head hard. "No. He wasn't the one outside my door that night. That fella was tall. This man"—she pointed at Doug— "was across the street when I ran to my balcony to see what that awful noise was the next day. He was every bit as horrified as I was to see John's shattered body lying on the street like that."

"Horrified might be a stretch." Doug used his right hand to crack the knuckles on his left hand, then switched to repeat the process on the other side. "Shocked was more like it. Especially when I realized it was that lying, cheating sack of . . . you know."

She tried to make sense of what she was hearing, but it didn't add up. Not entirely anyway. "I was here, in the shop, when you pretended to read about John's murder in the paper. But the details you read aloud weren't anywhere in that paper except Dixie's name. Why would you do that if you weren't trying to cover something up?"

He straightened his right hand then raked it through his hair as pinpricks of pink appeared on his cheeks. "I found my mother's diary a few weeks ago and read the page where she talked about the hurt and humiliation she felt having fallen for that creep. At a loss for what to do, I ripped it out of that book and sent it to him with my return address clearly marked on the envelope."

Doug's eyes returned to the ceiling, albeit briefly. "I guess I actually thought he'd realize the error of his ways and apologize. Stupid, huh?"

When no one responded, he continued, his voice void of anything resembling emotion, except perhaps exhaustion. "So when I heard nothing, I decided to make him apologize . . . under extreme duress, if necessary. I'd been telling my staff for weeks that I was going to make him sorry for hurting my mom, but I hadn't done a thing other than talk a good game. So I took advantage of a window of opportunity I had in between vendor meetings at the Connecticut store that day and I drove back down here with the sole purpose of roughing him up a little."

Finally it made perfect sense.

John's murder, coupled with the threats Doug himself had uttered aloud, would have had a number of fingers pointing in his direction if he could have been placed in or around the scene of the crime on the day in question. Especially when he'd told his employees he was out of state at the time.

Tori felt Margaret Louise's eyes on her yet couldn't make her head turn to meet them.

They were down to just one suspect and that suspect's gender didn't match the one on the other side of the neighbor's peephole.

Chapter 31

Tori had just emerged aboveground at the corner of Fifth Avenue and Fifty-ninth Street when her phone started ringing, a cruel reminder that the alone time her friends had insisted she take was only good for as long as people allowed her to be alone.

The ringing continued as she crossed the street and followed a stretch of sidewalk that was becoming all too familiar in much the same way the Big Apple as a whole was becoming much too familiar.

She missed Milo.

She missed her job.

She missed her bed.

She missed her cottage.

She missed Georgina and Melissa.

Yet now, thanks to her three distinct strikeouts earlier in the day, the prospect of going home was farther away than ever.

The phone silenced, only to begin ringing again.

One ring.

Two ring.

Three rings.

Midway through the fourth ring, she gave in to its intrusiveness, if for no other reason than to make it stop once and for all.

"Hello?"

"Hey, sugar, it's me."

She managed a small smile in spite of her foul mood. "I'm on my way."

"Hallelujah!"

"I don't know why you're Hallelujah-ing. This is a colossal waste of time and we both know it."

"You'll have a reprieve from the ongoing war between Rose and Leona, right?"

"Theirs would be preferable to the one going on in my own head," she mumbled between footfalls.

"You're enjoying the quiet calm that is New York City in the early evening at this exact moment, are you not?"

"I'm not. I'm on the phone . . . with you."

"You'll be surrounded by books and book-lovers once you finally get here, yes?"

"I suppose."

"And, sugar, you'll be with me, Charles—your personal ray of sunshine during your darkest hours."

Her laugh lasted all of about five seconds. "I don't know why I let everyone talk me into going to this dumb book club. It doesn't matter if Barbara "Steely Eye" Letts was spying on John and Dixie from behind a potted plant or sitting at the table *with* them—she doesn't match the description of the person pounding on his door and threatening to rip him limb from limb the previous night."

"So? She didn't match the description the entire time she was on the list yet you kept her there."

"That's because she was at the Waldorf that morning . . . and near the crime scene that afternoon . . . and you were able to place her as one of John's cons . . . and she had the opportunity in the bathroom that morning to slip the piece of ripped scarf into Dixie's purse."

"And none of that holds anymore?"

She stopped several feet shy of the next corner and pressed her back to the concrete wall that separated the sidewalk from the park. "I—I guess it still does . . ."

"Of course it does, Victoria. John Dreyer conned a lot of women. That means he earned himself a lot of enemies along the way. There's no reason the one who pounded on his door the night before has to be the one who pushed him to his death the next day."

Charles was right.

Ms. Steely Eye had made her way onto the top of Tori's personal suspect list for a reason. It was time to stay the course, not abandon ship.

She crossed the street at the light and turned right and then left, the McCormick's sign midway up the block returning the brief smile from earlier to her lips. "Okay, I'm coming up on the store right now. I'll see you in a few."

Tori settled into a folding chair just over Steely Eye's left shoulder and took a moment to really breathe.

So much of the past few hours had been about keeping up an encouraging pretense for her friends while simultaneously trying to hold back any sign of the panic that was threatening to paralyze her every thought. But now that she was there, away from her friends and barely more than an arm's length away from her lone remaining suspect, she needed to be sharp. Ready.

Charles's Academy Award–worthy greeting when she'd walked through the door had been a big help in clearing her head, of course, but now that the book club was moments away from starting, he seemed preoccupied.

Charles is fine . . . focus on Steely Eye. She's Dixie's ticket to freedom . . .

"She better be," she mumbled.

Ms. Steely Eye glanced in Tori's direction but turned away as Vanny joined the group. "So what did everyone think? Is it truly possible to find love after sixty-five?"

A wisp of a woman with white, cottony hair

two seats down from Tori nodded emphatically. "Of course it's possible. You read all the little pieces, those women were just like all of us or"— the woman winked at Tori and Vanny—"the majority of us anyway. They, too, had been resigned to the fact that they were going to live out the rest of their life alone, just like I was before reading this."

"You really think this book changed your outlook?" Vanny posed.

"I finished the book four days ago. Three days ago, I joined an over-sixty-five exercise group that meets three mornings a week for a nice, long walk in the park. There's at least a half-dozen men in there who are single, just like me. They're out there, they really are."

"Oh, they're out there, all right."

Tori heard the edge in Ms. Steely Eye's voice and slid forward on her chair as Vanny turned her focus in the same direction. "You say that with a good deal more skepticism, Barbara. Do you disagree with Mr. Rollins's book?"

"Disagree?"

She caught Charles's raised eyebrow behind the counter and knew the woman's bristling response wasn't in her imagination. Ms. Steely Eye was agitated, though at what exactly, Tori couldn't quite be sure.

"No, I suppose there are women who manage to find good men. The personal stories sprinkled throughout the book that Mavis just mentioned prove that. But let's not forget the other stories, too."

Tori looked down at Rose's copy of the book and then back up at Ms. Steely Eye. "Other stories? What other stories?"

Ms. Steely Eye became Ms. Exasperated Eye. "Did you read the book, young lady?"

Her face warmed at the answer she was forced to give. "I read most of it."

Ms. Exasperated Eye became Ms. Rolled Eye.

Vanny waited for Barbara's inaudible mutterings to stop before addressing Tori with an encouraging smile. "That's okay, it happens to all of us at some point or another. How far did you get?"

She located the end of her bookmark and then opened the book to its marked page. "I had to stop two chapters shy of the end."

Ms. Rolled Eye reclaimed her title of Ms. Steely Eye. "Then you read the stories I was referencing. The ones from the viewpoint of a real live, silver-haired con man."

Confusion pulled Tori's focus back to the book and the final chapter she'd read before giving in to sleep. "Those were just conjecture on the part of the author . . . to illustrate the kind of men who might see fit to prey on a lonely soul."

Ms. Steely Eye released a disgusted sigh. "Readers today disgust me. If it's not something they can watch on a movie screen or get a synopsis of from Ledge Notes, they just can't follow what's going on."

All her life, Tori had prided herself on being fairly even-tempered. Did she get scared? Certainly. Did she get frustrated? More times than she cared to count. Did she imagine clever retorts she wished she'd uttered at appropriate times in life? All the time. But until that moment, the sharp-tongued ones had always been confined to her imagination.

"Barbara, right?" Without waiting for a confirmation head nod from Ms. Steely Eye, she took the one offered by Vanny and a sheepish Charles and unleashed every ounce of frustration she'd been harboring since Dixie was led from her room by Officer Pollop. "Say the name of virtually any author you've ever read and I'll tell you the names of their books. Utter the name of a favorite character and I'm fairly certain I can tell you not only the book that made them famous but also the author who brought him or her to life.

"And while I can tell you which ones were made into movies, my knowledge comes from my lifelong love of books and my chosen career as a *librarian*."

The silence that met her first-ever tirade was quickly drowned out by the pounding in her ears and the mental chastising in her head.

"I'm sorry. I didn't mean to get so . . . so—"

Ms. Steely Eye became Ms. Misty Eye and then

Ms. Closed Eye, before returning to Ms. Steely Eye with a lot less steel. "No, I'm the one who's sorry. I shouldn't have said what I did. I guess I'm just so disgusted by this." Barbara waved Gavin's book in the air then slammed it onto the empty chair to her left. "What a fool I was to pay twenty-eight ninety-five to the same person who stands to earn millions off my foolishness!"

"We don't want you to be unhappy with your book, Barbara, you know that." Vanny rose from her chair and walked toward the book, stopping shy of her intended destination with the help of Barbara's hand.

"No. I bought the book because I was curious, just like everyone else. The foolishness I'm speaking about was falling for the trap Mr. Rollins set in order to write the damn thing in the first place."

Tori looked to Charles for any sort of indication he was following what was going on, but the confusion on his face told her otherwise. "Gavin Rollins set a trap for you?"

Barbara closed her eyes again, this time leaving them closed as she began to speak words that sounded vaguely familiar. " 'You caught me today. Caught me red-handed as we walked past your apartment. At first I tried to play it off, to introduce you to my latest target in such a way neither of you would be the wiser, but it didn't work. I'd like to say the near eardrum-shattering tirade that ensued taught me a valuable lesson, but it didn't. I am a con man and lonely, rich women are my con.' "

"Wait. That's one of the scenarios Gavin talked about in the book." Tori flipped to the correct page, compared Barbara's words with those on the page, and then looked up to find Barbara's eyes still closed.

"It wasn't a scenario, it was a firsthand account, just like the ones earlier in the book from women who found love after sixty-five."

"But those ones from the women were italicized . . ." She held the book into the path of the overhead light only to discover yet another pitfall of reading until six thirty in the morning.

"And so were the ones from John."

She heard Charles's gasp, knew it was an echo of her own. "John? As in John Dreyer?"

Barbara opened her eyes to release a single tear from each one. "He was writing about me in the entry I just recited."

She tried to make sense of what she was hearing, but it was too much. It simply didn't fit. To prove it, she flipped to the copyright page that listed the current year. "But Barbara, if the book was released last month, it was in production for at least a year and took at least a year before that in order to be written."

"I met John two years ago this past January. Trust me . . . it's me."

She shot a questioning look in Charles's direction. "Two years?"

"What can I say?" Charles shrugged. "I'm good with faces . . ."

She swallowed over the lump in her throat and the realization that she didn't want John's killer to be Ms. Steely Eye anymore. The woman had been hurt and humiliated enough.

Still, she had to know.

"Did—did you push him off that balcony, Barbara?"

This time Charles's gasp was echoed by Barbara instead of Tori. "Good God, no! Why would I do that? I needed him . . . I needed him as proof that Gavin Rollins is making a sport out of humiliating older women and then turning around and making millions off countless others just like them!"

"But I saw you that morning. You were at the Waldorf spying on my friend who was having breakfast with John. Then I saw you again, later that afternoon, by John's apartment."

"I was gathering proof. I was going to take my pictures and my suspicions to the newspapers and the news stations and watch that man's career explode in front of his face." Barbara tried to steady her breathing, but to no avail. "I wanted John's help, and after seeing the way he was with your friend, I thought maybe he'd see my proposal as a chance to get out . . . to change his

317

ways before he ended up all alone just like the women he was being paid to con. But—"

Tori knew Barbara was still speaking, even knew it was probably something she should be listening to, but it was hard to hear over the clanging in her head.

Being paid to con . . .

Being paid to con . . .

John wasn't making his money from the women he met on the Internet. Not the bulk of it anyway.

Sure, maybe he stuck around long enough to get a few nice gifts and eat in a few fancy restaurants, but the bulk of his money came in the form of a steady paycheck. For services rendered.

"Victoria, did you hear what she just said?"

At the sound of her name, she turned toward Charles, only to have her eyes guided back toward Barbara by his index finger.

"No. What did I miss?"

"Barbara left the bathroom before Dixie did that morning. She used those moments alone with John to tell him what she was going to do. He told her not to bother, that she didn't need to tell the world she'd been conned. He said he'd e-mailed Gavin the night before telling him it was time to stop. He was tired of hurting women. He said it had started out as a game years ago but became something far too big when he met Gavin. He told him it had to stop or he'd have to come clean—for both of them."

Tori held off any further explanation from Charles with her hand and addressed Barbara directly. "So why didn't you say anything when John was murdered? Why did you let my friend go to prison if you knew this was going on?"

Confusion clouded Barbara's eyes, chasing all remnants of her silly alias from Tori's mind. "Because I figured John had lied to me that day just like he lied to me two years ago. Only I figured this southern woman had the guts to do what so many of his cons only wished they had done."

"And the newspapers? Why didn't you take what you knew about Gavin to them?"

This time, Barbara's eyes disappeared behind her hands. "Because I thought about what John had said that last morning. About the world knowing I'd been conned."

Tori almost pointed out they were about to find out anyway, but she let it go. Maybe they wouldn't have to know after all. Murder was, after all, a far bigger crime than anything else Gavin may have done.

Chapter 32

Tori was putting the second to last folding chair on the cart when she finally felt settled enough to share her hypothesis. "He put that scarf in Dixie's bag when we were at the studio that day. He heard what she said to Melly and Kenneth on set and to the rest of us at some point or another in the Green Room and he realized he had the perfect scapegoat."

Charles, who'd been looking at the door off and on since before the meeting started, let off a little yelp.

"What? You think I'm wrong?" she asked. "Charles, it's all right there."

"No . . . I think you're right. It's just that I've only seen murderers on TV and on one field trip to the county jail when I was about seven." He held his finger in the air then retrieved a still-full lunch sack from the shelf beneath the register and dumped the contents, which included a crustless sandwich, an overripened banana, and a purple Pixie Stix, onto the counter, and held the bag to his mouth.

One breath in . . .

One breath out . . .

One breath in . . .

One breath out . . .

He moved the bag to the side and continued. "But right here . . . in the bookstore? That's another matter entirely."

Her eyes narrowed. "What are you talking about, Charles?"

"Gavin. He said he might try to show up tonight. To surprise the ladies in the book club."

The final chair slipped from her hands and clattered onto the tile floor. "He's coming here? Tonight? Why didn't you say anything?"

"It was supposed to be a surprise!" he fairly wailed.

"And in the twenty minutes or so since we pinned him as a murderer?"

"I've been trying to figure out what we should do!"

Indeed.

Looking around the store, she made a mental note of the secondary exit located on the far wall of the adjacent café. Only a handful of people still remained in the store, with all but one of them engaged in conversation over a latte or a soda. The one actual book browser was seemingly oblivious to everything but the story unfolding between his hands.

"Do we call the police? Tell them what he did?"

It was the smart way to go even if it wasn't her first inclination.

"Are you sure he's coming?"

"No."

"The book club's already gone home for the evening," she pointed out while bobbing her head around the nearest bookshelf to gain a view of the front door.

"But that's because of everything that happened. They're usually here long after we close."

"Gavin doesn't know that."

Charles nibbled the left side of his mouth. "Yes, he does. I told him myself when he was here for his talk and I mentioned tonight's book club."

So much for that theory . . .

But even as a part of her worried along with Charles, another part of her—an even larger part—welcomed the opportunity to give Gavin Rollins a piece of her mind.

For Dixie.

For Barbara.

For Doug and his mom.

For Caroline and Susie.

And for all the other women who'd had their hearts manipulated and broken so he could climb the ladder to fame and fortune.

"You have Al's number on your phone?" she finally asked. "You know, the cop who arranged it so we could spend some real time with Dixie?"

Charles nodded between glances at the door and an occasional breath or two in his brown paper bag.

"Go in the back and call him. Tell him what's going on and tell him to get some cops here ASAP."

Slowly, he pulled the bag from his mouth and relinquished it to the counter in exchange for the purple Pixie Stix. "Then what? Do I come back out here?"

"Just stay back there until help arrives."

"You know the ladies will have my head if they hear I left you out here with a murderer all by—"

The bell that announced the comings and goings of customers from the building clanged and Charles scurried off into the back room like a frightened rabbit, leaving Tori alone with a few clueless customers and her own pounding heart.

She lifted the final chair up off the floor and held it to her chest as Gavin came around the corner with a smile and a nod.

"Still in the Big Apple, I see."

"Not for much longer." She tried not to flinch at the acidic sound in her voice and instead used her grip on the chair to find the calm she knew she needed for however long it took for the men in blue to arrive.

If Gavin noticed her tone, though, it didn't show. "I'm sorry your friend won't be going home with you as you'd hoped. That has to be a really tough pill to swallow."

"It would be if that were the case, but it's not."

His surprise was fast, fleeting, but she saw it

323

nonetheless. "They're letting her leave the state?"

She placed the last chair on the cart and wheeled it behind the counter and over to the door behind which Charles had disappeared. Inhaling quickly, she opened the door, made eye contact with a stunned Charles long enough to earn her the nod she sought, pushed the cart inside, and returned to the shop and a still-bewildered Gavin.

"My friends and I have known since day one that Dixie had nothing to do with John Dreyer's murder. We knew it just as surely as we knew we'd eventually figure out who *did*. And we were right."

The door-triggered bell sounded twice and then once again as a pair of coffee drinkers and the lone reader headed out into the night, leaving Tori alone with Gavin, two remaining café hold-outs, and an utterly silent Charles in the back room.

Gavin glanced over his shoulder then back at Tori, his voice clear and professional as it left his mouth for the benefit of the holdouts. "McCormick's is now closed."

Her eyes darted toward the café as the pair seated at the far table slowly rose to their feet and headed toward the door, their awareness of the world around them stopping with each other.

The bell chimed once, twice, and then fell silent as the reality of the empty bookstore descended around them. She could run, maybe even reach the front door, but then Charles would be alone.

And besides, he'd nodded when she opened the back door.

He'd called the police.

Throwing caution to the wind, she placed the counter between herself and Gavin and had her say. "Do you have a mother, Mr. Rollins? A grandmother?"

"The reason you're asking?" he snapped.

"Because I'm just trying to figure out how someone could take advantage of lonely women, dupe them for money, step on their hearts, and take notes while they're doing it."

"I didn't take any notes."

"You're right, you didn't. You just hired someone else to take them. Someone who finally wised up, realized it was wrong, and threatened to expose you as the fraud you are."

His jaw tightened along with his fists. "My book *helped* women."

"You think hiring someone to break women's hearts is helping women? Please. That research helped you sell books to the same exact demographic you've been hunting down for years simply so you could sell a book. And then, when you're faced with exposure because John finally realized what he was doing to people's *hearts,* you wiggle out from under it by murdering him and trying to pin it on my friend? No way. The jig is up, Gavin."

He lunged forward so fast she had no time to back away before his hand closed around her neck. "For you it is, sweetheart."

The door to the stockroom slammed open and Charles ran out, brandishing his purple Pixie Stix in the air. "Get your filthy, disgusting hands off Miss Victoria right n-o-w."

With one powerful and well-aimed blow, Gavin's hands dropped to his side as a line of purple sugar crystals hit their emerald green mark at the exact same moment the door-mounted bell signaled the arrival of not one, but ten members of the NYPD.

Chapter 33

Tori knew it was silly, but she just couldn't make herself let go of Dixie's hand. She supposed it made sense on some level—particularly the one that had linked going home to Milo with Dixie's exoneration of any wrongdoing in John Dreyer's death. But she also knew it went further than that, to a place deep inside her heart that wasn't truly content unless her loved ones were safe and sound.

And as implausible as the notion might have

been some two years earlier, Dixie Dunn had wormed her way into Tori's heart just as surely as anyone else seated in their tiny circle at New York's LaGuardia Airport.

"You doing okay, Dixie?" she asked quietly.

"I'm trying to. But it's mighty hard to swallow the fact that the man who made me feel young again for one glorious morning didn't really care about me at all."

"But see, that's where I think you're wrong. I think you were different than all the rest. You had a real date with real smiles and real laughs."

Dixie tugged her hand from Tori's grasp and dropped it into her lap. "Based on what? A personality that wasn't even mine? It was Margaret Louise's, and Beatrice's, and Rose's."

"But it was *you* who shared that breakfast table with him. *You* he took for cupcakes. *You* he took to the zoo. And *you* he wanted to see again that night."

She saw the fleeting hope that lifted Dixie's shoulders ever so slightly and prayed it would be enough in the end. In the meantime, she reclaimed the woman's hand and held it tightly as the pockets of conversation that had accompanied their arrival at the gate broke in favor of one loud voice.

"Can you believe it? We're finally goin' home!" Margaret Louise tugged her tote bag onto her lap and smiled the kind of smile that belonged on her face the way two eyes, a nose, and a mouth belonged on everyone else's. "It's officially time to pee on the fire and call in the dogs on our time here in New York City."

Leona rolled her eyes. "Must you always be so earthy, Margaret Louise?"

"Ah, Twin, put your stinger away, will ya?" Margaret Louise said as she reached into her bag and extracted her vibrating phone. "Will you look at this . . . it's the studio callin' to wish us well, I reckon."

A hush fell over the group while Margaret Louise took the call.

"Hello . . . Yes, this is Margaret Louise . . . Oh, hello there, Zelman . . . Yes, we're at the airport and Dixie is with us . . . Of course we're glad it's all over."

Tori felt Dixie's hand inside her own and squeezed ever so gently, a misty-eyed smile her reward in return. Dixie had been thrilled beyond belief when they showed up at the jail to bring her home for good. She'd laughed and she'd cried, and laughed and cried some more, but in the end, she'd mostly just been quiet.

Reflective, even.

As if her week-long stay in a New York City jail cell had changed her somehow.

"I think that's mighty sweet, Zelman, and I can see why the show's ratin' would soar if we came back, but I think I can say for everyone here that we're not all too eager to come back."

Heads nodded around the circle.

"No, we don't blame the city . . . we just want to go home is all . . . where we belong . . . What? Say that again? . . . Well, I'll be! . . . Let me check."

Margaret Louise pulled the phone from her ear and covered the mouthpiece with her free hand. "Melly and Kenneth want us on the show again. This time with Georgina and Melissa as part of the circle, too."

The answer came in unison with nary a look at anyone other than Margaret Louise. "No!"

"Zelman said they can tape on location if we want—in Sweet Briar."

This time, gazes mingled, shoulders shrugged, and an occasional head or two nodded. "Should I tell them we'll get back to them?"

Tori squeezed Dixie's hand once again. "Dixie? I think this is your call to make. Do we do it or don't we?"

"I rather like our sewing circle being just for us and no one else. Less chance anyone can mess it up, I guess." Dixie looked at each member of the group before settling finally on Margaret Louise. "Tell Zelman thanks but no thanks."

With a single nod of her head, Margaret Louise delivered the news to Zelman and then tossed the phone back in her bag. "I sure am gonna miss

Charles, though. That young man was a hoot and a half, wasn't he?"

"If that's better than being a single hoot, then I'm oh so very flattered!" Charles poked his head around the corner and then sashayed his way into the circle, his infectious smile brightening their tiny corner of the gate immeasurably.

For only the second time since Dixie's release, Tori let go of her hand long enough to stand and hug Charles, the gratitude she felt for the eccentric bookseller more than she could ever articulate. "I had no idea you were going to be here."

"I couldn't let my southern friends leave without a proper send-off, now could I?"

"A proper send-off?"

Charles looked left and then right before motioning for everyone to come closer. When they did, he pulled a large black tote bag from behind his back and held it out for Dixie to see. "Do you see that appliqué right there? It's an apple . . . to remind you of my city."

Rose turned the bag just enough to get a proper look. "Did you sew that on yourself, young man?"

Charles beamed. "I did. Last night after I got home from the bookstore. I guess I got kinda sad when I realized you'd all be leaving and that's when I decided I wanted to send you all home with some memories." He turned his focus back on Dixie and placed the bag on her lap. "*Good* memories."

"I don't know what kind of good memories there can be," Dixie mumbled, not unkindly.

"Well, why don't you look inside and see."

Reaching into the bag, Dixie pulled out an envelope with a gift card to CupKatery inside. "They ship anywhere in the United States, including Sweet Briar, South Carolina," Charles explained.

Dixie nodded. "They were very good. Especially the pancake batter ones."

"They'll deliver those." Charles nudged his chin toward the bag. "Now keep going . . ."

Again, Dixie reached inside the bag, this time pulling out a stuffed sea lion. "Victoria here told me that sea lions are your favorite animal so I thought maybe you'd like one for yourself."

Tori blinked back the tears Dixie was unable to hide. "This is too much, Charles. You don't even know me."

"I know enough just by how determined the rest of these ladies were to get you out of that jail." Charles pointed to the bag one last time. "There's one more thing in there."

With her left arm wrapped tightly around the soft gray sea lion, Dixie slipped her right hand into the bag and extracted seven purple Pixie Stix tied together with a bright purple bow.

"There's one for each of you . . . so you'll never forget me."

Tori looked around at her friends, the same teary haze that made it hard for her to see clearly having the same effect on each of them. But just as she was about to speak, Dixie beat her to the punch.

"How could we forget one of our own?"

Charles swallowed. Hard. *"One of our own?"*

"Of course." Dixie looked down at her Big Apple tote bag and back up at Charles, a genuine smile lighting her face for the first time in days. "You *are* an honorary member of the Sweet Briar Ladies Society Sewing Circle, aren't you?"

Sewing Pattern

Zipper Flower Pins

Makes two flowers

Materials

one 24-inch metal zipper
small piece of felt
pin back
scissors
needle and thread
jewelry pliers (optional)

Instructions

Unzip the zipper and cut it apart by cutting the metal stop off the end. Remove the zipper pull.

Also cut the metal piece from the opposite end.

Cut three 6-inch zipper pieces.

Cut one 5½-inch zipper piece for the bud of the flower.

Sew and overlap the ends to form a petal with zipper teeth on top. The seam goes in the middle.

After all three 6-inch pieces are done, stagger the petals like a star, then sew them together.

Cut a circle from the felt to form the flower base. Attach the felt to the back of the flower.

To make the bud, start in the center. Hand sew as you go, so it is tight, and continue to coil around.

Sew the bud securely to the petals. Press hard in the center as you go around and sew.

Sew the pin back onto the felt to secure the flower.

Hint: Use jewelry pliers to push and pull the needle and thread through the flower as it gets thicker.

Reader-Suggested Sewing Tips

From Shirley L.
via my Fan Page on Facebook:
- As we get older, and our vision decreases, knowing where to hold my fabric while feeding it through the machine can be difficult. To counteract this, I put a colorful piece of duct tape on the machine where I want the edge of the fabric to be in order for my seams to be straight. Since I have a hard time seeing the lines that are marked on the machine, this makes it much easier to follow the edge.

From Kat D.
via my Fan Page on Facebook:
- I keep an empty soda bottle by my cutting table and one by my sewing machine to hold broken or damaged pins and needles. Keeps me from finding them with my bare feet.

From Janet L.
via my Fan Page on Facebook:
- When making clothes for children, save the "scrap" pieces. When you have enough, turn them into a lap quilt.

From Charleen W.
via my Fan Page on Facebook:

- Clear, plastic boxes with handles help keep projects in order and are easy to carry around. Put all cut items, thread, and the directions together, then you will find what you need when you need it.

From Ian H.
via my Fan Page on Facebook:

- When cross-stitching, and a pattern asks for two threads, I only cut one and double it over, threading the cut ends through the needle. Then, I make the first stitch and catch through the loop left . . . that way I don't have any knots on the back of my canvas.

Center Point Large Print
600 Brooks Road / PO Box 1
Thorndike, ME 04986-0001 USA

(207) 568-3717

US & Canada:
1 800 929-9108
www.centerpointlargeprint.com